MW00569444

DEATH BY DEFICIT

Also by Richard Rohmer

Fiction	Ultimatum (1973)
	Exxoneration (1974)
	Exodus/UK (1975)
	Separation (1976)
	Balls! (1976)
	Periscope Red (1980)
	Separation II (1981)
	Triad (1981)
	Retaliation (1982)
	Starmageddon (1985)
	Rommel & Patton (1986)
	Red Arctic (1989)
	John A.'s Crusade (1995)
Non-Fiction	The Green North: Mid-Canada (1970)
	The Arctic Imperative (1973)
	E.P. Taylor (1978)
	Patton's Gap (1981)
	How to Write a Best Seller (1984)
	Massacre 747 (1984)

DEATH BY DEFICIT

A 2001 NOVEL

RICHARD ROHMER

Stoddart

Published in 1995 by
Stoddart Publishing Co. Limited
34 Lesmill Road, Toronto, Canada
M3B 2T6
Tel. (416) 445-3333
Fax (416) 445-5967

Stoddart Books are available for bulk purchase for sales promotions, premiums, fundraising, and seminars. For details, contact the **Special Sales Department** at the above address.

Canadian Cataloguing in Publication Data

Rohmer, Richard, 1924–
Death by deficit: a 2001 novel

ISBN 0-7737-2902-X

I. Title.

PS8585.03954D4 1995 C813'.54 C95-931224-2
PR9199.3.R65D4 1995

Cover Design: James Ireland Design Inc.
Printed and bound in Canada

Stoddart Publishing gratefully acknowledges the support of the Canada Council, the Ontario Ministry of Citizenship, Culture, and Recreation, Ontario Arts Council, and Ontario Publishing Centre in the development of writing and publishing in Canada.

Acknowledgements

The statistics, projections, and graphs used in this novel are primarily based on "2001: Canada's Fiscal Odyssey," a remarkable paper produced by the Canadian Manufacturers' Association and published at a media conference held in Toronto on Tuesday, December 7, 1993.

I gratefully acknowledge CMA's permission to use its material and for the cooperation of CMA's president, Stephen Van Houten, and CMA's chief economist, Dr. Jay Myers.

Similarly I thank Eric Malling and CTV's W5 for CTV's permission to utilize the manuscript of their excellent New Zealand program.

This novel is dedicated to
all finance ministers of Canada,
past, present, and future

Day One

Sunday, January 28, 2001

1

8:00 P.M.: The Prime Minister's Office

The swearing-in ceremony had taken place on Saturday at Rideau Hall, the Governor General's residence. Sunday had been cram day for the thirty new ministers, including the Prime Minister. Cram day: from early morning until half past seven that night deputy ministers and their teams had force-fed information to their respective neophyte ministers during the briefing on their duties, responsibilities, and major issues. As one civil servant had said, it was like ramming grain down the gullets of disoriented geese, fattened for the ultimate processing of certain of their organs into pâté de fois gras.

That evening the PM caught his first whiff of the crisis that was about to engulf him and his government. Peter Smart, the nation's top civil servant, had just finished briefing him in his Centre Block office, and he was about to leave for dinner when the Clerk of the Privy Council spoke.

"Sir, there's something I have to tell you. I'd just as soon someone else did this."

Surprised, the PM looked closely at Smart. He was a tall, gaunt man, sallow faced, with thinning brown hair behind a high narrow forehead and intense dark eyes. Smart was trying hard to please his new boss, a person whom he knew but with whom he did not yet have a rapport.

"Sounds bad."

Smart thought for a few seconds before speaking. "It is. It's about the numbers being used by the government during the campaign, the deficit and the debt."

"What about the numbers?"

"They were way off, much lower than they really are."

"Oh God. How much lower?" The PM felt his whole body tense as he waited for the bad news.

Smart gave him the real numbers — the deficit projection for 2001–02, the federal debt, the combined federal and provincial debt, and the projected interest payment on the debt.

The PM was in shock as he listened, his eyes wide like a little boy's listening to a horror story. "God, I knew things were bad — I didn't swallow all that campaign snake oil those bastards were feeding us — but those figures are unbelievable! We're in serious trouble. Canada's bankrupt! How the hell are we going to deal with this?"

"May I make a suggestion?"

Smart's cool manner, so typical of the man during stressful moments, calmed the PM somewhat. He nodded. "Sure. Feel free."

"You should consider calling a meeting of your financial people. Tonight if you can do it."

The PM shook his head. "I wish I could, Peter, but unfortunately I can't." He paced to the casement window and stared out into the darkness over the broad, treeless, snow-covered lawn of the Parliament Buildings. Across the street he could see the lightless windows of the squat, grey embassy building of the United States of America. The President, he thought, I'll probably have to go cap-in-hand to him for a handout.

He turned back to face Smart. "As I told you, I'm having dinner with the Governor General. I really can't cancel."

"But she was appointed by *them*!"

"That doesn't matter." He went back to his desk. "Make it a breakfast meeting tomorrow morning. Set it up for the conference room, eight o'clock. Give me a run-down on who'll be there."

"Your Minister of Finance, Mario Greco."

The PM had chosen the newly elected Winnipeg native for this important Cabinet post because of his solid banking experience and reputation even though he had never served in the House of Commons. "Also his Deputy Minister," added Smart.

"Who's that?"

"Paul Simpson."

"Yeah."

"Your Treasury Board President."

"Ann Carter. Yes, we've got to have her. She's a C.A., a Nesbitt Burns alumnus; got her M.B.A. at York University, her Ph.D. in economics at Harvard. She'll have to be there."

"And the Governor of the Bank of Canada, Jane Smith?"

"That inflexible bitch. Yeah. And if you can't get her, then get the Deputy Governor, whoever it is."

"Victor Barbeau."

"Barbeau? I thought we'd got all the Québécois out of the civil service. Imagine those Québec bastards saying we're separating but we want dual citizenship so we can continue to run the Canadian bureaucracy!"

"He's not Québécois. He's from Sudbury."

"Okay. And I want Simon there too."

Simon Camp was the PM's newly appointed Chief of Staff whom he had brought with him from his Calgary law firm. A full partner in the firm, Camp was in his mid thirties, and single again. He brought his skills as an excellent organizer and administrator to the demanding job in the Prime Minister's Office. It didn't matter that Camp had no prior experience at the federal level. What mattered was trust, loyalty, and total commitment to the boss.

The PM looked down at the names he had just jotted down, then returned his gaze to Smart. "I want the full details about this mess. I don't want you or your people to pull any punches. Got that?"

"Yes, sir."

The PM studied the other man for a moment before asking his next question: "Why didn't you tell me about this earlier, Peter?"

Smart shifted his body. He was visibly uneasy. "Well, the news is so bad. On top of that, I'm a holdover from the old régime, and I thought perhaps you might think I had some responsibility for this mess — as you put it."

The PM snorted and shook his head as he went into the closet to put on his heavy winter overcoat. "*You* responsible? No way. Forget it."

He went to the door. "Eight o'clock. And don't forget to tell Simon."

Day Two

Monday, January 29, 2001

2

8:00 A.M.: The PMO Conference Room

"When I became the leader of this party I thought there was hope that we could keep this goddam country together."

The Prime Minister ran a hand from his high forehead down his fatigue-marked face, and took his cleft chin between thumb and index finger. He supported his weary head on his arm, the elbow hard against the glistening surface of the long oak table. The ancient, elaborately carved piece dominated the conference room located next to the Prime Minister's office in the Centre Block of the Parliament Buildings.

"I thought there was hope we could keep the country from being bankrupted, destroyed, by government deficits and debt."

"We all thought the same thing," Mario Greco agreed.

"Sure. Well, Québec's gone. It was not our doing. We couldn't stop them, couldn't persuade them to stay. They had to be free and independent of us *maudits Anglais*." The PM shrugged. "It's been four years since Québec's declaration of independence . . ."

"On St-Jean-Baptiste Day, of course," Ann Carter added, "and we're still trying to sort out a debt-sharing deal with them." She had picked up French at Neuchâtel and during summers in France, so that she, like Greco, was bilingual.

"Unbelievable. My predecessor led the public to believe that Québec had agreed to a debt deal. The negotiations have all been behind closed doors. The briefing Peter and his team gave me yesterday was a real eye-opener, a real shocker."

"And, no question, Québec's separation hammered us badly, damaged our credibility in the world's money markets," Carter added.

"And our own domestic lending market as well," the PM observed. He signalled Simon Camp for more coffee, and by common assent everybody had refills, giving them time to organize their thoughts.

"Of course, Prime Minister," Greco said after a few minutes. "The fact remains that failure of the previous government to get Québec to agree on a division of assets and liabilities, particularly the national debt, is appalling. Now it's up to us to resolve that problem."

"According to these briefing notes, national debt is over nine hundred billion dollars." The Prime Minister's finger stabbed the sheet of paper in front of him. "Nine hundred and fourteen billion plus the provincial debts. The refusal of Québec to agree on its share of the debt — Québec went public with that information last Friday, as you well know — couldn't have happened at a worse time. If there was even a shred of international money-market confidence in Canada, the Americans, the Japanese, the Europeans . . ."

"Which there isn't." Paul Simpson, the Finance Deputy, shook his head in confirmation.

"Québec's public screw-you position has finished us off completely, the way I see it."

"Finish is a good word, sir," Simpson said. "The unresolved matter of Québec's share of the federal debt combined with the size of the federal debt itself . . ."

"Yeah, these two things have absolutely bankrupted Canada."

"What you're saying is we can't pay the interest on the national debt, right?" The PM paused. "Just how much is the interest?"

"Seventy-six point three billion for this fiscal year."

The PM put down his coffee cup and frowned as he wrote down the numbers, then he looked up. "Not inflated or deflated for political purposes?"

Simpson smiled. "Prime Minister, no question there were a lot of campaign distortions of numbers by the previous government. They tried to say they had the deficit under control, that sort of thing. Reminiscent of the Ontario campaign in the 1980s when the NDP won and Rae and company couldn't believe the deficit numbers they had inherited from the Liberals."

The PM nodded. "I recall what the previous government was saying. Until now I had no idea how bad the situation really is."

"Sir, it isn't bad. It's catastrophic," Greco interjected.

"You're fully aware of all this, Mario?"

"Yes, I am," the Finance Minister replied. "I went through briefings yesterday. Frankly, it's enough to make your hair stand on end."

"What's left of it."

"That goes for both of us," Greco said. "And I have even more bad news, Prime Minister, quite apart from the horror of our true deficit and debt numbers."

The leader of the Reform PC party, which now formed the government, reflected on past events while he waited for the other shoe to drop.

The Reform PC party was a power-driven coalition of the Reform party and the resurgent Progressive Conservatives. The PCs had come back from their humiliating 1993 defeat to win eighty-eight seats in the House (including ten in Québec) in the May 1997 general election. The Reform party had won forty-five seats, making incursions into Ontario and the Maritimes. But it had not breached by even one seat the thick, ethnically impregnable fortress walls of Québec.

In the 1997 election the formidable federal Québec-based and sovereignist Bloc Québécois party had chosen not to field any federal candidates. The reason? By that time the Bloc was content that the upcoming declaration of independence that was made legitimate by the earlier successful referendum made their presence in the House unnecessary and irrelevant. So there was no need to waste time and money now in that despised *maudit Anglais* House of Commons. Now was the time to concentrate on the climax of its efforts: the declaration and assumption of independence for Québec. Thus it was that the 1997 federal election resulted in the party that had won power in 1993 picking up all the seats in Québec except for the ten that went to the PCs.

And thus it was that well before the 1997 federal election the PQ, on the encouragement of the Bloc, had decided to hold their referendum sixty days after that Canadian voting day. (The PQ government could save a substantial amount of money by using the federal voters list.)

The PM turned to his Finance Minister, who was looking over his notes. Mario Greco, bilingual through his education in the French language school system in Winnipeg, was also fluent in Italian. He was a tall, swarthy, handsome forty-eight-year-old. With his greying, thinning hair and salt-and-pepper moustache, he was a sort of Caesar Romero type. In 1995 he had retired from the Canadian Imperial Bank of Commerce as its Senior Vice President for Western Canada. An economist out of the University of Manitoba (Master's) and Harvard (Ph.D.), he was regarded as one of Canada's top pragmatic experts in fiscal and trade matters. Despite Greco's lack of experience in the House of Commons the PM was confident that his appointee would be able to handle the finance portfolio and the Opposition. Finance was without question the most difficult, least desirable ministry. By its very nature it was designed to destroy the reputation and popularity of its incumbent if he or she aspired to be the prime minister.

Other factors had made the Winnipegger politically attractive to the PM. Not the least of those was that Greco was a strong Roman Catholic family man. His seven children were in the professions or at university. Unfortunately he had lost his wife, Jeanine, to cancer about eight months before the election campaign. When approached to be a candidate by the leader of the newly coalesced Reform PC party (and having recently left the CIBC) two years earlier, he was open to the invitation. In a tough fight he won the nomination in Winnipeg Centre and went on to win his riding handily in the January 2001 general election.

"Okay, Mario, give me the bad news."

"As I said, it's catastrophic."

"So we won't call this D-Day, Disaster Day. We'll call it C-Day. Catastrophe Day. Right?"

"The press, the media, may call it something else. But C-Day's an appropriate working title. I suggest we leave the additional bad news to the end and Paul and I can take you through the briefing book. Okay?"

"No, I've been taken through enough goddam briefing books in the last few days. Just tell me what's in it."

"Yes, sir. Actually, Paul's going to do the briefing. He's got some slides, some graphs. Any objection to those? They're all set up."

"No. Just don't take me through the book. Go ahead."

Paul Simpson was sitting at the conference table in the second chair to the PM's right and to the right of Greco. He stood, stepped to the slide projector, turned it on, then returned to his chair. "I mean no offence, Prime Minister, but before I get into the numbers I'd like to lay out some principles that might help to explain where my people and I are coming from."

"You mean the minister's people?"

"Yes, sir. The minister's people — not *my* people."

"No problem. Remember, Paul, I'm not an economist, I'm a lawyer and a politician. If you've got principles for me to understand, I'm listening."

"Good. As you well know, a government may create a deficit in its annual operations — that is, a short-fall, or the amount by which its expenditures exceed its revenues — so the government must be able to borrow on the domestic and international markets an amount at least equal to the deficit in that year."

The PM nodded his understanding, and the Deputy Minister continued.

"I apologize, sir. I know you and your Ministers already know the principles I'm talking about, but I want to make sure you agree with our approach. If the ability of a chronically deficit government to borrow disappears for whatever reason, it follows that the government will not be able to pay the interest on its accumulated debt."

Simpson stopped and looked around at the faces turned toward him. The PM and everyone else at the table were following closely what he was saying.

"If the debt load gets so high that the government can no longer pay that interest, it will collapse."

He paused as if expecting a question. Silence.

Paul continued: "Without lenders — both international and domestic lenders — to buy its bonds to cover its deficit, the government cannot meet its payroll; pay its pensioners; fund its social programs; maintain its defence force; transfer money to the provinces. Above all, as I said, it cannot pay the interest on its accumulated debt."

"Which is where we're at now, right?"

"Exactly, sir. The same concepts apply to the deficits and debt of the provincial, county, regional, and municipal governments and their agencies such as hydro and transit commissions."

"But we're not dealing with the provincial debts here."

"We're going to have to, Prime Minister. We can't avoid it."

"Just stick to the federal problem. Don't get into what the goddam provinces are doing. We, the Reform PC party, haven't created this C-Day thing. We've *inherited it*! Remember that!"

Camp put a cup of steaming black coffee on the table in front of his boss. The PM nodded his thanks but did not pause in his questioning.

"Okay, Deputy, what other principles do you want to tell me about?"

"Those are the basics, Prime Minister."

"So what about the catastrophe?" The PM was focussing his legal mind on the facts he needed to know in order to deal with the situation.

The Deputy Minister didn't have to consult any notes to answer the question. "The total debt of a little over nine hundred billion dollars — that's federal debt only — now exceeds the country's GDP, Gross Domestic Product. The debt's about 100 percent of GDP. Here's the debt slide." Simpson clicked on the projector's remote control.

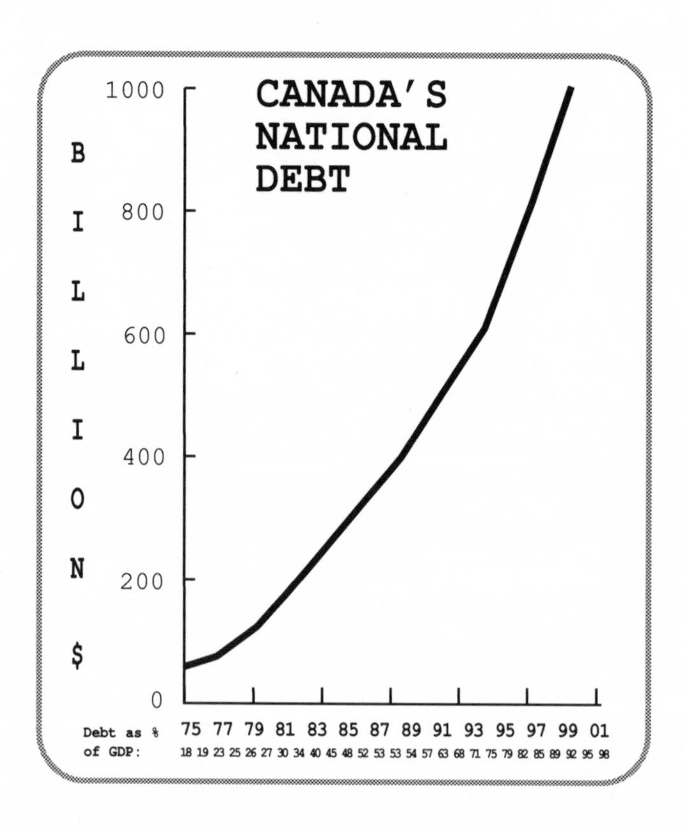

"In the 1993–94 fiscal year when Chrétien took power the total debt was only 485 billion, or 67.8 percent of the GDP. The Martin budget of 1995 was designed to eventually knock the deficit down to twenty-five million. He came close. But high interest rates the next year combined with the heavy fall in tax revenues because of the 1998–99 recession . . . well, the deficit just plain took off. So you can see how rapidly the situation got out of hand in only seven years. Here's the debt graph and it's federal. No other levels of government."

"What was the deficit in 93–94?"

"Forty-five billion."

"And now it's what?"

"Sixty-six point nine billion and rising rapidly. Here's a slide of the deficit from 1992 to 2001–02 showing the deficit widening." Simpson pressed the remote again.

"Like the mouth of a goddam shark," the PM muttered.

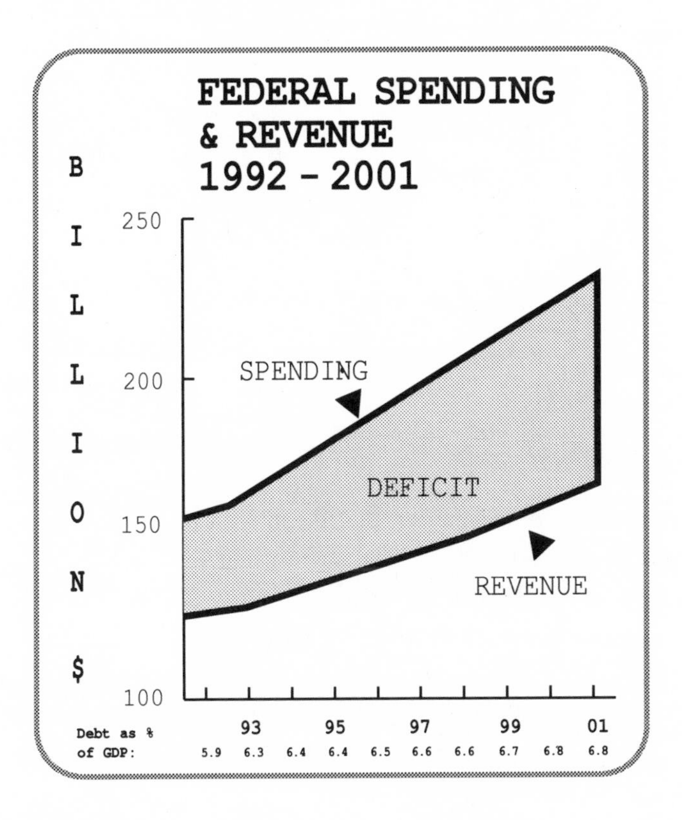

Several heads nodded in agreement, but the general reaction was shocked stillness.

"And here's the debt interest charges slide starting in 1975. The interest line is going up fast." With another click the projector advanced to the next slide.

"Looks like a rocket path!"

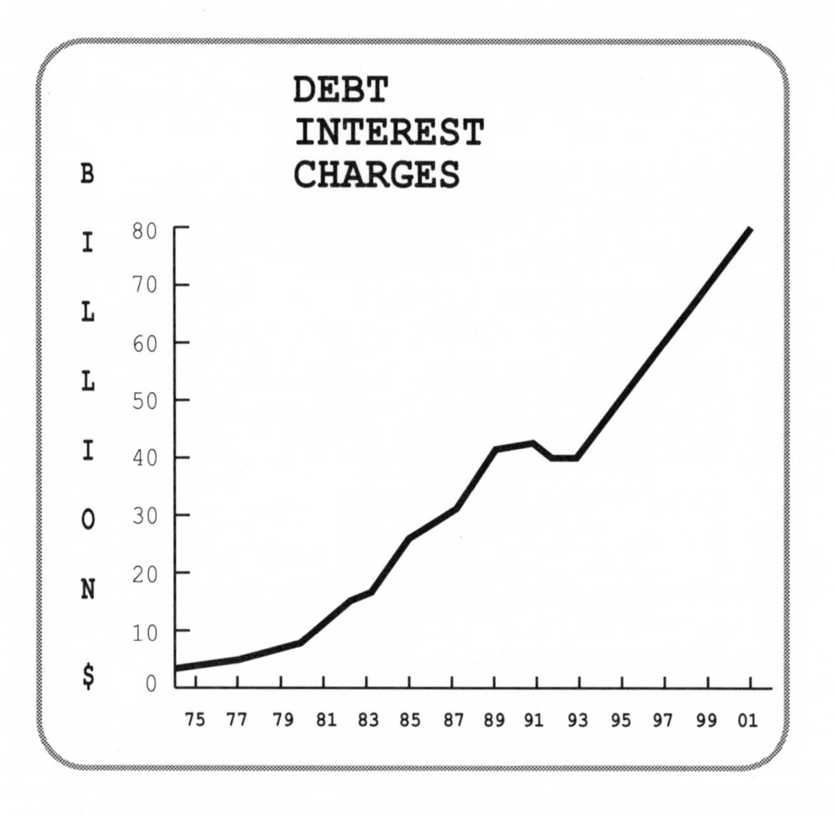

"You can see, Prime Minister, that the interest on the debt first exceeded the deficit in fiscal 1997–98. The interest that year was 56.1 billion and the deficit had escalated to 55.1. Canada had to borrow 55.1 billion that year in order to pay the interest on the money it had already borrowed."

The PM was still staring at the slide. He understood the implications of the numbers all too well. "So what you're talking about, Deputy, is a double deficit."

"I'm not sure what you mean, sir."

"Obviously there was a shortfall between the deficit of 55.1 billion and the interest payment of 56.1 — a clear billion-dollar deficit, as I see it."

"That's right."

"It's that deficit I'm talking about, the double deficit, the amount by which the interest exceeds the deficit. Where is it now?"

"The double deficit in 2000–01 is up to 7.1 billion, and next year it should be in the 9.4 billion range."

"And rising."

Paul Simpson was satisfied that the Prime Minister understood the situation. "Yes, sir. As you said, like a rocket. The brutal fact is that Canada is bankrupt."

The PM frowned as his brain analysed the facts Simpson had presented. "Even if international money markets won't deal with us, why can't the government borrow enough domestically to cover the deficit?"

"Because there aren't enough Canadian savings available from potential buyers of government securities like Canada Savings Bonds."

Ann Carter added, "And when the Canadian people hear about these true numbers you won't be able to give a Canada Savings Bond away." The pert, blond Treasury Board President had lots of street smarts and a razor-sharp mind as well as tongue — which made her a formidable ally or opponent.

The PM decided to sum up what he'd been hearing. "Let me see if I've got this straight. If I can't borrow in the foreign market, then I can't pay the interest I owe. And if I don't pay the interest I owe, I can't borrow in the foreign market — or domestically either. Sounds like a catch-22 situation."

As the PM was speaking, Camp's pocket phone rang. He quietly answered and went to the door to receive an envelope. It was addressed to Simpson, who was busy answering the PM.

"It is a catch-22, Prime Minister, and it's where Canada has finally arrived. The world's international lenders have no security for the five hundred billion plus dollars of debt we owe them. They only have Canada's promise to repay principal and interest. If we default they can't come in and seize assets."

Simpson paused, trying to think of something positive to say. Finally he said: "Fortunately you're not out of business — not really — because a government can't go out of business. The state will always function. It can print money for its domestic purposes."

When the Deputy Minister paused again, Camp handed him the envelope.

Simpson opened it and unfolded the note inside it. His face turned ashen as he read the contents. "Sorry, sir. I have to read this to you. It's a message from your Under Secretary at Foreign Affairs. It says:

```
Our ambassador in Japan has just reported that the gov-
ernment of Japan has ordered that no further purchases
of Canadian bonds or other securities will be made by
any Japanese financial institutions or corporations.
Japan has also ordered that any Canadian bonds or secu-
rities currently held in portfolio be sold immediately
and will indemnify any Japanese sellers against losses.
```

3

8:22 A.M.: The PMO Conference Room

For a long moment no one moved or spoke. Finally the Prime Minister broke the heavy silence.

"My God. This is what we were just talking about!" His voice conveyed his shock.

Simpson shook his head. "This is the beginning of the end. The Americans and the Europeans will fall into line immediately. They'll cut us off at the knees."

"Can the President do anything?" The PM was grasping at straws.

Carter responded. "In two words, not much. It's the market at work in the U.S., not the government. Unless you can persuade them otherwise, Prime Minister, the American and European financial houses — our main capital investors — will follow the Japanese lead."

"But surely the President . . ."

Ann Carter shook her head negatively. "He can attempt to persuade the market not to pull the rug out from under Canada, but that's about all he can do."

"I'll ask him to do that," the PM said firmly. He slapped his fist on the table. "I mean, Christ, we're the Americans' biggest trading partner!" He shrugged. "It can't hurt to put a little pressure on him — but the President would be putting only one finger in the dyke. We'll need a thousand fingers to stop the dyke from breaking wide open."

"It was all so predictable," Greco said. "We should have seen this coming. Everybody in the financial world could see what was happening starting at the beginning of the nineties and even earlier."

"Maybe the information out of Japan is wrong," Smart suggested.

"It has to be correct," the PM broke in. "Our people in Japan would have checked this one out from top to bottom!"

"Okay." Smart backed off. "Whether or not the news is correct, Prime Minister, you people, you and your government, are going to have to put together the biggest reorganization of government size, structure, and spending this country's ever seen."

"You've got that right," Carter muttered. "We'll have to carry the can."

Simpson lifted his hands, palm up. A sign of frustration. "The problem — there are millions of them — the problem is that, while the country's reorganizing, the interest clock on that nine hundred billion we owe still keeps up its compounding ticking."

The PM looked at the small group around the table. His face was stern. "The key word I'm hearing is *reorganize.* Reorganize the way we run the government, reorganize our spending programs, our overhead."

"Yes, Prime Minister," Ann Carter agreed. "Reorganize government programs so we take in more than we spend on absolutely everything, including interest payments."

"What I want to know," the PM asked angrily, "is, why wasn't reorganization done years ago, ten years ago?"

Simpson looked at him for a long moment. "The *why* doesn't matter now. The fact is, Prime Minister, it wasn't done. The reality is you've got to do it. It's your can to carry — as Minister Carter put it."

"Yeah, and it's filled with goddam worms." A wry smile accompanied the PM's words.

"Throw in a few snakes as well." Carter also smiled at her own repulsive contribution.

"As Deputy Finance Minister new on the job — just nine months," Simpson confessed, "I can tell you I'm still learning. So I've got to have time to put together a plan, a proposal, for your consideration."

"But there isn't time." The PM's voice was signalling his frustration. "You're telling me we can't borrow money, which means we can't pay our bills because we've run out of money. How are we going to pay the civil service, the members of Parliament, the judges, the armed forces, pensions, including OAS and CPP? There are hundreds of thousands of people on the government payroll."

"Over three hundred and sixty thousand. Far too many," Greco said. He couldn't be left out of this discussion.

"And on the provincial and municipal payrolls. Ontario has close to a million people at the government trough," Simpson added. "The provinces are in the same boat we are — even those that aren't running a deficit. They're going to be cut off, too. So every one of the premiers will be at panic stations today trying to figure out what to do."

"The premiers." The PM hadn't considered them. "Of course. As soon as we get our act together — and whether we do or not — I should have a videophone conference call with them. It's almost nine-thirty now. Do you think we'll be ready by four o'clock?" He put the question to the Clerk of the Privy Council.

"Should be okay, sir," Smart said. "You may have the first step of your damage-control program sorted out by that time. If not, you can postpone until the morning." He had selected the words "damage control" carefully. No reaction.

"No later than the morning." The voice of the President of the Treasury Board was calm. "We absolutely must do something today," Carter said. "This is C-Day, remember? The sky is falling. There's going to be a run on the banks. People will be lined up at every bank and trust company branch in Canada trying to get their money out. It's going to be chaos out there, Prime Minister. We can't wait."

The PM turned to his Chief of Staff. "Simon, line up the conference call for four o'clock, but let the premiers know we might have to delay. And find out where the hell the Governor of the Bank of Canada is. She was supposed to be here an hour ago."

"Yes, sir." Camp took his cellular phone to the quiet far corner of the large conference room, took out his telephone-number computer, and began his calls, starting with the Premier of Alberta.

"You were thinking about replacing her, putting in your own person," Greco reminded the PM.

"Too late now. Anyway, she's one of the best economic . . . one of the superior financial brains in the country."

As the PM was saying those words the huge oak door behind him opened just wide enough for the slim form of Jane Smith to slip through, briefcase in hand. Smith was trying to enter as unobtrusively as possible in order not to disturb the participants already engaged in deep discussion. By the look on her pale, round face (looking like a child hoping to avoid being scolded), it was clear that she hoped to sneak in, get to a chair, sit, pull out her working files, and be part of the discussion as if the PM hadn't noticed her arrival. Or her absence.

"Ah, there you are, Governor." The PM managed a momentary smile.

"Sorry, Prime Minister, I got tied up on the phone with the Bankers' Association and then I couldn't get into the building. There's a mob scene. CNN has reported the Japanese pullout — I'm sure you've heard about it. There are thousands of people out there shouting and screaming for action."

"Probably civil servants thinking their world's coming to an end." Carter's tone was derisive.

"It may well be." The PM turned to Greco. "Mario, please bring Jane up to speed on what we've discussed. We'll take a five-minute break. I have to take a trip. When I get back I want to know what we can do to meet our payrolls. Simon, keep going with that conference call and also see what the word is on the wire service. Got to keep track of what's happening. What a mess!"

The PM was back at the table ten minutes later.

As he sat Camp advised, "The conference call is set up for four, sir, conditional as you said."

"Good. I see you've got some stories off the press wire."

"Yes sir. From Toronto the word is that the TTC, the entire transit system, is going to be shut down. As of today the province doesn't have the money to subsidize the operation. The TTC's bank has withdrawn its line of operating credit. None of the other banks will finance the TTC."

"Even with the federal government's guarantee?"

"We haven't given a guarantee for the TTC," Carter told him. "It will be up to the province to ask us first."

"Bullshit. Why wait till then? Simon, call that asshole of a premier in Toronto and tell him we'll guarantee the TTC's line of credit."

"For how long?"

"Until we get this catastrophe under control."

"Before you do that, sir," Camp warned, "you should be ready to deal with another Ontario fire at the same time. Ontario Hydro's in exactly the same fix. The banks have pulled the plug. No money. Ontario Hydro will be forced to cut operations, shut down as much as it can. It can't pay its bills or its employees."

The PM was having difficulty keeping his anger in check. "Christ. Or the interest on its debt, right?"

No one gave an answer to the obvious.

"The Hydro shutdown can't be allowed to happen. The people and industries . . . the whole economic and social structure of Ontario is based on electricity. I mean, my God, if Hydro shuts down . . ." The PM's voice trailed off.

"There's more, Prime Minister," Camp said.

"What is it?"

"Ontario's GO Transit system, which feeds commuters into Toronto, will have to close down. It's totally subsidized by the provincial government. The Montreal feeder rail system is also stopping . . ."

"I don't give a damn about what's happening in Montreal!" the PM shouted, finally losing his temper. "Québec, that marvellous land of long-suffering French-Canadians, has a major share of the responsibility for this shambles, and they've formed their own goddam country!"

Camp, with an unerring sense of timing, broke the tension by quietly refilling the empty coffee cups. For a few minutes only the rattle of teaspoons and clink of china could be heard.

"These things are only the tip of the iceberg." Smith spoke up for the first time. "As I see it, every government-funded or subsidized organization in the country's going to be hit, as well as those in Québec. Every Crown corporation or agency that's into the banks for an operating line of credit is going to have that line pulled and loans called. The banks, all of them, are going to walk away from every level of government in Canada."

The PM put down his cup loudly. "When?"

"Today. They'll make an announcement before noon. They've already told me what they're going to do."

"Over my dead carcass! Parliament controls what the banks can and cannot do. I'll throw some back-to-lending legislation at those bastards that'll make their heads spin." The PM put the question to Smart, the expert, the Clerk of the Privy Council. "Peter, how quickly can I call Parliament?"

"You can do the paperwork today." Smart's answer was without hesitation. "The Governor General will approve the warrant as soon as it's drafted."

"Like in an hour from now?"

"Give me an hour and a half," Smart said. "This is Monday. You can open an emergency session on Wednesday morning."

The PM shook his head emphatically. "That's too late. I want the House and the Senate in session at four o'clock tomorrow afternoon. Simon, check out the availability of the Governor General."

The energetic Camp immediately took his telephone into the corner of the conference room to place a call to Rideau Hall. Nothing seemed to ruffle the efficient Chief of Staff. With his full head of jet black hair and matching black moustache, Camp was a handsome, robust thirty-four-year-old who reminded Ann Carter of that long-gone Clark Gable in his early days. For her, he was a pleasure to look at as he did his "thing" for the PM.

The PM put his next question to the Deputy Minister of Finance. "Paul, what can we do to deal with the bankers right now?"

"First of all, I suggest you get all the bank presidents and CEOs in here for a meeting," Simpson replied. "You'll have to lay down the law. I'm sure we can get them here by two or three this afternoon."

"Let's do it, but that may be a little early. How about four or five? I'll get Simon on that next." The PM turned to his Finance Minister. "Mario, you're a bank man. Do you feel uncomfortable if we take on your old cronies?"

"Sure I'm uncomfortable. I know where they're coming from."

"They have to protect their depositors, right?"

Greco nodded. "Exactly. But I'll back you, Prime Minister. I'm your Finance Minister. On the other hand . . ."

"On the other hand, what?"

"If it gets too hot in the kitchen, I may have to leave."

"I understand perfectly."

Greco had been thinking of a way to deal with the crisis. "Prime Minister, let me say something here. The Governor of the Bank of Canada and I haven't had a chance to discuss this, but the government can print whatever money it can't borrow, and it can use that money internally to pay its employees and pay its domestic bills. But of course printed money won't pay the massive amounts of principal or interest this government or the provinces owe to foreign creditors."

"That's right, we haven't discussed it," Smith replied, looking annoyed. "Printing money is also printing heavy-duty inflation. In my opinion, it's the last resort."

"Do we have any short-term choice?" the PM wanted to know.

"The question deserves a lot more than a split-second answer, Prime Minister." The Governor hedged. "I'd like to get the Bank of Canada's team together with Paul's as soon as possible to try to come up with a better answer than printing money — if there is one."

"You have until three this afternoon. That'll give me an hour before my conference call with the premiers. Is that enough time?"

"No, but we'll do the best we can. I'll call my deputy." She looked at her watch. "Paul, is eleven okay — my conference room?"

"Okay with me." The Deputy Finance Minister turned towards the head of the table. "Is that alright with you, sir? Will we be finished here by then?"

"I don't know. As this day unfolds I may have to turn this place into a goddam war room. Go ahead. Call your meeting for eleven."

Camp closed up his phone and went to the PM's side, saying, "The Governor General has several engagements today, but she'll make herself available to sign whenever the document's ready. We have to take it to Rideau Hall."

"I'll take it myself. Okay, Peter. Get going. Tell your people to prepare the warrant. And tell them to notify every member of the House and Senate *now*. Parliament meets at four tomorrow."

"Shouldn't you wait until the G.-G.'s signature's on the warrant?" Greco asked.

"No. We haven't any time to lose. The G.-G. will sign. Her signature's just a formality. Peter, use the phone in my office."

"I have my own phone with me."

"No. Use my office."

The Clerk of the Privy Council picked up his computer workbook and left the conference room.

"Now, Simon, the next chore, the bankers . . ."

As he spoke Smith took her telephone to the far corner of the room and dialled directly through to her Deputy Governor's private line. She spoke in a low voice. "Victor, as you've heard, we've got a crisis on our hands." In concise terms Smith explained that they would be meeting with Simpson and his people at eleven. "The PM wants answers. We're supposed to put our hands into the magician's top hat and pull out a rabbit."

Barbeau grunted. "There are only two things rabbits are good for. Eating and — "

"Victor! This is not time for — "

"Okay, okay. What are we supposed to do?"

"The PM wants to know what the alternative is to printing money. With the banks already pulling their lines of credit . . ."

"Yeah, after the Japanese pulled their yen plug. So is the only issue what happens if the government goes on a money-printing spree?"

"No, of course not!" Jane's voice reflected impatience. "The real question is, what can this new government do? What steps can they take to avoid an absolute disaster?"

"We've been telling them for years!"

Barbeau was not being very helpful, and it annoyed her.

"But not this government."

"Anyway, nobody's been listening. Well, they're going to listen now, even if it's too late."

"For government it's never too late," she told him sharply. "I'll be there at eleven or as close to eleven as I can make it."

While the easily irritated Jane Smith was talking with Barbeau the PM was giving Camp more instructions. "The next chore is to get those goddam bankers in here. I want them all, the top one or two people from each of them — Royal, Scotiabank, CIBC, Toronto-Dominion, Montreal . . ."

"What about the National?" Camp asked.

"The National is Québec's bank. It's been involved in the negotiations on the debt-asset split."

"That still hasn't been resolved," Carter pointed out unnecessarily. "And it's been four years since Québec went independent."

"Invite National. Sorry. 'Invite' isn't the word. I'm *ordering* all these bastards to be here."

"A couple of them are bitches, Prime Minister." Carter couldn't resist laughing. Her sense of humour always seemed close to the surface. That trait could be both welcome and irritating, depending upon the circumstances. The PM smiled to show he appreciated a moment of levity even in adversity.

"God, you're right!"

"The CEOs at the CIBC and TD are women. And the head of the Canadian Bankers' Association. Surely you have to bring her in, too."

"Of course. Simon, I want them here at five this afternoon. I'll meet them right here." He turned toward Simpson. "And what about drafting the legislation?"

Before he got an answer the PM waved at Camp. "Simon, go and set up that meeting with the bankers. You know what to say."

"What if they tell me to get stuffed?"

"If they're stupid enough to do that, they won't be telling *you* to get stuffed. They'll be telling me and my government. If they do that, they'll have to face the consequences. I'll dump all over them."

Greco was surprised. "Aren't you going to do that anyway?"

"You'd better believe it. But if they refuse to meet today I will dump on them in spades. The back-to-lending legislation I'm going to ask for can be amended very quickly, very easily. Penalties, conditions, nationalization. I could throw the book at them . . . Simon, do it." Camp took his phone to his own far corner of the room. Smith was just finishing in her corner space.

The PM turned back to the Deputy Minister of Finance. "Okay, Paul. Who will draft the bank legislation for us? We need a short act, short as possible. It'll tell the banks they're required by law to restore and maintain the lines of credit and loans to governments, Crown corporations, and government agencies. Will you get it going?"

"I'll get our chief draftsperson started right away. She can use as a model the back-to-work legislation the federal government's been using for decades in strike situations."

"I want the draft on this table by three so I can look at it and run it by the premiers at four."

"You'll have it, sir." Simpson took his telephone out of his briefcase. He stayed in his seat at the conference table but turned his back to be as much out of the PM's earshot as possible. He picked off his senior legislative draftsperson's number from his watch. In a few minutes he turned in his chair to report to the Prime Minister. "The draft will be here at three at the latest, sir."

"Great." The PM's piercing blue eyes went to Carter's sombre face. A fine-looking woman, he thought. Physically and intellectually highly attractive. Yes, what an outstanding person she was. He knew her remarkable record of achievement in her chosen fields of economics and finance. He saw her as a peer of such women as Sylvia Ostry, Marie José Drouin, and Wendy Dobson. What good fortune that she had persevered in the grubby game of politics to be available and willing to take a portfolio, the critically important post of President of the Treasury Board. All the more critical with this foreseeable yet unexpected fiscal calamity.

"Ann, what do you think about all this?"

A chartered accountant who had joined Nesbitt, Burns in 1994, Ann Carter was highly experienced in dealing with capital markets. She was an attractive, career-oriented thirty-nine-year-old woman, unmarried but with several affairs behind her. She had been recruited to run in the Rosedale riding in Toronto in the 1997 election. She had sometimes been nailed by the media as a latter-day Sheila Copps because of her on-call ferocity in the House when her party was the Opposition.

Never at a loss for words, Carter responded in her usual direct fashion: "Frankly, I'm having trouble putting my mind around the enormity of this situation. It's like being invited out for an innocent power lunch and going into a crowded restaurant where everybody's just been massacred by a crazy."

"We're the people in the restaurant," the PM said, going along with her analogy.

"Right, and the crazies are those lying incompetents we've just defeated." She shrugged. "I need a little more time to put my thoughts together. It's all going too fast. We should be going slow. Instead we're running at full tilt. I'll give you my ideas in a few minutes."

"You've probably got them listed already."

"Strange that you should think so, Prime Minister," she answered with a slight smile of satisfaction.

4

10:15 A.M.: The Prime Minister's Office

The muted buzz of Camp's phone could barely be heard amid the noise of the talk around the conference table. Again seated towards the far end, he was waiting for the next instructions from his boss.

It was George, the PM's secretary. "His wife's on the phone from Calgary." After the swearing-in ceremony on Saturday Olivia had flown back home to be with their daughter, who was to be married the following Saturday.

"Does he want to talk to her?" George asked.

"I'll have to ask him."

Camp thought that the PM would probably speak with her even though he was in the middle of this horrendous crisis. The PM enjoyed a close, loving relationship with his lawyer wife of over thirty years. She had been supportive of everything her husband had striven mightily to achieve.

Scratching out a quick note, Camp went to the PM's side and handed it to him. His chief was in full flight on a point he was making, but took the piece of paper and read it while talking.

He stopped in mid-sentence.

"Sorry people. It's my wife on the phone. We have a wedding coming up next Saturday. Our daughter's. I'll take it in my office. I'll be back in a minute."

He was back in three to report. "Everything's okay. My daughter's concerned about what's happening. Should they postpone the wedding, that sort of thing. I said no way. I'll be there come hell or high water. So where were we? Ah yes . . ."

The Prime Minister and leader of the Reform PC party was a Calgary-based corporate lawyer — a sort of amalgam of Peter Lougheed and Preston Manning, at least in looks. But most like Lougheed in forceful, effective political thinking and leadership.

The PM was a flat-stomached, fit, lean fifty-five-year-old. His now grey, naturally curly, full head of hair showed slight thinning at the part. He had an angular, lined face, with thin lips, a ready smile. His jaw protruded just enough to indicate a touch of determinedness sometimes judged to be stubbornness. Bushy dark brows set off minor pouches under dark brown eyes that could at one moment be mischievous or humorous and at the next be hard, even cruel.

He was from a family of modest means whose father was a lifetime sales clerk at Eaton's. By summer work on Alberta and Northwest Territories drilling rigs the PM had financed himself through the University of Alberta's law school. There he won the gold medal for top marks and the first prize in moot court competition.

Then it was onwards and upwards into a prestigious petroleum-industry law firm in Calgary. In less than a decade he had made partner. He specialized in handling hearings before the national and provincial energy boards, while moving onto the boards of directors of corporate clients. Over the years he had made money, a lot of money, not only from his law practice but also from stock options from his directorates and prudent investments from "on the street" rumours that were part of the business lifestyle of oil and gas people in Edmonton and Calgary.

But by the time the recession arrived in the early nineties, this high-profile, super-energized lawyer was fed up and angry about the tax abuses, wasted money, mad spending, and irresponsibility of the politicians and bureaucrats in Ottawa with their anti-West attitudes. He was so unhappy that he told his wife: "To hell with it, I'm going to take those bastards on. I'm going to see if I can find a riding that'll have me. And run as a Progressive Conservative! Been a Conservative all my life, like my Dad before me!" She applauded his decision and joined him on the hustings as often as she could.

In the 1995 by-election, his first time out, he trounced the incumbent in Calgary North. The Reform candidate was a distant third. The NDP woman lost her deposit.

The fledgling MP from Calgary North was introduced to the Speaker and took his seat with the two other PC members just in time to gain a few months' experience in the House of Commons before the traumatic 1997 departure of Québec from the confederation known as Canada.

The separation of Québec was to have a dramatic effect not only on the nature of Canada's form of government but also on the political career of the member from Calgary North.

The Parti Québécois had taken power in Québec after the 1994 election in that province, as it then was. The new Premier of Québec immediately began to implement his party's elaborate plans for separation and independence from Canada.

The PQ Premier was in no hurry. With a substantial majority in the Québec National Assembly he was under no pressure to act precipitately. Instead of calling an early referendum on the question of independence/sovereignty for Québec — yes or no — he chose to lay the legislative framework that would produce a nation state that was de facto independent from Canada but not yet so in law. The referendum would come later. And when it did come it would promise an offer to Canada of a political and economic association *after* a successful vote for independence.

Prior to the referendum the PQ government established mirror entities of those in the federal government's structure, such as: the Bank of Québec; the Armed Forces of Québec (and legislation in which all the military units and their bases located in Québec were to be designated Québec Armed Forces on the date of independence); the enlargement of the Québec Ministry of Transport to include jurisdiction over marine and aeronautics — to name but a few institutions.

By early 1997 the PQ stated that with its successful referendum out of the way it would declare Québec's independence about thirty days after the federal election, which had to take place sometime in '97. The PQ had opened extensive negotiations with the federal government (led as usual by Québecers) in preparation for and leading toward Québec's departure. Central to the negotiations was the difficult issue of a formula for Québec's assumption of a share of the enormous, escalating national debt. By the spring of 1997 that issue had not been resolved.

The then federal PM called his election for Monday, May 12, 1997. The ruling party (now with a leader from Ontario) won, but with a slim majority. The Reform party had its forty-five ridings, while the PCs came back with eighty-eight, in effect replacing the Bloc Québécois. The Bloc had disappeared from the House of Commons when the goal of Québec's independence had been certain of success in the upcoming referendum.

As for the NDP, they held on to only six seats in 1997.

As promised, Québec's Declaration of Independence was made on June 24, 1997, St-Jean-Baptiste Day. The recorded vote in the earlier referendum was 62.31 percent for independence/sovereignty, a smashing victory for the PQ. At high noon on St-Jean-Baptiste Day the premier stood in the crowded National Assembly to read Québec's unilateral Declaration of Independence. The Declaration was then approved by a unanimous vote of all members of the Assembly.

The deed was done.

In that instant the independent Republic of Québec was born. The Premier was transformed into being the Prime Minister of Québec. The new state would continue with the parliamentary form of government under a president appointed by the government of the day.

That moment of Québec's independence had a significant impact on the face of the federal government of Canada. The Québec-based members of the ruling Cabinet, including the Prime Minister, had just lost their electoral right to be seated in the House of Commons of Canada or to serve in the cabinet.

In the same way, the leader of the federal Progressive Conservative party, also a Québecer, was deprived of his seat in the Commons. He immediately resigned as leader of the PC caucus and as leader of the national PC party.

Another phenomenon also occurred: the hordes of Québécois employees of the federal government, who until Québec independence had had a numerical stranglehold on the top-to-bottom mandarinate positions in Ottawa, were dismissed from the Canadian civil service.

The PQ had cried foul, claiming that all Québécois were entitled to dual citizenship and therefore the Québécois civil servants in the federal government were entitled to keep their jobs and run Canada's bureaucracy.

But the party in power in Ottawa, with the unanimous support of the PCs, Reform, and the NDP, said absolutely not. There would be no dual citizenship, period!

A PC leadership convention, convened by the PC party executive, was held in Winnipeg in August of 1997. From it, and to his own surprise, the lawyer from Calgary North emerged as the new leader. He won on his track record and his dedication to rebuilding the party as a potent political force in a unilingual Canada.

A short time after the convention, and before the new Parliament was to be convened, the new leader of the PC party made his move. He proposed a coalition with the Reform party, which, among other things, was still struggling with its right-wing, mainly Western focus and image.

The timing was right. The Reform party leader was tired and disillusioned by the neverending political mayhem of Ottawa, as were many of the significant members of his caucus. Instead of a coalition, he proposed a merger of the two parties into the Reform PC party.

On the basis of the number of members each brought to the new party, it followed that the leader of the PCs would become the head of the merged party and Leader of His Majesty's Loyal Opposition in the House of Commons.

That was the scenario in the House when the new Parliament, now operating in the English language only, convened on Monday, September 15, 1997.

The Prime Minister, the new leader of the governing party, who had replaced the departed Québécois Prime Minister, was from a riding in Metro Toronto, his main political power base. That base had been badly eroded by the resurgent PC forces in the election results. It was an erosion that had given the opposition PC leader much encouragement. It was the trigger that had moved him to propose the reform coalition and to accept the merger counterproposal.

He was certain that the new government would be highly vulnerable in the election that would have to take place in 2001 or even earlier. In that certainty the new leader of the Reform PC party was absolutely correct.

By November 2000 the government was in a state of disarray in all aspects, but there were three major problems confronting it. The most ignored as to action, yet the most talked about, was the apparently unstoppable cancerous growth of the annual deficit. Equally ignored yet also heavily discussed were the gigantic, ever-increasing national debt and its voracious consumption of intolerable payments of interest. When the now defeated party had first come to power in 1994 it had recognized these three growing problems. All were clearly visible, like performers spotlighted on a dark stage. Then there was the bloated supporting performer also spotlighted on the blackened stage: government spending.

At the beginning of its tenure in 1994 the government had made much noise about how it would direct the main performers and the supporting actor. What drastic measures it would take in order to get all four off the national stage! It required draconian spending-cut actions that would have sliced through every government department and social program like a scythe slashing through a field of dry, golden overripe wheat. But those actions were politically unacceptable to the caucus of the party in power.

In November of 2000 a beleaguered, weary prime minister, his majority lost in late fall by-elections, called upon the Governor General to ask her to dissolve Parliament. The general election was called for Tuesday, January 16, 2001.

The federal election campaign that followed was a tough and dirty one.

During that campaign members of the Cabinet performed like masters of sleight of hand and mouth. They trumpeted that by their ceaseless efforts the annual deficit was under control, yea, was even decreasing. They sang the words unisonally like Toronto's marvellous Mendelssohn Choir. Their politically lyrical rendition sent a message to every voter that the party was as close as a beaver's twitching whisker to balancing the federal budget, thus eliminating the dreadful deficits that had been part and parcel of the Trudeau and Mulroney years.

Even the Reform PC policy people and that party's leader were somewhat taken in by what their in-power opponents were saying. During the campaign the government party bigwigs were out on the hustings like cure-all snake-oil salesmen in the old days, pitching to slack-jawed innocents who had no apparent reason to disbelieve what the pitchmen were telling them about the magic of their fiscal products.

Then it was done; the election was over. The Reform PC party had won with a substantial majority.

After the Saturday swearing-in of the Cabinet had come the time for the new Prime Minister to gather in his hands the countless reins of government power. Some of those reins were like thick and heavy leather for the strongest teams of horses. Other reins were so thin and wispy it was hard to tell they were in hand, let alone to what remote, many-legged government body they were attached.

Now it was C-Day, Monday, January 29, 2001, when all the sleights of hand, the misrepresentations, the false interpretations of numbers, the deceits of those now gone from power, had been revealed to the new Reform PC Prime Minister and his Cabinet. The financial catastrophe had struck them with the appalling force of an unheralded Silkworm missile. It had exploded on target, but the rattling sound of the rocket's approach was heard not before but after its impact — heard only, of course, by those who survived its detonation.

By mid-morning of C-Day the PM was in high gear, listening to the ideas and suggestions of this team, analysing his options, making decisions.

"We haven't got the time to start putting blame on those lying assholes responsible for this mess," the Prime Minister made it emphatically clear. "We can do that later. So, okay. We're calling Parliament into session. That's underway. We're getting the bankers in here at five. Jane, you and the finance team, Paul and his people, are meeting at eleven."

"And we're back here at three."

"With some intelligent recommendations."

"You'll have to be the judge of that, sir."

"What we have to do *right now* is get a handle on the damage that is being done to our economy, to our financial system, to the whole goddam country. Being done even as we speak. We've got to get the best advice, absolutely the best advice, we can find anywhere in the world on how we can cope with this." The PM looked around the table. "Any suggestions?"

"Yes." Carter's response was immediate. "Get on the phone to the President of the United States. You've already had your meet-and-greet TV phone conference with him."

"Yeah. On Saturday. He's a remarkable guy. Last night I thought about calling him, but I wasn't sure it was a good idea. Now I do. Are you suggesting I ask for money?"

"Not yet. Say you want to invite Al Weinstock, the Chairman of the Federal Reserve Board, to come up to Ottawa for a discussion. He's my counterpart in the United States. I know him, he's brilliant. Went through the Mexico crisis. You should get him to come up here this evening if he can make it. Weinstock can bring his best people with him. We need no more than one day of bludgeoning their brains."

"Not picking?"

"Too late for that."

Wasting no time, the PM turned to Camp. "Simon, get the President's Chief of Staff on the phone. Tell him it's an emergency. He'll already know. The whole bloody world knows."

Simon went to his corner, dialing. The PM went on: "Tell him we'll send one of our jets down for Weinstock wherever he is."

Smart was back at the table. He responded. "We've only got three government jets, Challengers, left in operation. I'll have to see what's available."

"Simon can do that. Simon?"

Camp was still in his corner on the telephone but not speaking into it. "Yes, sir, I'll do that. I'm trying to get through to Washington, to Spratt, the President's Chief of Staff."

"Has he answered yet?"

"No."

"Tell him I desperately need Al Weinstock, the Fed Chairman, and his team up here, today if possible. Will the President agree, or should I talk to him? Got that?"

"Yes, sir."

"Tell him we'll send an aircraft down to Washington to pick them up. It can leave here in an hour —if we have one, and Simon . . ."

"Sir?"

"If you can't get through, at least leave a message, then do three things. One: tell my secretary to put the President or Spratt through if they call back. Two: find out if we have a government plane available to go down immediately to pick up Weinstock. And three: hold all my calls on pain of death unless it's the Governor General or the Chief Justice. Or unless my secretary thinks, get that, *thinks* whoever's calling just *has to* speak with me."

"Yes, sir," young Camp muttered as he held the phone to his ear in his corner of the long, artisan-carved stone chamber, impatiently waiting for

Spratt to come on the line.

Carter decided it was time to make her move. She passed copies of a three-page document to the PM and everyone at the table saying, "This is an inventory of what I think we have to do in the short term.

"Some of these measures are draconian, to say the least. It's like trying to cure the patient by cutting off his arms and legs, then inviting him to celebrate by making love with his grandmother."

"Good god, Ann! Where in hell do you come up with those horrible images of yours?" Mario Greco said it for everyone.

"I dredge them up from my how-to-get-their-attention handbook."

"You're the author?"

"I'm still writing it."

"Okay, Ann," the PM cut in. "You've got our attention."

"Good. These aren't necessarily in order of importance. I think you can read my writing. Didn't have time to get this typed."

"It's okay. We can read it. Go ahead."

"Fine. I'll go through these one at a time. One: the federal civil service will be cut by one-third over the next six months, with an immediate termination of 25 percent across the board."

"Wait a minute, Minister," Smart reacted. "The cut in the civil service has already happened. When Québec went independent, all the Francophone federal employees in Québec went with it. Plus all the Québecers in the civil service located in Ottawa and outside Québec."

"Give me some numbers," Carter demanded.

"Total number of federal government employees — these are ballpark — before the Québec exodus was in the range of 360,000, with about 73,000 of those being Francophone. Of those, about 60,000 were Québecers. They got the axe so we have 295,000 people left on the federal payroll.

"So the civil service was cut by about 15 percent in 1996 and '97 with the Québecers gone. Are you talking about firing a third of what's left, 98,000 people?" To Smart the proposition was unbelievable.

"Absolutely, right across the board." Carter was emphatic. "Give them termination notice plus one week's pay for every year of service."

"But we're broke. That'll cost us billions," Simpson protested.

"In the short term, yes, about six billion dollars. But in the long run the savings will be enormous. A big whack at the deficit."

"Where will we find six billion?"

The Prime Minister answered Simpson's question. "As the lady said, print it."

"We haven't decided to do that," Greco protested. "Jane's and Paul's people are going to talk about that later this morning."

"I know that," Carter said. "Believe me, Prime Minister, they're going to tell you to print it."

"What about the pensions of the people you're going to terminate?" Smart asked.

"They'll take that part of the pensions they've paid into according to length of service. But only what they've paid. The pension pot is not funded — which means it has to be funded out of general tax revenues — so no entitlement beyond what they've paid in."

Carter waited a moment, then went on. "As of today, all existing federal government pensions must be cut back so they match the extent to which the pension pot is fully funded. On top of that, no more indexing for inflation."

Both the Clerk of the Privy Council and the Deputy Minister of Finance began sputtering with fury at the same time. Smart got it out first.

"Jesus Christ, you can't do that! Some government pensions will be cut in half. Maybe even more."

Carter's smile was cruel. "Tell me, top civil servant, is your reaction so violent because your personal pension is about to be gored?" Her face went hard. "Pity."

His face beet red with fury, Smart was about to retort, when the PM cut him off. "Okay, Peter, cool it." He spoke again to Camp, who was still waiting for Spratt to come on the line.

"Simon, you'll have to assume that Weinstock will be coming. He'll bring a team of maybe four. That's a guess. Book some rooms at the Chateau."

"Somebody should go to the airport to meet them," Carter said. "What about Oscar?"

"Yeah, Oscar would be a good choice." Oscar Fleming was the newly designated Minister of Foreign Affairs. He was a dapper sixty-year-old tenured professor of political science at the University of British Columbia. "He'll make Weinstock feel important and comfortable."

Camp said, “I know where to find him.”

“Do it. Gimme a sheet of paper, Ann.” When it was in front of him on the table the PM, pen in hand, said, “Okay, this is the way the schedule’s shaping up.”

He began to write in his vertical, highly legible hand, saying what he was putting on paper so that everybody could hear and add any input if necessary.

“It’s now what — ten-thirty. That gives us a half-hour until Paul and Jane are out of here for their meeting in the Bank’s conference room.”

Greco said, “I’d like to make a suggestion about that.”

“Okay.”

“Now that we have word that the Japanese have pulled the rug, we have to rethink our approach. We don’t have to speculate about what foreign lenders are going to do.”

“Right.”

“That means we have no choice: we have to bring in a new hack-and-slash budget and it has to be ready for the printer tomorrow night at six at the latest if we’re going to have five hundred copies the next morning. I don’t think anything useful’s going to be served if the Governor and my Deputy Minister go off for a two- or three-hour private meeting.”

“So what d’you suggest?”

“I think they should stay right here. They can tell their top people to be at their desks, available for immediate comment or research input by phone or fax. But Jane and Paul should stay right here and all of us should get on with trying to put together a budget.”

“Anybody disagree with that?” The PM looked around the table. No response. “Okay, that’s what we’ll do.”

Camp broke in to report that a Challenger jet was available and would depart as soon as the order was given.

“The next thing is what — the conference call with the premiers at four, after I get the warrant signed.”

“You’re looking for the draft of the bank legislation before three.”

“Right. The bankers are going to be here at five. And we’ll have them all in right here. They can sit at the far end of the table, the whole gang, and you can all stay and put your five cents’ worth in.”

"It has to be a dollar's worth. A dollar today is equal to five cents twenty years ago." That remark by Carter elicited a few smiles. "And now that we're going to have to print money, I mean *really* print money, the inflation rocket's going to be launched like we've never seen it before."

"Yes, Ann," the PM said. "Then there's Weinstock and his people. I've got them down tentatively for eight tonight and tomorrow morning at nine if need be."

"The need will be, count on it." Greco was resigned to the crisis grind that lay ahead.

"We'll see. But what if Weinstock can't — or won't — come? Maybe he's on vacation, or sick or whatever. We may have to deal with this mess ourselves."

Carter was in emphatic agreement. "We've got the talent and the experience. I think you should do what you're doing, Prime Minister. Set an agenda right now and get on with it. If and when Weinstock gets here, he can comment on what we've done."

The PM liked what he was hearing. "I agree."

The next minutes were spent in discussing and listing the items that had to be dealt with.

Finally the PM declared, "Okay, here's the agenda, and it's enough to choke a goddam horse:

(1) Prepare a press release and arrange a PM's press conference; purpose to calm and assure the markets and the people of Canada.
(2) Steps to be taken by Treasury, Finance and Bank of Canada to print money, supply money to cover all immediate government operations. Payrolls are top priority.
(3) Prepare new budget with massive program cuts across the board."

Carter picked up the document she had already passed around. "My cut proposals are right here. We can use these as a starting point and go from there."

"Okay."

"I promise you, Prime Minister, there's going to be a flood of blood on the floor. Yeah, a flood of blood."

The PM nodded. "The objective is for us to avoid being drowned in it. The next item on the agenda:

(4) The back-to-lending bank legislation."

Simpson said, "If you can persuade the banks, coerce them, pressure them this morning to restore the loans and lines of credit — maybe a conference call — if you can do that, the legislation may not be necessary."

Greco responded, "I think we should have the legislation ready anyway. It'll show them we mean business. They're liable to agree now and change their minds as soon as the next piece of bad news arrives."

Telephone to his ear, Camp walked toward the PM, saying, "Spratt is putting you right through to the President."

The Prime Minister took the phone and waited.

The President's voice was deep and resonant, reminiscent of the commanding, distinctive sound of the respected African American actor James Earl Jones. "Good morning, Prime Minister. Hear you have a big problem up there. A big problem. I understand the Japanese have just cut you off at the financial knees."

The American was at the beginning of his second term as President of the United States. He had been the Republican vice presidential candidate in the November 1996 elections. He and the presidential nominee working closely as a team had defeated their Democrat counterparts by a substantial margin.

In June of 1997 the new Republican President, a man nearing his mid-seventies, died suddenly of a massive heart attack.

At that moment the United States had its first African American president. So the new PM was dealing with a man in the White House who had been in power since 1997, was toughened by his three and a half years of dealings with a Congress that was reluctant even though it was Republican-controlled in both the Senate and the House of Representatives.

The Prime Minister knew that the American had a good grasp of the ramifications of the separation of Québec, of the enormity of Canada's federal debt and the potential for a financial crisis for the neighbour to the north.

"Financial knees is an understatement, Mr. President."

"More like at the genitals and the heart?"

"Both at the same time."

There was a sympathetic grunt from the Oval Office resident. "What can

I do for you?"

"I need, urgently need, advice on how to handle this situation. My people tell me I should ask you to send Al Weinstock up here along with his top advisors."

"I'm not sure Weinstock needs any clearance from me. But, sure, I'd be happy to authorize him to go. Can't order him to go, but I can authorize. You can tell him that."

"Wonderful. We'll track him down right away. One other thing, Mr. President." The PM mustered his most persuasive tone. "Is there anything you can do to influence Canada's bond and security holders in the States to not cut us off like the Japanese have done?"

There was no immediate response as the President turned that question over in his analytical mind. "I'll have to give that more thought. Yes, indeed, I'll have to think about it." He paused. "If the truth were known, I think it's too late. Wall Street already has the Japanese news. The lending institutions, the financial houses, will be reacting to it even as we speak. Neither Weinstock nor I have any power over whether the marketplace lends or doesn't lend to a friendly power."

"True. But if asked, could you say that it's in the interests of the United States — you know, in the interests of its commerce, trade, and prosperity — that the government of Canada should continue to be given financial support by American lenders?"

"Maybe I could do that. I have a press conference coming up shortly at eleven-fifteen. I'm sure there'll be questions about Canada's . . ."

"Catastrophe."

Another White House grunt. "Yeah. That's a good word."

"We'll send a plane down for Weinstock immediately. We'll put him and his team up at the Chateau — it's our best hotel."

"The Chairman would expect nothing less. My Chief of Staff will track him down now. Then he'll call you with Weinstock's number. Got that?"

The PM was within a split second of saying, "Yes, sir" in response to the former four-star general, Chairman of the Joint Chiefs of Staff, and now President. But the Canadian caught himself in time. It would be an embarrassing loss of face to say sir to his equal. "Yes, Mr. President. And I thank you for your support."

The President's Chief of Staff called back within fifteen minutes with Weinstock's office, home, and mobile phone numbers.

"Try the mobile phone," Spratt advised Camp. "The guy's probably on a golf course somewhere. He's a golf fanatic."

Camp took his advice. After two rings of the mobile phone a guttural New York–accented voice answered, "Weinstock here. Wait one minute. I'm just addressing the ball on the first tee."

There was no chance for Camp to respond. There was silence for a few seconds. Then he could clearly hear the solid "whack" as Weinstock's club hit the ball. That was followed by "Shit! I hooked it." A distant "Yeah, but you're okay" was heard, to which Weinstock replied, "Bullshit. I shoulda been right down the goddam fairway."

Another brief silence. Then, "Weinstock here. Sorry about the delay. So who's calling?"

Camp identified himself, quickly explained that the Prime Minister of Canada wanted to speak with him about the Japanese announcement and the crisis. Just before he took the phone to the PM, Camp asked, "Where are you?"

"I'm on the first tee at a fantastic golf course put together by a Canadian, Gordon Gray. It's Loxahatchee, near Jupiter, Florida. Got Joe Namath in my foursome. He lives here, the lucky bastard. And a couple of other crazy Canadians. One of them sells Christmas tree lights . . ."

The distant voice was heard again: "John Rice."

"Yeah, John Rice. And Chuck Magwood. Built the Skydome in Toronto. So let me talk to your boss. What's his name?"

Camp answered that question as he arrived beside the PM, then handed him the phone.

The PM explained the Japanese situation about which Weinstock had been informed by his own people as soon as the news arrived in Washington.

"So what do you want from me?"

"Two things. First I *urgently* need the best advice you and your team can give me about what steps we can take to stop our country from going right down the financial tubes."

The PM could hear the background chatter of the other golfers and the whack of the drivers against the balls.

"Well, my friend, you're already in the throat of the tube and hanging onto the lip by your fingertips. Pretty tough for me to give you advice over the goddam phone. You say you talked to the President?"

"Yeah. I asked him for approval to get you and your best team up here right away."

"What did he say?"

"He said it would be up to you. He couldn't tell you what to do."

"Did he sound negative?"

"No."

The whirring sound of Weinstock's golf cart came clearly through the phone as the foursome moved off down the first fairway.

"If Canada crashes, if our biggest trading partner goes down the drain, it's bad news for the U.S." Weinstock was thinking out loud. "We have our national interest at stake here. Washington should be doing everything it can to help. And that includes me and the Fed. So how do I get up to Ottawa?"

"One of our government jets will be on the way within the hour. What's your closest airport?"

"West Palm."

"Finish your eighteen holes. The aircraft should be there by two, three at the outside. The crew, my staff, somebody will give you an estimated time of arrival."

"But clothes, man. It must be cold as an Eskimo's icebox up there. And snow. Here I am in Florida, dressed for eighty-five degrees."

The PM had to smile. "On the way back north the aircraft can stop in Washington to pick up whoever you want to bring with you. Can somebody pick up your winter clothes at your house?"

"Yeah. I'll talk to my wife. Ruth can get that organized."

"Any idea how many people will come with you?"

"Well, I don't know." There was a moment of silence from the other end of the phone. "The fewer the better, I'd say. In fact, probably just one. Abigail Black, my director of international studies. She monitors disasters in other countries, how they've handled financial crises: Mexico, Argentina, Brazil, New Zealand."

"And now Canada."

"Abbi is one of the best-looking women you'll ever see, and one of the smartest. She got her Ph.D. at the London School of Economics, spent ten years with the IMF before I stole her."

"Great. She sounds like just the person we need."

"I'll start tracking her down now. I'm sure she'll be easy to locate. Gimme your phone and fax numbers so I can give you any other details as they develop. By the way, I can only give you until tomorrow at four. I'm having dinner at the White House with the President. Black tie state dinner for the King of England."

"Right. I heard about that. He rarely comes to Canada."

"You're not invited?"

"No, and with this mess on my hands I couldn't have gone anyway."

"Just a minute. I'm away."

The PM could hear the whirring of the golf-cart motor stop, the rattling of the clubs as Weinstock selected one. Silence for a few seconds, then the sound of a solid crack, probably an iron, followed by the chairman's grunted words of satisfaction.

"That's better. I'm on the green about fifteen from the hole." The golf cart started up again. "I assume you people are busting your asses trying to put together a new cut-everything-to-the-bone budget?"

"That's the plan," the PM replied. "We're working on it right now."

"Good! And you'd better open the IMF and World Bank doors. At least knock on them to let them know you're coming." Weinstock gave him the names of the key players at both institutions. "You should go there yourself, see them face to face, as soon as possible. Wednesday. Thursday at the outside."

The PM looked down at his agenda. There was little room to manoeuvre. "I'm recalling Parliament and the opening session's tomorrow at four. New budget will be presented Wednesday morning. The only time I can go is tomorrow morning, if I can get an appointment that quickly."

"Yeah, go ahead, set it up. Leave me and Abbi to work with your Finance Minister and whoever else. You could fly down to Washington and be back by two."

The PM saw another advantage to making the trip: "Then I could work the IMF and World Bank meetings into my budget statement."

"Why not?" Weinstock said. "By the way, this won't come as any surprise to those bastards: They've been watching Canada's debt and deficits for a long time. They knew this was gonna happen."

"So when I arrive they'll tell me they've been waiting for Canada to show up at their door."

"And they'll lay it all out for you, tell you what you're gonna have to do. And I can tell you, Prime Minister, it's gonna hurt real bad. Like having your arm cut off without having any anaesthetic. It's gonna be real bad."

Again the noise of the golf-cart motor stopped. "Gotta go and sink this putt for a birdie. Have your people let me know what time the plane will be at West Palm. Namath's just hit his first putt. Hey, too bad, Joe. God, is this green ever fast!" The line went dead.

5

10:46 A.M.: The Prime Minister's Office

The PM handed the phone back to Camp, saying to everyone at the table, "Okay. You heard my end of the conversation. He said I have to get down to the International Monetary Fund and the World Bank as soon as possible. I've only got tomorrow morning to do it. Any comments?"

Greco looked at the other faces, waiting to see who would speak first. No one appeared ready. "I think it's absolutely essential. Seeing the IMF is critical. I'd leave the World Bank until later."

"Ann?" The PM looked expectantly at the President of the Treasury Board.

"I agree. By the time this day's finished we'll have trimmed a lot of meat off the budget bones. And with any luck we'll have had a session with Weinstock. Who's he bringing with him?"

The PM told them what he knew about Abigail Black.

"Sounds good," said Carter, not afraid of the competition.

"Weinstock gave me the name of the IMF man, the Executive Director, Aubrey Farnsworth."

"I met him the last time I was in Washington," Simpson interjected. "Great guy and, believe it or not, he's a Canadian!"

"I don't know whether that's good or bad," the PM retorted. "Simon, see if you can get Mr. Farnsworth for me. Weinstock thinks he'll be expecting a call."

Which was exactly the case. It took only a few minutes to set up a meeting for eight o'clock the next morning at the IMF headquarters. It would be with the Managing Director, Leif Tromso. Farnsworth would have a car at Dulles airport at eight. The PM and Camp would be back in the air heading for Ottawa by eleven, which would put him back in his office by one-thirty, two at the latest.

"You people can put together the basics of the Governor General's opening remarks in the Senate and mine in the House. Ann, can you take that on? Just rough ideas. I'll have to write it myself."

"Sure."

"And Mario, you and Ann will handle the meeting with Weinstock in the morning?" It was more of a direction than a question.

"No problem."

The PM consulted his agenda. "Okay. Next, we prepare a press release and set up a press conference. Then we'll go directly to the new budget, and we'll use your paper" — he looked at Carter — "as a starting point."

She nodded. The hint of a smile on her face said she was pleased.

"I drafted a press release while you were on the phone with Weinstock," Smart announced. "It's one page."

"Good. Go ahead and read it."

"Okay. Stop me if —"

"No, we'll hear it, then take it from there."

Smart cleared his throat and began to read: "'The Prime Minister of Canada' — and your name goes in here, sir — 'has announced this morning that in response to today's drastic actions of the government and financial institutions of Japan in withdrawing all loans and credit to the Government of Canada, the federal Cabinet under the Prime Minister's leadership is preparing a new budget designed to immediately and dramatically cut federal spending over a short period of time.

"'The Prime Minister and his new government have no alternative but to slash federal spending in all social sectors, transfer payments to provinces, defence, transportation, foreign aid, and spending programs in all government departments.

"'The Prime Minister expressed regret that within a few days of his taking office he and the nation are confronted with a financial catastrophe caused by the inability of the previous administrations over the past two decades to take control of government spending.

"'The Prime Minister and his Cabinet are pledged to do all things necessary to rectify the situation and to restore the world's international money markets' confidence in Canada.

"'Parliament is being recalled for an emergency session commencing at 4 p.m. tomorrow in order that the government can place before the House and Senate legislative measures and a budget designed to implement the absolutely necessary massive spending-cut policy.'"

Smart stopped reading. He looked at the PM, waiting for his comments.

"I'd buy most of that just as it stands. Simon, give it to my secretary. Ask him to cut a draft and make copies for all of us. While you're at it, tell the press gallery the release is coming and I'll hold a press conference at two this afternoon."

"At the Press Club?"

"No. It'll be a scrum right here. In the corridor outside the House entrance."

"They won't like that. They'll expect you over there."

"New Prime Minister, new game rules."

"Yes, sir." Camp left the room, his telephone and Smart's draft in his left hand, while the fingers of the right hand were punching in the press gallery's number.

"So now we're back to the number-three item on the agenda, the budget, which is really the number-one item. Ann?"

Carter took her list and also took charge. "We're ready to discuss cutting the civil service."

"And the pension reductions."

"Abatements. That's a softer word. Although we discussed the civil service cuts and pensions, we didn't reach a conclusion."

"Try consensus, Ann, instead of conclusion." The PM spoke softly. "If there's a consensus on a point, I'll make the conclusion."

Carter acknowledged his position with a slight movement of her head. "So let's start with the reduction of the civil service."

The battles began. The bureaucrats took full part, arguing their cases with no shrinking or deferring to the Cabinet ministers — except to the PM whenever he had to step in to control the debate or, as he had put it, to make the conclusion on a point.

By half past eleven a conclusion had been reached by the Prime Minister on the extent to which the deficit had to be reduced in the short term. The short term was to be either a year or eighteen months. He opted for the longer period.

As far as he was concerned, the true short term was Wednesday morning when the budget speech would be delivered. It was that budget to which the world's financial and monetary analysts and gurus would react.

Would those ephemeral, never-seen wielders of computer power be convinced that the bankrupt government of Canada had put a proposal on the table that was credible? Would they believe it? Would the tea leaves in the budget cup give the right signals? Signals sufficient to allow foreign investors, perhaps even the Japanese, to stay with Canada, not pull the rug?

For the PM and his tight few around the conference table the sole overriding question was, how do we shape the budget to send the right signals?

Also by a quarter past eleven a consensus had been reached on the question, should the cuts be of a certain percentage for every department across the board? Or should the surgeon's knife (Governor Jane Smith had said "substitute 'hacksaw' for 'knife'") be used ministry by ministry?

The consensus? Ministry by ministry.

The first to be laid on the surgical table was the prime candidate. It was prime emotionally and logically. It was the once-vaunted (in real and cold wartime) armed forces. The military no longer had a foreign enemy, just domestic — themselves. Yes, there was the wonderful task of peacekeeping under the aegis of the unbelievably inept and chaotic direction of the United Nations. The U.N. was the world body brought initially to life largely by that visionary Canadian and, later, prime minister, Lester Bowles Pearson. Then there was Canada's now-fictional involvement in NATO, the North Atlantic Treaty Organization, that rudderless, U.S.-dominated European structure. Yes, and NORAD, the American-controlled North American Aerospace Defence structure designed to protect the continent from bomber and nuclear-armed intercontinental ballistic missile incursions. And yes, the naval requirement for defence against foreign fisheries, "enemy" submarines having died in port for lack of fuel, be it nuclear- or petroleum-based.

The PM started the defence discussion by asking, "What's the military budget for this fiscal year?"

"Nine billion plus." Carter had the answer. "Same as it was in the mid-nineties, but without inflation added since then."

"Okay. That's today's number. Before we get into defence, let me make one thing clear. I don't want any philosophical discussion about whether Canada needs a military force. Take it as a given that we do."

"Just like Québec," Greco snorted. "They've got their own goddam army, navy, and air force."

"Are you suggesting we should keep ours so we can defend ourselves in case Québec attacks us?" Carter was joking. Mostly.

Twenty minutes later, with no consensus on defence, the PM made his decision.

"Next is Old Age Security and the Canada Pension Plan. And while we're at it, unemployment insurance and health care."

"Holy Christ, PM!" Smart reacted. "You're dealing with dynamite if you —"

"Try a nuclear explosion. I realize that, Peter. We have no choice and you know it."

"Yeah, but we've got millions of senior citizens out there who have nothing but their OAS payments, as well as millions of people on UI and welfare. We can't just cut them off!"

The PM raised his hand to contradict Smart. "It's not a question of cutting them off. It's cutting back. That's what we have to do. I've given all of you my deficit goal. Now we have to get the puck into that net." He turned toward his Treasury Board President.

"We'll do the OAS first. Universality. Payouts to taxpayers who don't need it."

"We've had the clawback in place for years. But maybe the clawback threshold's too high." Smith was thinking about her aunt in one of Canada's finest charitable homes for the aged. Aunt Helen had been in Thompson House in Don Mills for over ten years. That's all Aunt Helen had, her Old Age Security payment. If that meagre amount was cut back — all of it except a sustenance spending-money bit — Thompson House and the Ontario government that subsidized the place probably couldn't keep her.

"If the threshold was lowered to, say, twenty-five thousand, then people who really don't need OAS money can be used to keep payments up for the needy," Smith reasoned.

"That's a good starting point," the PM agreed, "but only a starting point. Keeping in mind my deficit target, is lowering the clawback threshold really enough?"

When the OAS controversy was put to rest — again by the PM's conclusion — the group moved on to unemployment insurance.

"I've gotta tell you, Prime Minister, this UI thing has been the biggest scam ever." Simpson was back in the fray. "People rip off the system from one end of the country to another. Why work when you can collect UI . . ."

"Or welfare?" Greco asked.

Simpson nodded vigorously. "Yeah, or welfare."

"But UI is supposed to be funded by employers and workers," Smith said.

"Supposed to be, but it's costing us, you heard the number, 25.2 billion a year," Simpson reiterated.

The PM stepped in. "What we have to do is simple. We can't borrow money to pay UI or OAS. We're cut off. Period. No international credit. Period. I'll say it again: to get that credit restored, to get *any kind* of a line of credit restored, we have to come up with a credible budget made with an axe, a big, sharp one, not with a delicate pair of nose-hair scissors."

He pulled at his loosened tie, then put his half-glassed spectacles on the table as he looked into the tired eyes of his reluctant decision-makers.

"Look," he said, "I don't enjoy this any more than you do, but we've got to be ruthless. It's axe time, so let's get on with it."

The message couldn't have been clearer. Before noon the OAS and UI cuts were made, both by consensus. No need for the PM to wield his personal axe.

Camp's phone rang quietly. He still had the ringer almost muted. It was the PM's secretary, George Pearce. "Simon, the warrant has just arrived. You know, for the recall of Parliament."

"Great."

Camp wrote a note and took it to the PM. It was read, then acknowledged with a nod and scribbled words on the note: "Tell the G.-G.'s people I'll be there at twelve, give or take five minutes."

Camp retreated to his corner, dialing the Rideau Hall number as he went. In less than a minute he caught his boss's eye and gave him a thumbs-up sign as he headed back to the table. Midway, the quick-learning young Chief of Staff stopped and turned back to his corner to make another call. "George. We're set to arrive at Rideau Hall at noon. Make sure the car's at the Speaker's entrance right away. I want him out the back door. Speaker's entrance, right?"

The PM rose and straightened his tie. "I have to leave now," he told the group. "The warrant's here for the recall of Parliament. I'm due at Rideau Hall at twelve." He looked at his watch again and started for the door.

"Give our best wishes to the Honourable Pearl." Greco smiled. "She's another Manitoba jewel in Canada's crown — without the fleur-de-lis."

"Okay. I should be back by one. Simon'll get some food in for you. Tell him what you want."

Camp asked, "Will you be having lunch here too, sir? If so, what'll I get for you?"

"What I'd like is Japanese emperor crab and a knife to put in the Emperor's heart." The PM gave a half-hearted smile. "If I get back in time, I'll have a green salad with vinaigrette and a glass of white wine."

"We'll make do with ham-on-rye, hold the mayo!" The PM, not sure who muttered that remark, ignored it and turned to Carter.

"Please carry on. Ann, it's your list, so you're the acting chair."

"What would you like us to tackle next, Prime Minister?"

"The transfers to the provinces. There are three major items. Give me the numbers, Ann."

She riffled through her papers to find the sheet she wanted. "Here we are. The first is CAP, the Canada Assistance Plan, in at ten billion this year. The next is EPF, Established Program Financing, at 16.6 billion. And last and, in my opinion, totally obsolete, is equalization at 13.5 billion. Even with Québec out it's 13.5."

"Do you have a breakout of all the numbers under each of the three headings?"

"Yes. And copies for everyone."

"Good." Another look at his watch. "I really have to go. Have all of those items decided by the time I get back." His voice had a sufficient hint of the facetious.

"Prime Minister, you've gotta be kidding!" Smart said it for all of them.

"Of course I'm kidding. Simon will be able to get me if there's an emergency. I was going to take him with me, but I think he's better right here with all the balls we've got in the air, the bankers coming, the press conference at two, Al Weinstock . . ."

"And the bank legislation at three *and* the conference call with the premiers at four." Carter added to the now familiar litany.

"Don't forget Nellie, for God's sake." The PM turned to Simon. Nellie was the tough, strong-willed, hard-talking Inuit and Norwegian woman who was still the elected head of government of the Northwest Territories. "If she's not in on that conference call she'll skin my you-know-whats with her ulu."

"An ulu?" Carter asked.

"Yeah. It's a half-moon-shaped knife that Inuit women use to skin seals, beluga whales, or anything else that has to be skinned."

6

12:05 P.M.: Rideau Hall

The Prime Minister used the ten-minute drive along snow-banked Sussex Street to hunker down in the back seat of his car — just a Chevrolet, no limousine for him — hunker down and think. Try to sort out the enormity of the crisis that had been dumped on him.

One thing was clear and unavoidable: As first minister, like it or not, he had the responsibility of pulling the country out of this mess before the economy went down the drain.

The economy. It was like being the pilot of an aircraft that was out of control, in a steep dive. Could he pull it out of the dive? How would he do it? How much time did he have? Or was it too late?

Were there precedents, guideposts he could look to, to see how other countries had handled a crashing government's house of fiscal cards? Mexico and New Zealand had gone through something similar?

As his driver eased the car through the stone entrance gates to begin the run up the long, stately, treed drive to Rideau Hall, he took his phone out of his inside overcoat pocket. "Simon, we need someone to give us a briefing on Mexico and New Zealand."

"Both of them?"

"Yes. New Zealand had a debt crisis back in the early eighties."

"That's right. I remember a program *W5* did on it. CTV. I think it was Eric Malling who did it."

"See if you can find Malling or someone at CTV. Get a tape or transcript of that show."

"Mexico had a big debt crisis in 1995. They had to go to the Americans and the IMF."

"Just as we're doing. Maybe that woman, Abbi Black, can give us a rundown on Mexico when she gets here."

"I'll call her and ask her if she can do it."

"Ask her about New Zealand, too."

"Yes, sir."

The car approached Rideau Hall's porte-cochère. There he was, the large Royal Canadian Mounted Police staff sergeant who had been overseeing the front entrance of the Governor General's residence for years. A fixture who had seen probably six G.-G.s come and go. With his fur cap square on his bald head, greatcoat brass-buttoned up to the neck, the staff sergeant looked every bulky inch the protective bulldog for the beautiful woman who was the current resident of Government House, the King's representative in Canada, the Honourable Pearl McConachie, PC, CC, CMM, CD.

The two men exchanged cursory polite greetings as the staff sergeant, saluting, opened the car door and the PM headed for the front door. It was held open by yet another saluting RCMP officer.

The Governor General was standing at the top of the flight of some eight carpeted steps that led up to the long, high-ceilinged reception area. Arriving visitors gathered after checking their coats and hats in the lower level of the residence.

The hatless PM handed his overcoat to the staff sergeant and, with the thick warrant envelope in hand, moved quickly up the steps to take the Right Honourable Pearl's outstretched hand.

As he approached he noticed that her usually upswept blond hair was hanging in natural waves to her shoulders, touching the collar of her dark, close-fitting suit jacket set off by a white buttoned-at-the-neck blouse. McConachie's garb signalled that she was ready for serious business with the Prime Minister.

But her broad, welcoming smile and sparkling green eyes showed only pleasure and delight at greeting this fellow Westerner who was now her first minister.

Taking her hand, he returned the smile. "Your Excellency."

"Prime Minister." With that she gently pulled his hand towards her. It was the vice-regal signal that it was appropriate to exchange kisses, but only on both cheeks.

Then her young military aide-de-camp, an air force captain, led the way through the Rideau Hall labyrinth of halls to the handsomely furnished library, or "study" as she called it. Filled bookshelves along with portraits and paintings lined the wood-panelled walls around the high-mantled log-and-flame-filled fireplace.

She motioned towards the settee and the low table in front of the fireplace. The aide departed.

"I have coffee if you'd like some, Richard."

"I'd love some."

She sat next to him and poured. "Dinner last night was great fun. But I didn't expect to see you again so soon."

He laughed. "And I didn't expect to be here." He smiled. "Just can't leave you alone."

"I wish." She returned the smile, then looked down at the envelope he had put beside him on the settee. "You have the warrant with you, I see."

He nodded and sipped his coffee.

"I have the Great Seal at the ready on my desk over there. Tell me what's happening. Why are you recalling Parliament in such a rush? Has it to do with the Japanese announcement — a financial crisis?"

The Right Honourable Pearl was an astute, experienced businesswoman. A pharmacist, she had founded her own chain of drugstores that had spread across the western provinces and into British Columbia. Widowed about six years before her vice-regal appointment at the beginning of the year 2000, she had become strongly independent and self-reliant.

One thing the PM had to give his predecessor credit for: When the term of the previous Governor General was up on January 1, 2000, he did something the *Globe and Mail* had been advocating for years — or, at least, a close variation of it. He asked the 150 companions of the Order of Canada to nominate three Canadians to fill the office. The final selection from the three would be made by the Prime Minister and recommended to the King for his consideration and his appointment as a matter of course.

The Right Honourable Pearl had been invited to fill the vice-regal post as a result of that novel, prestige-enhancing step.

The PM knew she would understand the grave situation that he explained to her in unhurried detail. She had many questions, good ones, as he talked.

"So there you have it, Pearl. We're in very serious trouble. I must bring in a new budget, a cut-to-the-bone budget."

"Sounds like an into-the-bone budget to me."

"It could even be through the bone, because I'm going to shut down three, maybe four ministries we don't need."

"Such as those that duplicate provincial departments?"

"Exactly."

As he spoke he caught her eyes, and they looked at each other for a long moment without speaking. She gave a soft sigh and looked down. She caught his eyes looking at her knees. Her skirt had slipped up well above them. She was about to tug the skirt down but decided that she enjoyed his attention. Why not?

Her voice was gentle as she took charge of the conversation. "As I told you at dinner, I have a formal visit scheduled this week for the Northwest Territories with Nellie. I'll be going to Yellowknife, Norman Wells, up the valley to Inuvik and Tuktoyaktuk."

"Yes, I remember." The PM cleared his throat. "I think you'd better stick close to home. I don't know what's going to happen. Do you think you could cancel?"

"Postpone, not cancel. Nellie's very practical. She probably has heard the news."

"I have a conference call set for four with Nellie and the premiers. If you call her between five and six she'll have the full story."

"Fine, I'll wait until then. But I'll let my own staff know right away so they can reschedule."

"Great. But don't cancel your flight arrangements with the air force or any bookings you've made until after you've talked with Nellie. Please?"

"Understood." Her hand touched his knee. "I'll sign the warrant now. You can apply the Great Seal."

"You have such a gentle touch, Your Excellency." His hand reached out and took hers. Then they stood up together, he a little more swiftly than she.

"I was thinking, it would be nice if you stayed for lunch."

The PM looked at his watch. There was so much to do. He really had to get back. Then he looked into those lovely green eyes again. "Of course,

I'd love to join you. But I can't stay long. I have a press conference at two."

"So you should be back by what? One-thirty?"

He nodded.

"Good. That gives us an hour. After all, Richard, we deserve a bit of private time together, don't we, the Prime Minister and the Governor General?"

He was following her to the desk, taking the warrant out of its manila envelope.

"We certainly do, Pearl."

7

2:05 P.M.: The Prime Minister's Office

The Prime Minister was late getting back to his office. He was almost running when he finally arrived at the conference room door. He burst in, struggling out of his overcoat, catching everyone by surprise and Ann Carter in the middle of an angry statement.

Obviously things hadn't been going well. Paper plates, plastic cups, knives, and forks were strewn over the conference table like white islands in a sea of documents.

"God, Prime Minister, are you okay?" Carter looked shocked.

The PM knew his face was beet-red. "I'm fine. Just the pressure of rushing because I'm late."

Camp took his coat and threw it over a chair at the far end of the table. The PM slumped in his chair tugging at his tie to loosen it.

"So, how are you people doing?" he asked Carter.

"Poorly. We did, sorry, we tried to do the equalization payments first and we're still at it."

The PM was astonished. "You mean you've taken all this time and —"

Greco stepped in to defend Carter. "Look, sir, transfer payments to the provinces are very complicated and politically sensitive. We have to be really careful. I mean, if we cut transfer payments unilaterally the way it was done in 1995 the have-not provinces could go belly up!"

The PM lost his patience. "For Christ's sake, Mario, the federal government's belly up right now! The goddam provinces are belly up along with us." He realized he'd raised his voice. "I shouldn't do that," he told himself, and sat back, trying to calm down.

"Okay, okay. Sorry. Can we start at the beginning, please? Somebody give me the number for EPF, the Established Programs. And give me some background."

The experienced Treasury Board President took up the challenge. "You probably know all this . . ."

"The number, please?"

"The budget for this fiscal year is 16.6 billion."

"Very big."

"Too big. The EPF was started in 1977. The name was changed to Canada Social Transfer in the 1995 budget. It's our main program for providing provinces with assistance in financing post-secondary education, health care, and welfare."

"It'll be a lot easier to handle education than health care. Do you have the numbers split?"

"Yes, 13 billion for health, 3.6 for post-secondary."

The PM did not take long to make up his mind.

There were looks of shock on some of the faces around the table as he gave his decision.

That scene was repeated when he gave judgment on the cuts in the second part of the Canada Social Transfer program. The intent of that program was for the federal government to support the cost of provincial health care, social assistance and welfare. The budget number given to the PM was ten billion.

Then it was on to Equalization, the idealistic, entrenched scheme by which all provinces, regardless of their fiscal capacity, should have sufficient revenues to provide reasonably comparable levels of public services at reasonably comparable levels of taxation. Alberta, B.C., and Ontario, traditionally the "have" provinces, received no equalization payments. Before its departure from Canada, Québec had been receiving about $600 per capita.

"The number?" the PM asked.

"Thirteen point five billion," Carter replied.

"Okay. So what we're going to do with Equalization is . . ." He stopped and looked around the table. "Listen, if any of you want to object."

There was some uneasy shifting, nervous body language, a throat clearing. But otherwise the room was silent.

"Well, then . . ." He gave his Equalization decree, then dealt quickly with Other Transfers: 5 billion; Territorial Governments: 1.1 billion; Municipal Grants: 650 million; and Fiscal Stabilization: 402 million.

Camp interrupted the PM. "It's five to two, sir. The press release has been handed out and the media are waiting for you at the bottom of the stairs."

The PM stood up. "The usual place?" He put on his suit jacket.

"Yes. The scrum's in front of the House doors."

"Okay, take a break, everybody. I'll give them fifteen minutes. We should be ready to go again at two-thirty." He ran his fingers through his hair to smooth it down. "Simon, any word about Weinstock?"

"The air force tell me the Challenger's on schedule. They'll pick him up at West Palm at two and his clothes and Abbi Black in Washington at three-fifty. They'll use the military airport." He was searching his mind for the name.

"Andrews Air Force Base." Smart gave it to him.

"Is Fleming organized to meet them?" asked the PM.

"Yes, sir."

"Good. Ann, I'd like you and Mario to come with me for the press conference. Okay? But would you both do something for me?"

"What's that?" Carter asked.

"If you'd both refer any questions they put to you . . ."

"To you. No problem." Carter was happy with that request.

As soon as Camp opened the corridor door to the PM's office, the noise of the gathered media scrum directly down the stone and marble flights of steps hit the ears of the PM and his two ministers like the snarls of a pack of angry pit bulls.

This would be his first confrontation as prime minister with the nation's television, press, and radio people. In ordinary times this initial press conference would have taken place at the "theatre" in the national press gallery. It would have been the happy third day of the PM's "honeymoon" with the media and the citizens who had voted him in.

As the PM began his walk down the wide noise-echoing steps, he wondered how the media would be, whether they would be friendly, courteous, respectful, or nasty, belligerent, angry with anyone and everyone who had anything to do with this national catastrophe.

It wasn't his fault. He recalled the months and years he had spent in the House, hammering the government about the absolute, urgent need to get spending under control and destroy the deficit. To no avail.

Partly on election day, and totally on Saturday when he was sworn in as prime minister of Canada, the situation had changed. The catastrophe, though not his fault, was now his responsibility.

He resolved to criticize and bitch about the previous government as little as possible. But he knew without doubt that somewhere along the line he would have no choice but to place the blame on his predecessor and that man's indifferent-to-debt government and party.

As they turned on the last landing for the final flight of steps, the cacophony of shouting voices and banging of equipment abruptly stopped. All eyes focussed on the descending trio, the inexperienced new kids on the power block who suddenly were the government.

It was a wrench for all the media who for years had been dealing with a prime minister who was irreplaceable, couldn't be defeated. The man *was* the PM! Suddenly here was this new face. It was a familiar one really. He had been Leader of the Opposition. But as the Prime Minister?

And that press release. Holy Christ, what is going on? What's going to happen?

Carter and Greco flanking him, the PM reached the second step from the bottom. He stopped there so that he could see out over the throng and the cameras, TV gear, lights, microphones, and notepads. It was an unsettling sight, all those faces and eyes turned upon him. It was like being sized up by a motley pack of pit bulls that hadn't eaten for a week.

It was a make-or-break situation and the PM knew it. His voice was strong, confident: "Good afternoon, ladies and gentlemen. You've been given our press release. In short form it tells you and through you it tells all Canadians that the moment of fiscal disaster the government's been putting off for so long has finally arrived. The federal government as well as the provinces have been running up deficits and debt, spending as if there was no tomorrow. I'm here to tell you that the Japanese government has decided to tell Canada there is indeed a tomorrow — and it is today. You all know what the Japanese have done."

The PM stopped speaking. He looked down at the CBC, CTV, and Global television commentators standing right in front of him. It was a silent invitation for questions. The TV lights and flashes of the cameras made it difficult to see.

The CBC person went first. "What are you and your new government — you've been in office for three days — what are you going to do about the Japanese action?"

The PM had to develop his reply. "The Japanese action is a *fait accompli.* What I'm deeply concerned about is what the American and European markets and investors in Government of Canada bonds and securities will do, how they will react. The reaction in London and New York, from reports we're getting in, is that the Americans and Europeans are going to follow the Japanese lead."

"Which means?"

"That as of today the entire world system of governments, banks, financial institutions, and investors have cut off the Canadian government — and that includes the provinces. No more loans, and the bonds and securities we've got out there in foreign hands will be dumped at fire-sale prices."

The Global woman jumped in. "How are you going to cover the federal deficit, sixty-six billion, if you can't borrow?"

"I'd prefer to answer that question when I bring in a new budget on Wednesday morning."

A heavy murmur of surprise welled up through the whirring of the TV equipment and the clicking of cameras. "A new budget? But Parliament isn't sitting!"

"It will be, as of tomorrow afternoon at four. I've called an emergency session. The Governor General signed the warrant at noon."

The CTV person asked, "It usually takes months to prepare a budget. Can you really have it ready for Wednesday? And you said you were going to deliver it. What about your new Minister of Finance here?" He pointed to Mario Greco. "Shouldn't he be delivering it?"

"Mr. Greco has had no experience in the House so it would be unfair for me to ask him to do it. On top of that, the budget is going to be the toughest one Canada has ever seen. It has to be, if we want to begin to restore the confidence of the world's lenders, confidence in Canada. So *I* will present the budget."

"And what about getting it ready for Wednesday?" came a voice from the rear. The PM tried to see who it was, but couldn't.

"We're well into the process. My colleagues" — a gesture toward Carter and Greco — "and I and our staffs are working hard on it."

From the back again, a new voice: "The Americans. Have you talked to the President?"

"Yes, but there's not much, if anything, he can do about the situation. It's not like Japan, where the government has a direct control button. The President was going to say something during his press conference this morning."

"He did," someone else called out. "He said he hoped that American investors wouldn't follow the Japanese, something like that."

"Good."

The questions came in rapid-fire order: "If you can't borrow, how are you going to cover the deficit? How are you going to pay the interest on the debt? What about pensions? What cuts are you planning on making? Will funding to the CBC be affected? Will the civil service be cut? How are you going to pay the civil servants if there isn't enough money? Have you been in touch with the IMF? The banks have cut off their lines of credit to government and Crown agencies; how are you going to handle that situation?"

The PM circuitously appeared to answer all the questions without actually giving specific answers to any of them, saying they would have to wait until Wednesday morning and the budget.

The TV network people were obviously frustrated and impatient with the novice PM's way of phrasing his responses.

The CBC man, a self-important, aggressive television broadcaster, finally said, his voice loaded with sarcasm, "You really haven't answered one single question, Prime Minister. Not one. Maybe you haven't got any answers. Maybe you haven't any idea how to handle this situation. You have a new, inexperienced Cabinet filled with people who don't even know how to find a washroom in this place, let alone know how to handle this crisis. Don't you think you should get some help, call in the best brains in the country?"

The Prime Minister looked down into the eyes of his challenger. Keeping his rising anger in check, he then looked out over the crowd. "I've just been asked the following question by that most clever CBC-TV representative standing in front of me." (He was about to add, "his hot, beery breath fouling my face with his every word," but restrained himself.)

He then repeated the question verbatim, ending with, "'Don't you think you should get some help, call in the best brains in the country?'"

The PM paused. He looked down again into the smug CBC eyes. "By the best brains in the country, you undoubtedly mean starting with a certified know-it-all whom I'm looking at even as I speak."

The crowd burst into laughter smattered with applause.

The Prime Minister went on but addressed his words to the throng. "You can rest assured we're getting and going to get advice and counsel from some of the best brains in this country. And we're going after the best mind in the U.S., the Chairman of the Federal Reserve Board, Al Weinstock. He and one of his senior staff people will be here this evening."

Another buzz of reaction to that news broke out, accompanied by the furious scribbling of almost every notepad-equipped media person in the huge corridor.

"What about the bankers?" A strong female voice threw the question from the middle of the excited pack. "They've all pulled their credit plugs on you."

"I've asked them to be here at three, the CEOs of all the major banks, including the National even though it's a Québec bank."

"What're you going to tell them?" the woman shouted.

"Restore our credit lines, or else."

"Or else what?" Several voices called this out simultaneously.

"I'll let you know later."

The CBC broadcaster was waving a sheet of paper at the PM. "My producer's just handed me a press release, a Canadian Bankers' Association release. It says they're not all coming, just the president of one of the major Canadian banks and the president of the Association. What d'you think of that? Thumbing their noses at you, aren't they?" He had a smirk on his famous face.

"Obviously not. Today is a high-pressure day for us and for the bankers. I can understand what they are facing right now. However, I can deliver my message just as strongly to two representatives as I can to the whole group."

Another question came from the middle of the crowd. Because of the light the PM had difficulty seeing who was asking it. "Is what the banks have done, is that one of the reasons you're calling Parliament into session?"

Good question, the PM thought. "Partly, yes, it's one of the reasons. But the absolute necessity of a new budget is overpowering."

He spoke to the whole crowd while looking directly into the CTV and Global cameras' lenses. Screw the CBC.

"My colleagues and I have to get back to work. But before I leave I want to say to the people of Canada that we will do our utmost, we will use our very best efforts, to restore the government of Canada's fiscal credibility. We will do our utmost to keep the drastic impact of this long-expected catastrophe to a minimum for the citizens of Canada."

He paused, listening to the whirring, clicking silence as his thoughts and image were recorded and transmitted.

"The pain that is going to be inflicted by the failure of previous governments to tackle the monstrous deficit and debt will be the most hurtful and traumatic in the history of Canada. No person will escape, no business will escape. The extravagant social support net of the federal government, a net that has survived on borrowed money, will have to be transformed from a net into a thin rope."

The Prime Minister looked down again at the CBC commentator. "Canada's ability or, for that matter, its *need* to finance a television and radio network, in the name of national unity, no longer exists. There is no longer any justification for the continuation of the Canadian Broadcasting Corporation and its enormous drain on the empty public purse."

He resisted a smile as he again looked out over the now slack-jawed journalists. None of them, even the non-CBC participants, could believe what they were hearing.

"I've given you the first clue as to what Wednesday's budget will be like, the kind of steps we're going to take, steps we have no alternative but to take. The action taken today by the Japanese, which the Americans and Europeans really have no choice but to follow, leave us, the new Reform PC government, with only one way to go. The situation is, of course, made worse by the intransigence, the reluctance, of Québec to come to grips with accepting the amount of its share of Canada's national debt on the day Québec's independence took effect four years ago."

Carter whispered in his ear. He nodded.

"I'm reminded that we have to get back to work. Thank you."

He waved as he turned and with Greco and Carter still flanking him he started up the stairway.

With every step until he disappeared on the landing he could hear (but ignored) questions shouted at him, screamed at him by the frustrated, near-panicking media.

As the trio turned the windowed corner on the first landing and were out of ear, eye, lens, and microphone range of the scrum, Carter laughed. Patting the PM on the shoulder, she exclaimed, "You really gave it to Oldman, that CBC ass. Fantastic. But we haven't even talked about what to do with the CBC. What you said came right out of the blue."

The Prime Minister of Canada stopped on the marble staircase, put his hands on the shoulders of his Treasury Board President and his Minister of Finance. Looking from one to the other, he said, "Haven't talked? We just did. And we've made a billion-dollar-plus-a-year decision that should've been made long ago."

8

2:33 P.M.: The Prime Minister's Office

The trio were met with applause as they went back into the conference room. Simpson, Smart, and the rest of the working group had been taken by George Pearce into the PM's office, where they had watched the scrum on the enormous flatscreen TV. Now they were back around the long oak table.

Camp, grinning from ear to ear, said it for all of them. "Christ, sir. Did you ever give it to that CBC guy."

"Try 'PITA' — pain in the ass," the PM countered, returning the grin.

"Your CBC announcement caught everyone with their pants down," Camp went on.

"Even Ann's." Greco laughed.

"Down, but not off!" Carter quipped.

"Okay, people," the PM said as he took off his suit jacket, loosened his tie, and settled into his chair. "We have to keep going. Let's finish off the social programs list. I'm going to use the index list in the Federal Spending book. Simon, did you get a copy for everybody?"

"Yes, sir."

"Okay. Let's start with the immigration program. We're still letting in more than two hundred thousand people a year and it's costing us over 1.2 billion, about 300 million of that to provide settlement and integration services, including income support and language instruction. So what are your suggestions for this program?"

Smith jumped right in. "This is somewhat outside my Bank of Canada terms of reference . . ."

"Feel free," the PM invited.

"Alright then. In the circumstances I think we should cut off immigration immediately," Smith said emphatically. "Shut the gates until we get this debt mess resolved."

The PM played the devil's advocate: "That may take years."

"So be it. For decades we've been taking in people from literally every country in the world and it has cost us, is costing us, billions of dollars. Borrowed billions," she added, as if anyone needed reminding.

"Anybody else have a different viewpoint?" The PM looked around the table.

"Yeah, I don't agree with that position at all." Mario Greco shook his head. "My parents are immigrants. Like hundreds of thousands of Italians, they came to Canada after the Second World War. They all made a tremendous contribution to the building of this country — just as newcomers from other countries have done and still do. I say we need new people and their productivity."

Then the others joined in, arguing pro and con for cutting off all immigration or limiting the numbers, with a corresponding budget cut. Again it was the PM who ultimately had to make the decision.

Smith's cellular phone rang. She left the table to consult quietly in a corner. Meanwhile the discussion continued.

"Now it's on to Indian and Northern Affairs. The number here is 3.6 billion or about fifteen thousand dollars a year for every Indian and Inuit living on a reserve or Crown land."

On that one they reached a relatively quick consensus.

"Here's the tough nut," Carter announced. "National Health and Welfare. OAS and other old age items are now up to 27.8 billion, out of total program spending of 157.8 billion . . ."

"And the 157.8 billion, that's without interest payments on the debt, right?" Greco the novice had to be sure.

"Right," Carter replied. "The interest will be another 76.3 billion on top. Add those two together you get a total expenditure of 234.1 billion."

"And the revenue is what, Ann?" Greco asked as he wrote down the figures.

"Only 167.2 billion, leaving a deficit of 66.9 billion. And we can't borrow to cover it."

"Which means we can't pay the interest on our borrowings." Carter finished the sentence. She shook her head in frustration. "I wonder what's happening to the Canadian dollar?"

The Governor of the Bank of Canada, now back in her chair, winced when she heard the question. "That phone call I had a couple of minutes ago. It was my deputy, calling to report that the markets are dumping our currency everywhere. The dollar's down from 69 cents U.S. to 52.33 and still falling."

The PM shrugged. "What else can we expect? With the dollar in the pits, we can't even think about how we can pay off our foreign debt, let alone the interest on it."

It was time for a touch of soothing, Carter thought. "Prime Minister, dear Richard, right now you have us taking the first step, I mean the *first* step, upwards, out of this hellish mess. Let's not stop and worry about the goddam Canadian dollar. Let's do this budget."

"You're right, Ann. God knows, we've still got a long way to go," the PM said. He stretched wearily, then looked at his watch. "Hey, it's almost three! Where the hell is that banking legislation, Mario? Your people were going to have it here by three."

"It *is* here, sir," Camp spoke up, glad to have something positive to report.

"Let's see it."

His Chief of Staff passed him the document. "I've made copies for everybody. It's not very long — one page, as a matter of fact."

"Great. The shorter the better. I'd like the banks to understand they're getting a powerful legislative enema."

When the PM judged that everyone had had enough time to read the draft bill, he broke the silence: "Looks good to me."

The bill ordered the banks to restore all the lines of credits and loans to the government of Canada and all provincial and municipal governments and their agencies, including Crown corporations, to the same extent and under the same conditions as those that existed as of Sunday the 28th day of January, 2001.

"Wouldn't the wording be better if it was cast in the negative — easier to get an injunction?" Smart asked. "And you couldn't hit the banks with a money penalty. It would be meaningless."

The PM, casting back to his law-practising days, grunted. "You're right, Peter. I'd forgotten you're a lawyer."

"Yes, sir. With fifteen years in practice in Montreal before I joined Justice . . ."

"And went to the top of the civil service. Okay, Peter, rework this in the negative. Delete any reference to monetary penalties."

Smart got up from the table. "It'll be back in half an hour. I'll make the amendments myself, right now."

The PM checked the time again. "I have just a little over an hour before that conference call with the premiers."

"And Nellie," Carter added.

"Yes, Nellie and the Yukon leader of government. I know what to tell them." He reached up to scratch his head. "That's not a problem. It's the IMF thing that's beginning to worry me. There's no Canadian precedent for this. I have to figure out what to tell that fellow — what's his name, Tromso?"

Simpson had an immediate response. "You won't be telling them much of anything. They'll be telling *you.*"

"So I understand. According to Weinstock, the IMF has been waiting for years for Canada to darken its threshold."

"Darken, that's what you're doing tomorrow morning, sir." Smith was frowning, looking at the backs of her flat-on-the-table hands. "They'll be telling you what Canada absolutely must do, if we want the IMF's support, its resources."

Carter broke in. "But surely the PM should take with him as much up-to-date information as possible. You know, a balance sheet, a fact sheet on the debt, the deficit, how much foreign paper's out there already and at what rates, the projected revenues for the balance of this fiscal year."

"Just two months away, March 31," the PM murmured.

"That's right. And for the next two years. We asked Paul to get those projections while you were at Government House."

"That's a good idea. They're absolutely essential for the budget process. So Paul, would you get your people to prepare a brief for me containing the items Ann suggested? And anything else, any other information they think I should take."

"Yes, sir. But what the IMF will really want to know is what the new budget is going to look like."

"Well, at the rate we're going I'll be able to tell them what my objective is and what cuts will be made in the items we've covered."

"That should be enough," Simpson said. "I'll get my team working right away on what you need."

The PM had another thought. "You might also find out what is going on in the American market. Are there any signs yet of the extent to which they're following the Japanese lead?"

Simpson looked grim. "As a matter of fact, the signs are very clear that's what's going to happen both in the U.S. and Europe."

Smith nodded her agreement with Simpson. "The Bank of Canada has a bond offering of ten billion Canadian that was scheduled for noon today. Interest rate at a premium. Authorized by the previous government, of course. On Friday we expected it to be snapped up by New York traders as soon as the offering was released."

"And?"

Smith shook her head. "There are no offers. None. The reality is, we're at a dead stop. Dead in the water." She hesitated. "There aren't even the usual Canadian bidders."

The PM angrily slapped his hand on the table. "Huh! The goddam banks!"

"The financial houses are simply watching and following the banks."

"And the banks are watching and following the Japanese." The PM turned to the Governor of the Bank of Canada. "Jane, you're the expert. The government's broke. It has no credit. How are we going to pay our employees? How are we going to make unfunded pension payments, OAS payments, you name it?"

"No choice. We've already talked about it. We have to print money and hand it out."

"So you really mean it. We have to print money. Literally?"

"On a big scale. We can have the Mint print thousand-dollar bills by the tens of thousands, even print a ten-thousand-dollar bill. The computer will tell us how much money we'll need every day."

Smith looked to Simpson for his reaction to what she was saying. He gave a slight nod of approval. She went on.

"The Bank of Canada will accept the cash from the Mint and deliver it to the banks. It's legal tender, so they have to accept it, and they have to honour the pay, pension, and other government cheques that have been issued against the government's account."

"Is this normally a function of the Bank of Canada?" the PM asked.

"No. Traditionally the government has used all of the major Canadian banks. No trust companies. I would prefer to continue to use the commercial banks. Dump the cash into them.

"So, we, the Bank of Canada, can be the nominal recipient of the printed cash. We will then cover all the government cheques presented to us by the commercial financial institutions."

"How will you honour those cheques?"

"By daily shipping to each bank cash equal to the value of the cheques it has cashed and presented to us." A gesture of uncertainty came in the form of a shrug. "I'm not sure of the day-to-day mechanics. I mean, there's no precedent to follow. No book of rules."

The PM, thinking out loud, muttered, "The more cash you print, the less the purchasing power of each dollar. Hardly an ideal solution to the crisis, is it?"

Smith nodded. "You've got it. It's called inflation *in extremis*."

Reluctant to accept such a desperate measure, the PM asked once more, "Do we have any choice?"

The answer was, "In the short term, absolutely none, if all the information we're getting about the foreign markets is correct."

"We have to assume that it is," Simpson said, holding up some computer print-outs.

"How do we get this money-printing system up and running immediately?" the PM persisted.

"Just tell Paul and me to do it, sir. I've already told the banknote-printing group to stand by. They've already computer-designed a ten-thousand-dollar bill."

"They should do a fifty-thousand bill while they're at it."

"They already have."

The PM made his decision and looked into the faces around the table. "Okay, do it."

The Governor of the Bank of Canada turned to Simpson. "My phone is dead. Could you call Barbeau for me?"

The Deputy Finance Minister handed his phone across the table to her. "Be my guest."

9

3:45 P.M.: The Prime Minister's Office

At quarter to four the team was only partway through a review of the natural-resource-related programs: Agriculture Canada; Energy, Mines and Resources; Environment Canada; Fisheries and Oceans; and Forestry Canada. Transfer payments plus operations totalled 10.22 billion.

With only fifteen minutes before he was due to have his conference call with the premiers and the two territorial heads of government, the PM decided to tackle the toughest of these first: Agriculture Canada was another hot political chestnut, as he put it.

"As a westerner and a politician I can live or die with what we do to or for farmers. I mean, my God, look at these programs that have been created — 'grown up' is maybe better — grown up to protect the farmers. All of them are too costly."

His eyes ran down the list: Crop Insurance, Farm Income Protection Act, Western Grain Stabilization Act, Gross Revenue Insurance Program, Net Income Stabilization Account, Special Grains Assistance, Deficiency Payments to Canadian Wheat Board, Farm Debt Review Boards, and under the heading of "Other" the tab was almost half a billion dollars. The PM shook his head in wonderment as he read that number.

The Crow Rate grain transportation subsidy for Prairie wheat to the tune of $577 million a year had been axed in the 1995 budget. The PM had opposed the action but at this moment he was pleased that Martin had done it then so the deed would not have to be carried out now.

"I've been thinking" — Greco looked over the top of his horned rimmed glasses at the PM, then at Carter — "I've been wondering if we should have the responsible minister with us when we're eviscerating his or her budget. I mean . . ."

The PM pulled off his own spectacles as he leaned back to wearily rub his hand across his forehead.

"A good point, Mario, but a little late, don't you think? We've worked our way through a good part of the budget already."

"Well, I mean wouldn't it be fair to have the Minister of Agriculture here. What's his name?"

"Flude. Greg Flude. He's from the Moose Jaw area. A farmer. That's why I picked him."

"So couldn't we have him here while we do this?"

The PM smiled. "Sure we could. But two things. Flude doesn't have a handle on his portfolio. He's as green as the wheat sprouts that'll be starting on his farm this spring. Second, and more important — we haven't got the time to be entertaining arguments from my individual ministers."

"Most of whom don't know anything about their portfolios." Carter made the point for the PM.

The sensitive Greco asked, "Does that include me? I'm the ultimate political novice."

"No, no," Carter quickly responded. "C'mon, Mario, you have plenty of finance credentials. You know what I mean. Take the . . . try Alex Garvey, the Minister of Defence. He owns a shoestore in West Vancouver. Never been in the military. What could he contribute to this process?"

"Nothing," the Finance Minister admitted.

The PM chose to ignore Carter's remark about the Defence Minister. She looked defiant as she said, "So let's do this goddam agricultural list of transfer goodies. Get your scythes ready."

They had finished Agriculture and were about to start into the much smaller program of Energy, Mines and Resources at 1.6 billion, when Camp intervened: "Sorry, Prime Minister. It's five to four. You're going to do the conference call in your office."

"Right. George'll be getting them on the line right now. Okay, people, take a break. God knows, you need one. Don't know how long I'll be. These people are big talkers."

"Give 'em hell, Richard." Carter raised her fist. "Remember they're a part, a big part, of the debt problem on top of ours. Like, to the tune of several billions, even though most of them have cut back to a zero deficit."

"Yes, I know. If I'm not back by twenty after four, you people go ahead with the rest of the natural-resources-based programs. Okay?"

The PM and Camp then went to the ornate, rich wood-and-carved-stone Prime Minister's office where so many of this first minister's predecessors had held the sway of power, often fleetingly.

As they passed through the secretaries' office, George Pearce was furiously punching telephone buttons while barking into its mouthpiece. He turned as his boss went by. "I've got them all, sir, except Nellie. She's somewhere in Tuktoyaktuk. The Inuvik operator's found her. Ya. Is that you, Nellie?"

George heard the click of the PM's phone as he picked it up.

"They're all on the line, sir."

"Okay, George. Good afternoon, everybody." He didn't wait for the twelve to respond. "Let me explain to you what's happening, at least from my perspective. Then you can have at me with comments or questions." He did not ask for any words of approval but went straight on. "This is what's happening."

The PM took them through the entire catastrophic scene, opening with these words:

"I know that two of you are members — as are your governments — of the same political persuasion as the party we just defeated. So I'm sorry to say that the fiscal mess they've left us with is beyond beleif. No doubt you know what mess I'm talking about."

When he had given his rundown on the actualities of the day he then switched to what he and his Cabinet (Finance and Treasury Board meant "Cabinet") were doing about the situation: a new budget; the call of Parliament; an emergency debate on the crisis and the budget; the arrival of the Chairman of the U.S. Federal Reserve Board; the Canadian banks and legislation; the printing of money to cover government payrolls and other payments.

"What about us?" the Ontario premier asked. "Will you cover us too?"

"Of course. Good point. We haven't overlooked it. The same applies to all of you."

"Nellie here." The PM had known the amazing Nellie for years. "That's great. But I can tell you, Richard, don't even think about cutting my budget. Your goddam Ottawa bureaucrats have already squeezed us so hard, God, it's like squashing a polar bear's nuts. All we can do is howl, and we're so far north, so remote, no one in Ottawa can hear us!"

"I hear you, Nellie." He had to smile at Nellie's way of expressing herself. "The polar bear's nuts won't be squeezed or squashed, but we may have to shave the hair off his balls."

Nellie laughed. "I might even hold 'em for you. The only ones of any kind I've held in years."

"Bullshit, Nellie," was the PM's retort. "Now let me finish. I go to Washington in the morning for a preliminary discussion with the International Monetary Fund. Parliament meets at 4 p.m. The Governor General gives her Throne Speech in the Senate. Then we get underway in the House with a full emergency debate on the crisis. Then the next morning I present the new budget."

"What's your deficit target?" the Ontario premier asked.

"I'll tell you on Wednesday."

"I think we should know now," was the belligerent response.

"Sorry." The PM was adamant. "I'll tell you, Canada, and the world on Wednesday morning."

Ontario couldn't leave it alone. "Look, Prime Minister. You've been in office for three days. Most of us, the ones you're talking to now, have headed up our governments for years. We know you. But you don't have any track record at governing. Frankly, we don't have any confidence in you or your neophyte team. None whatever."

The PM could feel his hackles rising. "And I have zero confidence in you, with good reason. You've allowed the Ontario deficit to grow by eight billion a year minimum over the last two years. Alberta's been the only province with the guts and brains enough to try — with pain, much pain — to slay the deficit dragon. I don't mean shrink it, I mean kill it!"

"Alberta here." A new voice broke in. "Thank you for that, Prime Minister. D'you know what the combined provincial debt is right now, thanks to my big-spender colleagues right across the country? Except Québec, of course?"

The PM surprised his listeners. "Goddam right I do. When Québec separated, its debt was 86.8 billion. The debt of the remaining provinces was 191 billion, of which Ontario's share was 106 billion. Now Ontario's at 126 billion."

"Right on. Alberta's deficit is zero!" its premier shouted in his honed radio voice.

"But you still have a debt of 23.7 billion."

No denial from Alberta.

"Alright," the PM said. "I've told you people all I can up to this point. If I need your advice I'll ask for it."

"Screw that. I'm British Columbia. You're going to get my suggestions whether you like it or not. I'll fax you something by morning."

"I'll be glad to have it."

"Whether you read it or not's another thing. But you'll have it. Keep in mind one thing, Prime Minister."

"Yes."

"We can separate just the way Québec did."

"That's not news."

"We're Canada's window to Asia and Japan, the Chinese and Hong Kong. You lose us and the chances of our going American are nine out of ten."

The PM could feel the tension as the other premiers were listening and waiting for his reply.

"So what is it you're threatening — independence or a join-up with the States?"

"I'd have to run a plebiscite for my citizens before I could answer that."

"You'd better get ready to do it," the PM growled. "Don't forget to put 'Stick with Canada' as a choice on the plebiscite."

Silence for two seconds.

"Maritime premiers and Newfoundland. Have you any questions or input?"

"Newfie here. Do what you have to do. We're in such bad shape that nothing you do could have much of an impact."

"What about Hibernia?" It was Ontario butting in.

The Premier of Newfoundland laughed. "What a farce. Billions of Canadian taxpayers' dollars thrown at a project where the only beneficiaries will be the American oil companies and their American customers. The jobs and contracts for Newfoundlanders have been next to nothing. Everything goes to foreigners or mainlanders."

Saskatchewan entered the fray. "What about the CBC? You've just told that big press conference you're going to kill the CBC. Surely we should, all the premiers . . ."

"And us too," Nellie shouted.

"Everybody should have a say."

"No way. You, all of you, have had your say about the CBC. The government we've just replaced had its say. Between you, you've broken the bank, every bank in the goddam country. We're broke. There is no money — get this — *there is no money* to finance the CBC. Québec's gone, so there's none of that national unity bullshit to spread around. The U.S. stays united without a government-paid-for radio and TV. Canada will now do the same. You and my predecessors made this unbelievable mess and I have to clean it up, and I'm going to do just that. You can join me, fight me, or sit in your offices and suck your self-serving thumbs. It's up to you."

Another silence. This time it was long. Seven seconds.

"One more thing: I have to meet with your friendly bankers, the people — great Canadians all — who pulled your lines of credit this morning. I'm doing something about it to help you."

Brave Nellie asked, "What are you going to do?"

"I'm going to tell them to restore every line of government credit now, immediately."

"If they say no?" she dared to ask.

"I'll tell them the first order of business before the House tomorrow will be legislation that will squash a polar bear or a banker's balls."

Nellie roared with laughter.

The PM fielded more questions — Manitoba, New Brunswick, P.E.I., and Nova Scotia, all of whom were hostile. He deflected them, saying the answers would come on Wednesday. He signed off by again inviting their suggestions or comments by fax.

Ontario had the last outside word. "That invitation is as hollow as a rotten maple tree trunk. Just present your budget on Wednesday, Prime Minister. I'll probably announce a referendum the next day."

"A referendum on what?"

"Going the Québec independence route or . . ."

"Or?"

"Ontario joining the U.S."

The Prime Minister hung up muttering, "Go to hell!"

10

4:20 P.M.: The Prime Minister's Office

In the short time between his conference call with the premiers and the territorial leaders and his scheduled five-o'clock meeting with the bankers, the PM had continued to drive his weary budget team through the remaining programs related to natural resources.

He had driven them and himself far enough for everyone to be on the verge of stress exhaustion. They all needed to get out of that room and be part of the real world again. Feet up for half an hour, a drink, dinner.

"Okay, gang. In a few minutes I have to go and put the lash to the bankers."

"Don't be too hard on them," Carter sarcastically cautioned.

"I'll be a mean pussy cat. What I want all of you to do is break until eight. Have a good meal, take it easy, but do what you have to do with your respective staffs."

"In your absence, PM, we instructed all our people to go for dinner at about five-thirty and be back at their desks by seven-thirty, and not to leave until we — that is you — release them," Greco said. "They've all got plenty to do, considering the questions we've been putting to them."

"Great. Simon, what's the word on Al Weinstock?"

"He and Abbi Black will be arriving at the airport at ten after six. They'll be at the Chateau Laurier by about ten to seven. They're having their dinner on board. They'll be here at seven-thirty or quarter to eight."

"Is Oscar Fleming meeting them?"

"Yes, he'll be there."

"Good. Ask him to get them here at eight. We'll all be back by then and ready to go."

"Yes, sir."

"You have the bios on our people, but do you have résumés on Weinstock and Black for us?"

"No, sir."

"Better get all the information you can."

"But everyone knows Weinstock."

"Sure. But we don't know anything *about* him, where he's coming from. And nobody here has ever heard of Abbi Black. Call Weinstock's office. They'll fax the stuff to you. If you can't reach anyone there, try the President's Chief of Staff . . . what's his name?"

"Spratt."

"Yeah, Spratt. He'll organize it. See if the *Globe and Mail* and the *Financial Post* can give you any recent articles on either or both of them. If so, make copies for everyone."

Simpson stood up, getting ready to leave. "A question, Prime Minister. What do you really think Weinstock's going to contribute to what we're doing?"

"His presence."

"Pardon me?"

"Even if he doesn't say a goddam word, the fact that he is here will be reassuring to the financial powers-that-be in Japan, America, and Europe. He'll help us begin to restore our credibility as a country that can borrow and be relied upon to repay. Got it?"

"Yes, sir."

"But that's only one of the reasons for inviting him to come. He can also tell us what he would do if he was in our shoes, tell us what he thinks about what we're trying to do."

Carter added, "He has to have access to the President and Congress. If there's something he thinks the U.S. government can do . . ."

"To bail us out?" Greco put the question on everyone's mind: What can the Americans do to help us?

"Look," Simpson responded, "the Americans have been fighting their own debt and deficit battle for years. They've got enough problems without getting tangled up in our mess. They tried to help Mexico, President Clinton did, and got a lot of negative crap and criticism for his trouble."

The PM countered, "The Americans are already tied up with our mess. We owe billions to their financial houses — how much is it, Jane?"

The Governor came up with the answer quickly: "At last count, around 450 billion."

Carter reminded the meeting: "They have a major chunk of their automobile-manufacturing plants here — Windsor, Oakville, Oshawa."

"Thank God for that," Greco intoned.

"The reality, Prime Minister," Carter summed it up, "is that the Americans have an enormous ownership, investment stake, in Canada. They own or have a piece of just about everything except the banks, newspapers, radio, TV, and our airlines. What happens to Canada — this financial disaster — has to be a major worry for them."

"Absolutely!" the PM agreed as he stood up. "See you people at eight. Oh, and let Simon or George know where we can find you if I have to get you back here in a hurry."

"Have fun with the bankers, boss," Carter shouted as the PM went out the door.

"You gotta be kidding!" was his parting shot.

The Prime Minister sat tensely behind his desk with Camp, his witness, in a chair by the windows to the PM's right.

The two people facing him at the moment were part of a powerful enemy. In his opinion the banks were a Canadian economic force that rightly and properly should have been totally supportive of the government of Canada, regardless of the political persuasion of the party in power.

Instead, this pair and the massive financial institutions they represented had this day turned their backs on the people of Canada and all of the nation's governments and agencies. Which is exactly what the Prime Minister told the high-profile bank representatives who sat uncomfortably across from him.

And he also remarked on the absence of the other bank heads. A very poor showing in this crisis. He asked if the rest of them were too ashamed or afraid to face him. What excuses could the absentees possibly have? He was extremely annoyed that only two turned up, and told them so.

He looked into the flushed face of the small, immaculately tailored chairman and CEO of Canada's largest and most profitable bank, into the obviously nervous eyes of a man hauling in a salary of about two million a year for his efforts.

Then, as he talked, the PM shifted his gaze toward the masculinely dressed, tough, but femininely attractive woman who was the president of the Canadian Bankers' Association, the group that lobbied members of Parliament to vote in favour of any and all legislation that benefitted the Canadian banks.

"So today you people pulled the financial rug from under the very government to which you owe your protected, coddled existence. Why?"

"We didn't have much choice," the bank chairman said defensively.

"There's a western word for that. It's bullshit. What you mean is, you decided not to stick with Canada. By the way, Mr. Waters, I see you're wearing your Officer of the Order of Canada pin."

"Yes, sir, I am," the CEO replied as he stiffened in his chair.

"I suggest that when you leave this room you take it off. If you continue to wear it you should be ashamed of yourself."

The banker hadn't been talked to that way since he was a teenager. "Now wait a minute. You may be Prime Minister . . ."

"There's no *may* about it, sir. I *am* Prime Minister. You bankers and the weak-kneed governments, the blind, irresponsible politicians you've been dancing with for the last ten years have driven this country — what's left of it — into bankruptcy."

The banker bristled angrily. "We haven't had anything to do with the ballooning debt, the horrendous deficits. Government has done that, not us. The Japanese pulled the rug today, not us!"

"Again, bullshit." The gloves were off, and the PM came out swinging. "They pulled one corner of the rug, and in the wink of a computer's eye you pulled the other corner. How long was the emergency conference call you and your fellow CEOs had this morning before you decided to pull our credit? Five minutes . . . ten?"

"Actually it was more like half an hour. Some of my colleagues wanted to stay in, but the majority decided in favour of pulling out. We have to protect our depositors and shareholders."

"Your shareholders aren't just the people on your stockholders' records.

Your real shareholders are the people of Canada. You owe them and your depositors a high level of loyalty and responsibility, although obviously you don't understand that." The PM paused. "As a lawyer I know I shouldn't ask a question unless I know what the answer is."

"Before you ask it, I'll tell you." His jaw thrust forward, the banker said, "I voted in favour of pulling out."

"Of course you did. Because of your duty to your depositors and your shareholders." The sarcasm in the PM's voice was unmistakable. "Well, I'm here to tell you, sir, and your banker colleagues with their combined assets of hundreds of billions — maybe a trillion — I'm here to tell you that I want, the government of Canada wants, every single line of credit restored by midnight tonight."

"As president of the Association, sir, I must point out that we really need more than the few hours between now and midnight." Her voice was firm as she addressed the PM. "It's after business hours and trying to track down busy CEOs —"

"Come off it!" The PM waved his hand to cut her off. "Your constituents took half an hour to decide to shove the knife into the heart of their own country. I'm giving you over six hours, for God's sake."

The Prime Minister was tired. He was angry. He was in a mean mood. He articulated his words slowly, emphatically.

"Get this straight, you two. I want a positive response, or else. And I want you people to hold a press conference first thing in the morning to tell the world you're backing your government. Just like you would do it if you were in Japan and were Japanese. Understand?"

"You used the words 'or else.' What do you mean by that?" The woman asked the question knowing — she thought — what the answer would be.

"'Or else' is simple." The PM reached in his desk drawer to pull out the redrafted, ready-to-go bank legislation. He threw it across the bare, highly polished desk.

"That's the 'or else.' I've recalled Parliament, and if you force us to pass this act tomorrow, that's when we'll do it. It will be the first order of business. Then the Canadian banks and their leaders are going to be confronted with all manner of new regulations and legislation. You people will be kneecapped at every opportunity."

The banker was appalled. "You're threatening us! This is blackmail; you can't do this!"

"I can, and I will." The Prime Minister stood up. "I have important things that deserve my urgent attention. If you will please now leave, Mr. Camp will escort you out."

Just as his Chief of Staff was opening the soundproofed oak door to let the two visitors out, the Prime Minister spoke. "One final thing. You can tell your patriotic, nationalistic colleagues that if you force us to pass this act, then in the public interest there will be a cap legislated on the salaries Canadian chartered banks pay their chief executive officers. The amount you people are paid is, in a word, *obscene*!"

11

7:35 P.M.: The Prime Minister's Office

When the bankers had gone, the PM decided he had to get out of the office for a short break. His driver took him to his apartment building close to the centre of town and was told to wait.

A quick shower and complete change of clothing refreshingly restored his energy. A glass of white wine in hand, he talked with his Olivia in Calgary about the upcoming pre-wedding parties that he now had to miss, and, of course, how his crisis-fighting plans were shaping up.

By 7:35 p.m. the Prime Minister was at his desk, wolfing down yet another sandwich, when the call came from Oscar Fleming at the Chateau Laurier.

"I'm with Mr. Weinstock, sir. We've put him in the Royal Suite."

"What about Miss Black?"

"She's in the suite next door. We should be at your office in about fifteen minutes, at ten to eight. Is that okay?"

"Perfect."

"Mr. Weinstock can't get over all the snow here. And the cold."

"Yeah. It's a long way from Loxahatchee. See you shortly."

As he hung up the PM finished off his tuna sandwich, washing it down with a glass of chilled Point Pelee white wine.

Coat jacket off, he went to the sofa and lay down. Fifteen minutes stretched out and physically, not mentally, relaxed would give him enough of a boost to get him through what promised to be a long and brutal session.

Then he had to be on that Challenger for Washington at what . . . 6 a.m.? Which meant that he had to be up and dressed by five. No problem — he was an early riser whose juices started flowing the moment his feet hit the floor.

The PM's family always claimed he could sleep on the head of a needle. Yes a needle, not a pin. His eyes closed . . .

He woke up when there was a firm knock on the door.

It was Camp. "Sir, Mr. Weinstock and Ms. Black are here — and Mr. Fleming."

"Fine." He pulled himself off the sofa saying, "I just have to get my suit jacket on. There we are. Okay, bring them in."

Oscar Fleming made the introductions and then said good night.

To the PM, Weinstock's flat, craggy face, high forehead, and wavy salt-and-pepper hair looked just like his pictures. But he was shorter than expected. He looked rather like a reworked, much younger Henry Kissinger.

It was Abbi Black who was the sight to behold. The PM's male hormone computer told him she was one of the most strikingly beautiful women he had ever laid eyes on. His computer went up a further notch when she slipped off her heavy coat and white scarf. This tall, high-heeled, long-legged, slim beauty was wearing a tight-fitting black woollen sheath with a gleaming row of golden buttons running down from the discreetly low-cut bodice that covered firm breasts (just the right size, according to that computer).

His eyes swiftly took in the cascade of wavy ebony hair and the smooth, unlined forehead, the black, well-shaped eyebrows arched over eyes that held deep-brown pupils in their centres. Her nose was perfectly shaped; her high cheekbones led to a wide, full-lipped mouth with exquisite teeth.

The PM liked — very much — what he saw, but there was serious business at hand, and he switched off his internal computer as he shook Abbi Black's soft, well-manicured hand.

Then he waved towards the sofa and the high-backed, soft, maroon-leather chairs positioned around the room. "Please, have a seat. May I get you anything . . . coffee, soda, wine, whatever?"

Weinstock chose a chair and replied, "I don't know about Abbi, but I don't need anything right now. This is one helluva culture shock, after walking off the eighteenth green at Loxahatchee, with fifty bucks of Namath's money in my pocket, and here I am in the coldest, snowiest place I'll betcha south of the North Pole."

Black, now gracefully relaxed on the sofa, also refused. "Maybe coffee later."

The PM went to his desk to pick up the list of people who would be joining them and a short bio on each.

"We already have this," Black said in her distinctive, cultured low voice.

"Sir, I faxed all this to them in the aircraft," Camp said.

"Good. That saves us time."

Weinstock leaned forward and looked the PM in the eye. "Now, what d'you really want from us? I mean, man, you have a full-scale disaster on your hands. Tell us what you have in mind."

"We need all the advice and suggestions you can give us. No holds barred."

The American gave a chuckle. "I've never shrunk from giving advice, have I, Abbi?"

"Never, even when it hasn't been asked for." She smiled, as if to soften her words.

"Keep in mind, Mr. Prime Minister, that gratuitous advice is worth what you pay for it."

The PM reached into his trouser pocket. "Here's my retainer. It's a Canadian dollar." He passed the coin to Weinstock. "Today it's trading at —"

"Yeah, I know, fifty cents on the U.S. dollar." He shook his large head in negative gesture. "So what's your plan, Mr. Prime Minister?" He turned the coin over between his fingers as he waited for the answer.

"I'll tell you that in a minute. I'd like you to come into the conference room with me. My team is there. We'll give you as full a briefing as we can on all the factors, the elements, that have brought us to this shambles. Are they all there, Simon?"

"Yes, sir."

"I understand you're working on a budget." Black shifted her position and crossed her long legs.

"As hard as we can. I want to bring it in on Wednesday morning."

"Your budget." The Chairman lifted his bushy brows. "It's probably the only key left to open the credit door. If it isn't right, if it doesn't fit in all the locks in Tokyo, London, and New York . . ."

"Then what?"

Weinstock shrugged. "We'll talk about it."

Black added, "And we'll also talk about New Zealand. I'll run you through what happened there, starting in 1984, and I'll use Canadian material to do it. And Mexico. I'll go over the Mexican scenario as well."

"I was hoping for that. We were looking for one of Canada's best, probably the best, TV news magazine producer, Eric Malling. He went to New Zealand back in '93. Did a great job. But we can't track him down."

"We did, sir," Simon interjected, "but he's in Japan. Went yesterday. According to his staff he knew something like this was imminent."

"Okay, Ms. Black. Instead we have you."

"As a matter of fact, the Canadian material is —"

She was cut off by Weinstock. "Believe me, she knows every rock in the Mexico and New Zealand paths."

"And the rocks and the path are very similar to what you're going through. Very," Abbi added as she stood to follow the PM into the conference room.

"As I started to tell you, I pulled Malling's manuscript, his *W5* New Zealand manuscript, off my computer. That's the Canadian material I was referring to. It really adds a gritty flavour to what went on. There's been some criticism of the program but it's okay for our purposes."

"Do you have copies?" Camp asked.

"Just two."

"I'll have some made." He held out his hand and she gave him one copy.

They trooped into the conference room behind the PM. Introductions were over with quickly.

The PM seated Black on his right, the Fed Chairman on his left. His own team was divided nearly equally on each side down the table, with the appropriate staff sitting next to their individual ministers. Camp joined the group late, handing Black a stack of paper before he took his seat.

From the head of the table the Prime Minister first cautioned his American guests about the need for secrecy. Then he launched into his comprehensive briefing on the budget cuts and deficit target, inviting the guests and his own group to come in with questions or relevant information. He spoke without notes. The depth of his understanding and grasp of details visibly impressed the two Americans.

"When you're finished with this job, Mr. Prime Minister, and if I'm still

Chairman, you can come and work with us any time."

The PM smiled. "A great compliment, Mr. Chairman."

Weinstock grinned. "Well, it's no bullshit. I haven't been exposed to a briefing like that in years." He looked across the table at Black, who nodded in agreement, then at his host. "As I told you, your budget is the key. You've got the makings of exactly what the foreign markets want to hear, must hear."

"The question is, can you sell it to your own party group . . ." Black looked at the PM for assistance.

"The caucus."

"Yes, the caucus, because there's going to be so much blood, so much controversy, you'll be lucky if you get all your caucus behind you. Really lucky."

The PM couldn't disagree. "Over half of my newly elected members have no parliamentary experience. Many have never even been to Ottawa. So you're right. I'll be lucky."

Greco spoke up: "I'm the Finance Minister and this is my first time in the House. What we're going to have to do, I suggest, is get the caucus together tomorrow night after dinner and the PM's going to have to read them the riot act — tell them they have to support him and his budget, no matter what."

Weinstock wanted to get away from the mechanics. "There are a couple of things, a couple of comments, I want to make about the budget — at least, as far as you've put it together."

"Go ahead."

"I think your deficit target should be at least five points lower."

"That means a complete —"

"And why not? Go for it. The markets will love you."

"Good advice. Why not."

The Chairman's face scrunched up. "Unfortunately, I think you've got a problem that a single budget, not even ten or twenty of them, is gonna fix." He gave another of his shrugs. "I know you inherited this case of cans of worms, but you gotta carry them."

The room was silent, waiting for the guru to speak.

"Frankly, with a debt that's 100 percent of Gross Domestic Product, I can't see how you're ever going to pay off your federal debt of nine hundred billion, let alone what the provinces have on top of that. I mean even if you killed the deficit and started running a surplus tomorrow of, say, 10 billion a year, it would take Canada ninety years to pay off nine hundred billion. See what I mean?"

"Absolutely. Clear as a bell. Is there a solution?"

"Join Abbi and me for a drink at the Chateau and I'll tell you what it is."

The PM looked surprised. "You don't want to discuss it in front of my people?"

Weinstock shook his head, smiling. "These are all very bright and pleasant people. But what I have to say is for your ears only."

"You're on." The PM turned to Black. "Are you ready to give us New Zealand and Mexico?"

"Sure. New Zealand first. You won't like much of what I'm about to tell you."

12

8:15 P.M.: The Prime Minister's Office

"New Zealand," Abbi Black began. "Financial catastrophe faces the brand-new 1984 Labour party, the socialist government of Prime Minister David Lange. An unsuspecting David Lange, unsuspecting as to the real state of the nation's finances."

"Just like us. Brand-new and unsuspecting," the PM commented.

"Rather than give you a dry lecture on the New Zealand crisis, I'll give you the copies Mr. Camp made of the CTV *W5* program that Eric Malling and his people put together. It was shown on Sunday, February 28, 1993."

"That's eight years ago," Carter said. "I remember seeing it and probably many of us did. But I can't remember its details."

Black glanced at the intense President of the Treasury Board. "This will refresh your memory." She looked around the table. "Why don't all of you read it to yourselves; then perhaps we can have a discussion. Sorry I don't have a video. It would have been easier."

There was general shifting about in chairs as people made themselves more comfortable; then, except for the slight rustle of turning pages, the room was quiet.

W5

PROGRAM	W5
NETWORK	CTV
DATE	Sun 28 Feb 93
TIME	19:00:00 ET
END	19:55:00 ET
GUEST	DAVID LANGE, New Zealand Prime Minister, 1984–1989; RICHARD PREBBLE, New Zealand Assoc. Finance Minister, 1984–1989; HENRY VOORDOUW, New Zealand Dock Worker; MYLES GAZLEY, Car Salesman; GENEVIEVE WESTCOTT; REV. RICHARD RANDERSON, Social Researcher; DR. PETER ROBERTS, Intensive Care Director; SIMON UPTON, New Zealand Health Minister; MAUREEN FLETCHER, Community Councillor; DAVID CAREY, Sheep Farmer; BRUCE BOLT, Farmer;
TITLE	New Zealand: W5 looks at how New Zealand is coping with a similar debt crisis to the one that threatens Canada.
HOST	Eric Malling

Show #19, Sunday, February 28, 1993
W5 *with Eric Malling*

ERIC MALLING

Another load of imports from Japan rolls off the boat. They don't run too well. There's a reason for that. These aren't new cars, they're used scratch-and-dent specials. Get sick and get out the chequebook. The country that practically invented medicare now charges

$50 a day to be in hospital. Pay farmers to raise sheep they can't sell? Not a chance. The subsidies vanished almost overnight. It all happened when New Zealand, a country a lot like Canada, suddenly realized it was going broke.

SIMON UPTON

The only difference between an African Third World state and a Canada or a New Zealand is that they actually hit the end of their credit limit very quickly. We're given more rope to hang ourselves with.

RICHARD PREBBLE

They say that hanging clarifies the mind. Now being told you've got no credit also makes you suddenly realize that you can take tough decisions and you have to take them.

ERIC MALLING

So Brian Mulroney is on his way and for the next six months there'll be nothing but politics on television. First the leadership race, then the election — good theatre. I suppose, like a pennant race in baseball. But in my opinion none of it really matters. Economists are predicting that sometime in the next year, maybe two years, the deputy minister of finance is going to walk into cabinet, and it doesn't matter whose cabinet, and announce that Canada's credit has run out. Now that matters. Our lives will change dramatically. Scare-mongering? Well, Canada now has more foreign debt than any other developed country. We're getting down there with Mexico and Brazil, and their credit ran out. Can't happen to us? Well it did happen to a country very much like ours, New Zealand. It's a little strange to be doing an hour on another country's economy but have a look and you might see yourself in the mirror.

NEW ZEALAND

ERIC MALLING
Way down under and on the other side of the world, people just like us. Remuera is a suburb of Auckland. Blink and you could be in Vancouver. With a million people, Auckland's not quite as big but it looks just as pretty. And here on Clonburn Road, Earl and Mary Bowers have roses year round. But when it rains, raw sewage from the ditch behind overflows into the garden and with it comes diarrhea, impetigo, the threat of typhoid.

EARL BOWERS
We've got used condoms.

ERIC MALLING
In your garden.

MARY BOWERS
In our garden, right across.

ERIC MALLING
What did council say when you wanted it fixed?

EARL BOWERS
They now had no money to do it.

ERIC MALLING
They're finally getting a minor repair. But a few blocks away, here's a million-dollar view, looking over the city of sails. The richest man in New Zealand, brewer Dougie Myers lives along here. But at the edge of the bay what's this eyesore? A deteriorating old viaduct, the main sewage line for Auckland. When it leaks they patch it, when it stinks they tolerate it. But this in the best neighbourhood in a gorgeous city, in a country where Greenpeace is God?

PAULINE FELL

It's purely expense. They just keep probably hoping to keep it working as long as they can.

ERIC MALLING

Don't have the money.

PAULINE FELL

No, don't have the money.

ERIC MALLING

Across town at the Auckland City Zoo, a blessed event last spring. You think kittens are cute. What about a baby hippo? Kids were in love with it.

CHILD IN SCHOOL

I am very, very sure that the zookeeper has shot the hippo.

ERIC MALLING

What, shoot the baby hippo? That's right. No room at the zoo and they couldn't expand the hippo pen because the government has no money. But this is New Zealand, which for many years had the third highest standard of living in the world, right after the U.S. and Canada. And not just rich but a pioneer. Women got the vote here 100 years ago. Medicare and welfare go back to the '30s. It was a jewel of a country, three and a half million people, about the size of B.C. or Greater Toronto, a little Switzerland down in the South Pacific. But then in 1984 everything changed. There were strange things going on here in the Beehive — what a great name for Parliament — disappearing government. Conservative politicians from all over the world come to the Beehive to crow about the triumph of hard-nosed, free-enterprise, businesslike, no-nonsense, slash slash, government. Well it's important to remember though two things. One, it wasn't a triumph for everyone and second, it wasn't started by conservatives at all but rather the Labour Party, New Zealand's version of the NDP, which was driven in the beginning not by ideology but by debt.

DAVID LANGE
We came in appealing to their hearts and minds, and then after the big drop we went for their bowels.

ERIC MALLING
The Prime Minister David Lange was a socialist all right. He threw out the U.S. Navy, broke with South Africa, championed women's rights, but with debt there was no choice.

DAVID LANGE
Can you imagine a labour party with a tradition of being at the heart of working class people, which was raised in New Zealand out of the trade union movement, suddenly being forced to behave as if it was to the right of Genghis Khan, making Margaret Thatcher look like Joan of Arc, Ronald Reagan look like some sort of Jesuit brother? I mean, we became tougher than any of them.

ERIC MALLING
Farm subsidies were gone, crown corporations slashed and then sold. Later, welfare and even medicare came under the axe. Personal incomes crashed. New Zealand had been topping up with borrowed money and its credit finally ran out. That sounds like Latin America or Africa. But how does a country like New Zealand, like Canada, eventually hit the wall?

RICHARD PREBBLE
In comes the Secretary of the Treasury, the Governor of the Reserve Bank, and you start off by saying, well why have you stopped all foreign exchange dealings. And they say oh, very simply, Minister, we have no foreign exchange. What?

ERIC MALLING

Richard Prebble was a new minister. His first cabinet meeting. Just the change in government was enough to expose the books. Lenders were spooked and firms like Merrill Lynch and Salomon brothers reported that New Zealand bonds weren't selling. Simple as that. Prebble remembers asking:

RICHARD PREBBLE

Well when's our next overseas loan due? And I still remember the answer. It was next Wednesday. So, well can we pay? And the answer was no, ministers.

DAVID LANGE

At one stage they even told me that they'd asked our embassies around the world to report back urgently to them on how much they could draw down on overdraft facilities at their banks. So using staff credit cards presumably to the limit.

ERIC MALLING

So you're telling me the New Zealand High Commission in Ottawa might have to go down to the Royal Bank and borrow some money to help out the government?

DAVID LANGE

Yes, the game was up.

ERIC MALLING

What happens when a country defaults on a bond?

RICHARD PREBBLE

That's what I asked actually. I said to the Governor, what happens if we don't pay? He said oh, all our loans are written so that if you default on one loan, you default on all of them. That means that our credit will be blown everywhere we're trading. We'd be basically a basket case.

ERIC MALLING

New Zealand's foreign debt back then was 47% of its gross national product. Canada's foreign debt today: 44% of GNP, almost as bad. It's money borrowed from the rest of the world to keep up our standard of living. Total government debt: 62% of GNP pushed New Zealand over the edge. Canada: 88%. Our total government debt today is worse, far worse. So when do we start shooting the baby hippo?

Will a government ever on its own take a stand and say we have to change, enough is enough?

DAVID LANGE

Not unless they have a strongly suicidal bent. Unless there is some extremely traumatic external threat to you, people are not going to believe that there is the need for this change.

ERIC MALLING

And whose fault? Well blame it on the sheep. They'd been the big dollar earner for New Zealand. Canada's fish, wheat and resources are all diminishing in value but sheep diminished all at once, back in 1973 when Britain joined Europe and New Zealand's main market for spring lamb was gone. The Prime Minister was Robert Muldoon, National Party, the conservatives. Instead of taking the hit, Muldoon borrowed money to keep up the standard of living. Borrow and hope. He subsidized the sheep and borrowed more for megaprojects besides. The steel mill. Cost $3 billion and eventually sold for a tenth of that. If that sounds familiar, see Canada's airplane companies, Canadair and De Havilland. Synthetic fuel plant — any price for energy development. See Hibernia and Canada's Western oil upgraders.

DAVID LANGE

You're talking about a country which was run like a Polish shipyard. It was bizarre. It was a whole series of pork barrel politics. It was using overseas debt to build up domestic expectation far ahead of any common sense view of what economic development should be.

RICHARD PREBBLE

They say that hanging clarifies the mind. Now being told you've got no credit also makes you suddenly realize that you can take tough decisions and you have to take them.

ERIC MALLING

It was like a national garage sale. They needed the money. Among the first to go, Air New Zealand, sold to the Australians no less. The state telephone company went to an American bidder, Atlantic Bell, for $4 billion. Government insurance, holdings in the biggest bank, gone. Next, three-quarters of the country's post offices.

RICHARD PREBBLE

I was the postmaster general and we closed 732 post offices in one day.

ERIC MALLING

That must have made you popular with the postal workers.

RICHARD PREBBLE

No, I'm actually unpopular world-wide. I went to Canada and I was addressing a conference, and the postal workers picketed outside the conference hall. And of course they didn't know what I looked like, so I went out there and said he's a terrible fellow too.

ERIC MALLING

You're an international villain.

RICHARD PREBBLE

I'm afraid so.

ERIC MALLING

And a socialist, no less.

RICHARD PREBBLE

Absolutely. Still am.

ERIC MALLING

The debt crisis went beyond government. Interest rates were punishing, real estate crashed. The New Zealand dollar was devalued 20%, a 20% national wage cut. In fact since the '70s their dollar has gone from $1.40 U.S. to 50 cents today.

People don't really care about what happens on money markets mostly.

DAVID LANGE

No, they don't, they don't. But they like to watch television, they like to use the video, they like to drive their car and they like to have petrol for their car. I mean that's pretty fundamental. If your credit card runs out you don't buy gas at the station. If the country's credit card runs out they don't buy gas from the tanker.

ERIC MALLING

Well, the ships still call at the port, although like everything else it's up for sale too. The Arabian Princess is unloading cars from Japan. What's this, cars that won't start? Who'd buy these? Well New Zealanders struggling with debt. Almost half the so-called "new" cars in this country are used cars from Japan, and not just executive driven but old delivery vans and Tokyo taxis.

HENRY VOORDOUW

Here we are, we're buying their problem off them and paying them good money at the same time.

ERIC MALLING

You're the garbage man.

HENRY VOORDOUW

That's about it, too. Is it only New Zealand doing this or are you going to take some of these as well?

ERIC MALLING

Well, who knows? We may have to start if we're not paying our bills. But it did bring down prices and only some of the old fogies seem to object.

MYLES GAZLEY

The 60 to 70-year-old people who are saying well we fought against these bloody Japanese, why should we buy something that they've cast off and no longer want?

ERIC MALLING

So this is a good buy for me.

MYLES GAZLEY

Oh, definitely. You'd look lovely in it.

ERIC MALLING

And what's this, behind the cars, waiting to be loaded up for Japan? Round logs, perfect pine. They come from the cherished national forest. Trees planted by relief workers in the '30s are now being sold off mainly to foreign companies. Rich countries aren't supposed to be selling things like round logs. You know, they should be taking them and turning them into sophisticated manufactured products. Well unfortunately the Japanese would prefer to make the chopsticks back home, and there isn't a lot New Zealand can do about it because it's just so desperate for money.

At the state railway, staff was cut from 22,000 to less than 6,000, a third. But now it actually hauls more freight than before. It's been called the most efficient railway in the world.

RICHARD PREBBLE
No one owes New Zealand a living and we've got to make a choice. Can we run a railway and be a railway museum or are we going to run a country? We decided to run a country.

ERIC MALLING
The railway is also for sale and they're courting America's Burlington Northern. New Zealanders don't like selling to foreigners any more than Canadians would but New Zealand needs foreign cash to keep up with foreign debt. TV New Zealand, their CBC owned by the taxpayers. It's not for sale, yet. But staff has been cut in half - in half - and it's forced by law to make a profit, $26 million this year.

TV BROADCAST
One Network News.

ERIC MALLING
But in place of home-grown drama, there are lots of game shows. Wheel of Fortune, kiwi-style, with their own Vanna White.

TV BROADCAST
We always like talking about your clothes.

ERIC MALLING
Current affairs. Try 60 Minutes. They get the original from CBS and insert some of their own stories.

TV BROADCAST
... and Genevieve Westcott.

ERIC MALLING

Genevieve Westcott. The former W5 reporter became a big star here, after moving down with her New Zealand husband.

GENEVIEVE WESTCOTT

When I got the clippings from home about what cuts had been happening at the CBC, I felt bad for them. But on the other hand, if they'd had to live through it here, they would have realized they probably got off pretty lightly.

ERIC MALLING

Dealing with debt has changed everything. Beyond the used cars, people hang onto their clothes longer, eat out less, holiday at home instead of zipping off to Australia or Fiji. Standard of living: it went from third in the world to 22nd today - steak to baloney, the legacy of debt. And there's a new problem here, unemployment. Look at the jobless in 1955 - 22. Everyone knew their names. 1974 - 650. Today, 200,000. Still not as bad as Canada but here a national shame.

REV. RICHARD RANDERSON

I was at a church that opened the first food bank in 1983. The media were fascinated. Nothing like this had ever happened in New Zealand before. The number of parcels that have been given out at food banks have multiplied by a factor of eight, just in the last two years.

ERIC MALLING

So for all it's been through, New Zealand is still ailing. That's the trouble with strong medicine. Even when you're forced to take it, you don't get better right away.

RICHARD PREBBLE

I think we've turned the corner but it's going to take a lot of hard work.

ERIC MALLING
How much of that was debt? You know, when I grew up in Canada I thought it was my birthright. We're all told we have the second highest standard of living in the world, and you folks did very well here too. I mean, how do you convince people that maybe they're not cutting it anymore?

RICHARD PREBBLE
Well debt's about like liquor to an alcoholic because he thinks look, I'll just have another drink and I'll be right. And if it hadn't been for our ability to borrow, we would have tackled these problems 20 years ago. I wish previous governments, including my own party, when it had been in office, instead of borrowing had said to the country, look fellows, we got to bite the bullet and we all know what has to be done.

ERIC MALLING
The tough Labour government in New Zealand actually got re-elected in 1987 despite putting the country through the wringer. But for all that, the books were still out of whack. Big business was supposed to drive the recovery but instead of building factories, the tycoons were putting their money into takeovers, speculation, new glass towers. Sound familiar? They couldn't grow their way out of it in New Zealand like Canada hopes to do. In fact, the minister of finance calls that "puberty economics" - give the kid enough time and the pimples will go away. It doesn't work that way, she says. In New Zealand they bumped their GST to 12 1/2% - still not enough money coming in. So in 1990 when the National Party, the conservatives, took over from Labour, they went after what had still been sacred, medicare and welfare, any government's big ticket items. That's coming up.

Most people agree that government debt in Canada is too high. But what do you cut? Take away his unemployment insurance but don't touch my medicare. Pull out of Hibernia but keep the wheat subsidies flowing. Everything is sacred. Well as New Zealand found out, things aren't so sacred if the borrowed money runs out. Here's what happened to government spending down under.

The travel magazines say come not just for the view but gourmet food. Lamb of course but also fabulous seafood and fresh vegetables year round. Beyond national pride, food is New Zealand's vital interest, almost half of its export dollars.

TV BROADCAST

Food poisoning, the health hazard rife in the nation's eating places.

Good evening. Eating out in New Zealand can be dangerous to your health.

According to the health department, hygiene standards in our restaurants and take-away bars are so lax, food poisoning is commonplace.

ERIC MALLING

They run twice the risk of Canadians. In Dunedin, the fourth largest city, a third of the restaurants failed to meet basic health standards. Budget cuts at the health department forced by debt eliminated 50 inspectors. Now there's only 83 for the whole country. At the local level it's the same story, stretched too thin. Now the tourists from Hong Kong, Singapore, Taiwan are warned not to drink the water in some towns. Filtration has broken down and there's no money to fix it. That would never happen back home in their newly developed countries. Third World? The Maori here used to be better off than natives in Canada. But now some of their towns look just as bad as a northern reserve and some old diseases are coming back.

REV. RICHARD RANDERSON

I was running a seminar in the far north of the country

last year, and people up there are reporting an outbreak of tuberculosis. TB is something which has been unheard of in New Zealand for decades.

ERIC MALLING
And now, in a country which had medicare 30 years before Canada, it costs the top half of income earners $50 a day to go to hospital, plus the drugs. A patient wakes up in intensive care after a car crash.

DR. PETER ROBERTS
He was sweating, he was covered with perspiration and we couldn't figure out why. We thought we had his pain and so forth adequately covered. We said what's the matter, and he wrote a note to us. It says How much do we owe already? This is not the sort of thing you should be worrying about when you're sick.

SIMON UPTON
There's nothing special or sacred about a hospital just because it's a hospital. It doesn't have to necessarily provide a free service.

ERIC MALLING
Health Minister Simon Upton, Rhodes scholar, considered a bright light in the conservative-minded National Party.

SIMON UPTON
Now there are some people from around middle incomes and upwards who are having to spend more, but those are the people we judge have got to be able to take it.

ERIC MALLING
And how does it work here? Like Canada, hospitals were free. Better yet, prescription drugs virtually free. But New Zealanders have always paid extra to see the doctor. So first step was to divide the country in two. Families

below $33,000 a year get the community services - for that read "poverty card." They'll pay less for everything. $33,000 is not a lot here, prices are high.

CLERK AT CLINIC

Do you have a health card?

PATIENT

No.

ERIC MALLING

A minister though is above the line, $31 to see the doctor, $50 a day up to $500 a year for hospital.

PEOPLE ON THE STREET

I was in for four days and it cost me $200, and I think it sucks.

I'm not paying it on principle.

Oh, I think it stinks.

ERIC MALLING

Pardon me?

WOMAN

I think it stinks.

ERIC MALLING

Down at the drugstore, $15 for each prescription, up to $300 for the year. And when people get the bill for drugs that had been free:

COLLEEN DICKINSON

You tell them what it is and they'll say well no, I won't take it, I won't come back.

DR. PETER ROBERTS

We get a call from the pharmacist saying which one of

these drugs can he do without, and we say none of them.

ERIC MALLING
Jack and Barbara Christie have lots of time to smell the roses. But Jack, who used to import power tools like Black & Decker, has emphysema. Ten days in hospital, medicine and doctor's bill cost $1,280. The good news, they eventually got 80% of it back from a private insurance plan like Blue Cross. But the twist: insurance premiums went up $1,000 to cover the government's new fees.

What do you think about these new charges, these new costs?

BARBARA CHRISTIE
No, not on people's health. Nobody wants to be sick, do they?

DAVID LANGE
You ought to expect a society where a doctor feels for your pulse before he feels for your wallet.

ERIC MALLING
Tough as he was on the economy, the former Prime Minister says the new Health Minister has gone too far.

He's saying that we'll look after the poor but the people who can look after themselves, they're going to have to put in a share.

DAVID LANGE
That's right, and it's a totally inefficient way of dealing with it. The best health care is provided by people who in effect have a de facto form of insurance by paying their taxes. And it's there as a right.

SIMON UPTON
When people write to me and say Mr. Upton, I've paid my taxes, now you're asking me to pay twice, I write back -

and it's often a wee P.S. on the bottom of the letter - by the way you didn't even pay once. What you consumed over your lifetime was in part borrowed and even today it still is. I can only say it, politicians can only say, but at the end of the day if people don't believe it, then someone will pull the plug.

ERIC MALLING

Next comes competition. Insurance companies are setting up their own boutique hospitals and now if a private hospital can set a broken leg cheaper than the general hospital, that's where the government will send the patients.

You can't run hospitals like you run department stores.

SIMON UPTON

I don't see why not. You can run GP practices, radiology clinics, rest homes, geriatric hospitals. All of these places are private in this country and they do very, very well.

ERIC MALLING

Public hospitals, now called Crown Health Enterprises, are squeezed for every dollar. So here in the capital at Wellington General, the hospital's public health vehicles have become rolling billboards. The local Toyota dealer pays $125 per car per year for the ad space. Sharp Electronics towers over Auckland. But this isn't company headquarters, it's the biggest general hospital. They rent out the roof for the neon sign. It pays the salary for one more nurse. A neighbourhood clinic on a suburban corner. Come right in, kind old Doc is waiting, and his sign at least is sponsored by the big drug companies. Everything has to pay. It's the same throughout government. Even the weather costs money.

TV BROADCAST
A big surge of cold air moving across the country. The snow crystallized out of that.

ERIC MALLING
That incidentally is like snow in August here. TV New Zealand has to pay the weather office $2,000 a week for this information. Fishermen and airlines get charged too. Public servants everywhere carry bulging briefcases, but in New Zealand they do work at home. No more job for life. The top 400 bureaucrats like these in the debt management office are on contract - deliver or else. In return they have a lot more flexibility to hire the best people, buy computers or pencils wherever they're cheapest. And it shows in Wellington where there's lots of expensive space empty. Departments are settling for cheaper digs. Welfare, pensions, unemployment benefits. Those under 25 cut back to $100 a week and told to move back home. Single moms. When the youngest child is 7 years old, look for work. The unemployed. Turn down two jobs and you're cut off. Severance pay. That's fortunate, so no benefits for six months, or until the cash runs out. And then pensions.

RICHARD PREBBLE
We had the world's most generous pension scheme, which means that when you were 60, even if you earned a million dollars a year, you've got a pension which was equal to 80% of the average wage.

ERIC MALLING
It was Richard Prebble's previous Labour government that started boosting the pension age from 60 back up to 65. And the well-to-do were cut off.

RICHARD PREBBLE
They went mad. They came in their Mercedes Benz to

Parliament and marched on us, one of the most extraordinary marches I've ever seen.

ERIC MALLING

There's still plenty of private wealth around and in places like Auckland's Mission Bay they don't want to share it with burglars. They needed a police substation, but no money.

MAUREEN FLETCHER

One businessman got in on the act and gave us $10,000 and we thought right, with this sort of money we can make a building. So we persuaded the city council to give us some land, raised the money and the Lions built it free of charge.

ERIC MALLING

Not a thing of beauty but with the station in place, the city did send out an officer. Next, get a local dealer to donate a car.

MAUREEN FLETCHER

And he gave us a little Honda which was brilliant, with lights and horns and whistles and everything. But when the lights and the sirens were on, the car just absolutely died. It wasn't powerful enough to cope with everything.

ERIC MALLING

So donate a bigger car and with that comes a bigger sign advertising the good-hearted dealership. It's a touch of the frontier spirit and some of the cutbacks people don't seem to mind. But the charges for health care are different. According to the polls they all hate that cash register at the hospital.

It could cost you the government, it's that unpopular.

SIMON UPTON

Well I'd have to say, and I think quite a lot of politicians in New Zealand since the mid-'80s would say this, that the survival of the country is actually more important than just winning an election and putting our children and grandchildren further into hock. Sorry, folks, we told you you could have things which we didn't ever pay for. We have to break the bad news, that's just not possible. It was always a fairytale and we really are at the edge of the cliff.

ERIC MALLING

Well now a lot of Canadians I think are getting a view of the cliff too. But we just can't seem to deal with it. But apart from no choice, New Zealand does have a couple of advantages, no Senate and no provinces, so the government can on its own deal with things. And of course both main parties, Labour and National, agree that debt is a disaster. Of course we're probably getting to that point too when you hear what NDPers Bob Rae in Ontario and Roy Romanow in Saskatchewan are saying about debt these days. I suspect there's very little Preston Manning would disagree with. Curiously in New Zealand, the only party that says they can start spending again is Alliance, an alliance of far-left wingers and on the far right, Social Credit. It actually still lives in New Zealand. When we come back, farm subsidies - gone.

Headline in the paper this week said farmers got a 64% increase in direct aid from the government last year. Farmers said they're still not making do. What happens though when you have to make do? Coming up.

Of all the subjects we deal with on W5, I suspect none is touchier than farm subsidies, like motherhood. But according to the OECD, the international economists, about a third of everything Canadian farmers take in is subsidy. It comes as payments from government and payments from consumers who get soaked by marketing boards for milk, eggs and poultry. The bottom line: When you take farm profits, what farmers have to live on, they're getting more from subsidies than they are from farming. Used to be that way in New Zealand too.

Bosnia? Belfast? Beirut? Wrong.

TV BROADCAST

All around France, farmers blocked roads with their tractors ...

ERIC MALLING

The French are among the most pampered farmers in the world, and still they explode over any threat to their subsidies. Saskatoon in January. Saskatchewan wheat farmers have been getting $20,000 a year from government but here they're demanding a lot more.

FARMER

By dammit, we need money today!

ERIC MALLING

Their prices are down. Russia's not buying, and these days Europe exports more wheat than Canada. But if farmers anywhere ought to be protesting, it's in New Zealand. Market price for wool, nothing more. Here during the debt crisis in 1984, farmers suddenly lost every penny in a system that had subsidized not only sheep and wool but fences, fertilizer, farm interest.

DAVID CAREY

The farmers of the day really enjoyed it but there has to be a day of reckoning.

ERIC MALLING

And that came with foreign debt. Beef and sheep farmer Dave Carey.

DAVID CAREY

Financially this country was really and truly in the mire. I don't know the position of Canada but I would suggest —

ERIC MALLING

Worse if anything, worse.

DAVID CAREY

Well I haven't got a choice.

ERIC MALLING

New Zealand farmers do have a big advantage. The grass grows year round and the sheep look after the rest. But when Britain joined Europe 20 years ago, the arse went out of her boy, as they say in Newfoundland. Dave Carey and the others had lost their main market for lamb and wool. But instead of having them grow something else, the government laid on the subsidies. Social security for sheep. Like Canada, one in three farm dollars was coming from subsidy. The nation's freezers were bursting with unsold lamb, and so they started destroying it.

DAVID CAREY

Melt it down.

ERIC MALLING

For what?

DAVID CAREY

For tallow and for some of the stock foods, so they're actually fed back to the stock to eat. We didn't mind, farmers didn't mind. Couldn't care, we were getting paid. The rest of New Zealand was starting to have a bit of a stomach full of farmers getting more money than what they were through subsidies. And indeed, in the place we've got here now, we've got a swimming pool here. It was bought by subsidies. They had to spend it.

ERIC MALLING

It's the problem with subsidies. The ones who get the most often need it the least.

You cut those farming subsidies.

DAVID LANGE

We didn't cut them, we slashed them.

ERIC MALLING

But the real motive back in 1984, David Lange's Labour government was broke, too deep into debt.

I'm sure you watched the news every night and said farmers are going to be thrown off their land, people were committing suicide.

DAVID LANGE

They burnt me in effigy, take my car, they pinched the flag. Massive protests, but there was at the same time an appreciation that the party couldn't last forever and someone had decided to call a halt.

ERIC MALLING

In New Zealand it's not just the sheep who know about being sheared. All of the subsidies were gone in just three months. The price of a lamb fell from 23 down to just $8 because of the glut. Land prices which had been driven sky-high by subsidies fell by half. Like farm incomes.

Bruce Bolt had just bought this spectacular 1,200 acres for a million dollars, and a lot of it was borrowed so the bank moved in.

BRUCE BOLT

We were within a few days of being sold off.

ERIC MALLING

Bolt convinced the creditors he was worth a lot less dead

than alive, and besides he had a plan. Bulls. He calls them "soccer hooligans." They're rowdy but they grow a lot faster and leaner than males that have been fixed, turned into steers. Bruce Bolt looks after 1,000 of them by himself because of electric fences. High-tech farmer. These boys would eat ordinary barbed wire for breakfast if they took a hankering to visit Daisy next door. Bolt still has 2,000 sheep and went up in the hills to capture deer. He's bred them into a commercial herd and there's a rich market for them in the finest restaurants of Germany. Now he's making $180,000 a year, no subsidies.

BRUCE BOLT
With subsidies sometimes you seem to get the wrong thing produced in the wrong place for the wrong reason.

ERIC MALLING
But it wasn't easy here. Farmers work harder, fewer hired men. They share machinery. But most important: produce a premium product. Carey's lambs are worth $50 each and will be flown fresh to France and Britain for Easter Sunday.

DAVID CAREY
Our farmers, instead of going out and growing fat lambs, they're now growing prime lean lambs. The whole, that word "fat" has gone away from the farmer vocabulary. It's not there.

ERIC MALLING
So you've had to be smarter.

DAVID CAREY
For sure.

ERIC MALLING
That's why New Zealand lamb comes to Canada in neat little packages perfectly trimmed and almost half the price

of home-grown. And the bulls? Some of them end up here. Talk about selling ice in the Arctic. New Zealand sells Canada 200 million burgers a year. That's eight for each of us. The hooligans are too stringy for steak but perfect in lean ground. What else has changed? Well in the old days, farming for subsidies meant clearing and grazing every last acre, even cliffs which soon started eroding.

DAVID CAREY
There was a lot of land which had never, ever been touched, never.

ERIC MALLING
Now it'll go back to this or be planted for commercial forest, another cash crop. Fertilizer: They used to spread and spray it everywhere just to keep more sheep on welfare.

DAVID CAREY
That suddenly got into all of our waterways and only now, and it's probably 6 or 7 years after those subsidies have come off, that our waterways etc. are starting to come right.

ERIC MALLING
And when the farmers got efficient, they pushed their suppliers to lower costs, trucking prices were cut in half, and next the packing plants, "the works" as they're so elegantly called here. Dave Carey and 700 other farmers built their own plant in partnership with a local Maori council. Rigid union job categories are gone in New Zealand, so the Maori on the floor all get $15 an hour and farmers can give a lamb "the works" for six bucks, half of what the old plants had charged. And it's so efficient this one plant could handle all the lamb in Canada. So the farmers survived, prospered even. But what about the predictions that the countryside would be empty? Surely it's better to keep farmers on the land than pay them welfare in the cities.

DAVID CAREY

That was an argument before our subsidies had been removed. There are probably more farmers on land now than what there was then.

ERIC MALLING

But the argument is, you know, everybody else is doing it. Should any country cut its own farmers' throats in order to get rid of the subsidies unilaterally?

DAVID CAREY

It is not as bad as what it's made out to be. We are now getting probably the best prices that we ever had for our lamb, best price that we ever had for our beef.

ERIC MALLING

Because you've produced a better product, the world will pay more for it.

DAVID CAREY

Sure, for sure.

ERIC MALLING

But you know, another argument is when something goes wrong on the farm, it's usually God's fault. It's drought, it's grasshoppers, and we should all pitch in to help out.

DAVID CAREY

The government used to come in and pay drought relief. That's gone. Farmers cannot be propped up simply because they're farmers, because other industries also have some hard times. So if you look after one, you're going to have to look after the rest. And so basically now we're getting to the stage where everybody is getting treated the same. And why not?

ERIC MALLING
And last word, a little advice for Canada, when we come back.

Canada as you know has more debt for its size than New Zealand did when it hit the wall. We're running higher deficits. But it's one of those things that's "someone else's" problem. It's the politicians' fault, and for politicians the rule is it's not a problem if you're in opposition and then when you're in government it's the only problem where some people think excuse. We'll be right back to see what New Zealand politicians have to say.

If you've stuck with us this long, you'll want to hear the last word, some advice for Canada from two New Zealand politicians who've been nailed to the wall because of debt. And remember, these are implacable political foes. First, Health Minister Simon Upton, the farmer who went to Oxford, the conservative cabinet minister who savaged medicare.

You know, when Canadians hear apocalyptic talk about debt, they say well, that happens to Mexico, that happens to Brazil, that happens in Africa. It can't happen to us.

SIMON UPTON
It just takes longer in rich countries, that's all.

ERIC MALLING
Was it the same here?

SIMON UPTON
Yes, absolutely. And the only difference between an African Third World state and a Canada or a New Zealand is that they actually hit the end of their credit limit very quickly. We're given more rope to hang ourselves with.

ERIC MALLING
So what's the lesson for us in what's happened to you?

SIMON UPTON

Well I can't judge for Canada. But when your credit rating is on the line, that focuses the mind. And what New Zealand governments have had to confront and try to communicate to the people is this: listen, we can't ask other people to fund our living standards forever. Eventually they'll say no.

ERIC MALLING

But living standards are interesting. I mean, I grew up in Canada believing that the second highest standard of living in the world was our birthright. Did New Zealanders feel the same way?

SIMON UPTON

Of course they did. But was it your birthright to enjoy those living standards when people in Asia were working two to three times harder than you? Was it your birthright to go on borrowing from other more productive countries to sustain your living standards? No, of course it wasn't. The real challenge comes in the second half of the 1990s in New Zealand. If we get 3, 4, 5% growth we'll start to run budget surpluses. Now that's when the real courage is needed because politicians are going to have to say to people, folks, there's a budget surplus and it's a healthy one and guess what? We're not going to spend one cent of it. It's all going to debt retirement. And that's the real test.

ERIC MALLING

Richard Prebble is a socialist lawyer in Auckland. He lives in a kind of ramshackle house with a fish cart out back. His constituency sells fish on Saturdays in the market to raise campaign funds. Prebble remembers that first cabinet meeting just after his Labour Party won the 1984 election.

RICHARD PREBBLE

I couldn't see how any government could get re-elected, the books were so bad. And so I met with the other finance ministers and said look, let's set politics aside, let's forget everything we've done in our whole adult life and let's actually decide to do what's best for the country. And we did it. We were certain we were going to be lynched, and we went up in the polls. That was a great surprise to us.

ERIC MALLING

But what does that tell you? I mean, in Canada people can talk about debt, and they're all concerned about debt until you take away my rail line or touch my pension or fiddle with medicare in any way.

RICHARD PREBBLE

I don't believe Canadians are any different from New Zealanders. If a politician actually went on TV, forgot about his media advisors and told the truth, the real truth, what he would find to his astonishment is that that person will become the most popular politician in Canada.

ERIC MALLING

Oh politicians have been telling us we're sinking into a sea of debt for ages.

RICHARD PREBBLE

But then they don't do anything about it. And then they wonder why they're unpopular. No, no, you can't just say look, we're sinking into debt. You've got to give the real facts and then say hey, the only way we can turn this around is we got to raise more revenue as a government and we've got to spend less buying votes. And we're not going to buy votes from anyone. Tell all the privileged groups frankly to go to hell and then you'll be surprised, you'll get a good response.

ERIC MALLING
We're pre-empted next week, back in two. I suspect some of you may want to write to us. Our address is CTV-W5, Box 565, Station F, Toronto, Ontario M4Y 2L8 or fax us at 416-609-7427. Good night.

The PM finished his speed-reading, then sat back to monitor who would be the last to finish. Judging from the expression on each face, it was clear that all his people were translating the New Zealand crisis into Canadian terms and measuring what the extent of such damage would be in their own lives, their own country.

Finally the PM opened the response to what they had just read. "Pretty rough stuff, the way I see it. Perhaps I should use 'horrendous' instead of 'rough.'"

"'Horrendous' is a good word," Black acknowledged. "I'm afraid what happened in New Zealand was child's play compared to what's about to happen here in Canada."

"Yeah, but we're not going to have condoms coming down the hill out of sewer pipes we don't have the money to fix." Carter was emphatic. "Know why?" She paused, knowing no one would have the answer. "Because there won't be a soul in Canada who's going to have enough money to buy a condom."

Weinstock's face was expressionless. "That's not really as unreal as you think. The image is that incomes — the buying power of the dollar — are going to be reduced to rat shit. Combine that with the knocked-down value of your dollar against ours. Skyrocketing interest rates. I mean . . ."

"Plus inflation, once we start printing money," Greco added.

"That used Japanese automobile thing" — Simpson's voice had a tone of surprise — "it had never, ever occurred to me . . ."

Black picked up on it. "Think about it. With the FTA and NAFTA in full force, there are no import duties on used cars out of our country into yours. You can wind up in exactly the same position — well, similar anyway. You'll continue to produce new cars in the Ford, GM, and Chrysler plants here."

"But the only buyers will be Americans."

"Exactly. All your people will be able to afford to buy will be our used junk — like the New Zealanders."

Jane Smith shook her head sadly. "This can't be happening."

"This is only the beginning," Black told her. "The best thing you can get out of the New Zealand experience is that the human spirit isn't easy to break. Bend it, yes. Break it, no. The collapse or withdrawal of credit to New Zealand was theoretically expected for a long time. But no one — not anyone, not for a minute — believed that someone would call the loans and pull the plug. But that's what happened."

"And that's exactly what's happening to us," the PM admitted. "Almost exactly. Now what do we do about it?"

Black turned the question away. "Before we deal with the 'what do we do about it?' question, I suggest we take a look at the Mexico shambles that began at the end of 1994."

There were no notes to refer to.

"The collapse of the Mexican peso was like the situation here. It was totally predictable yet totally unexpected."

"Like our situation," the PM commented.

"In short, Mexico disregarded the on-going advice of the International Monetary Fund, particularly with regard to exchange rate readjustments. The result was an enormous trade deficit — enormous.

"From 1991 to 1993 foreign funds poured into Mexico as international investors looked for countries to park their money in during the global recession. They bought 15 percent Mexican bonds and securities and hundreds of millions of shares in the Mexican stock market.

"At the same time, Mexico was following some, but not all, of the IMF's advice. It sold state-owned companies to private buyers and it started to get rid of trade barriers."

Carter muttered, "NAFTA, the famous North American Free Trade Agreement."

"Exactly."

"A smoke-and-mirrors deal for Canada. NAFTA did little more than increase our trade wars with you people," Carter complained. "Anyway . . ."

Black shrugged and went on. "The main point about Mexico is that its government succeeded in meeting an IMF goal that Canada just can't seem to reach. It balanced its budget. Its deficit was zero. I'll come back to the debt situation."

The PM had started to make notes. Others followed his example as Black spoke.

"Mexicans took the great piles of money that were flowing in and did the human thing. They spent it buying far more goods from abroad than the country could pay for with the proceeds from its exports. In fact, their trade deficit was horrendous — at a rate of three times the biggest American trade deficits of the 1980s."

Black looked down the table at her scribbling Canadian audience. "In 1994 the inflow of international money to Mexico stopped. Higher U.S. interest rates that we — the Federal Reserve Board — permitted made it more attractive to invest in the U.S. than Mexico. The global recession was over. Political violence in Mexico turned off investors.

"When the money tap turned off in '94, the Mexican government spent 20 billion U.S. in six months to defend the peso's value in relation to the U.S. dollar. When they ran out of reserves, they had to unpeg the peso, which immediately lost roughly 30 percent of its value."

"Just like our loonie," Smith said.

Black continued: "Mexico was in the middle of an economic disaster. They needed outside assistance desperately. The U.S. Congress balked at Clinton's forty-billion bailout plan, so he came up with his own scheme independent of Congress. It was a combination of loans and loan guarantees available over three to five years that would give Mexico up to twenty billion to help restructure its debts.

"His plan called for loans of a further 17.8 billion from the IMF — its biggest ever to a country in financial distress."

Black stopped. Her eyes looked into the face of the PM, then moved momentarily to the other listeners, as she emphasized what she had just said. "Remember that number. It's only 17.8 billion. Your debt is over 900 billion. And you think the IMF's going to bail you out?"

Black didn't expect an answer. "Mexico's debt in 1995 at the time of its bailout was eighty-six billion; that's a long way from where you are.

"By the way, if 400 billion of your debt is in U.S. dollars, with a 50-cent

Canadian dollar it will cost you 800 billion Canadian to cover that U.S. debt. So I think your nine-hundred-billion debt estimate is somewhat low in real terms."

Black shrugged her shoulders again. She was finished.

There were no questions, just stunned silence.

Weinstock waited for a moment. "Mr. Prime Minister, before Abbi did Mexico you asked the question, what can we do about it? My answer is, by doing what you're doing. You're gonna bring in a new axe-everybody budget." His eyes rolled from side to side as he talked. "You're gonna keep paying people on the government take, you're gonna print money to cover them . . ."

"And the armed forces."

"Sure, and you'll just dish out increasingly valueless money to all the foreign lenders."

"If they'll take it."

"They won't have a choice. The foreign lenders who hold your paper right now, they'll be delighted to get whatever they can, interest first, principal a close second."

"Even if we print it?"

"So print it. Your dollar will have a foreign exchange value and the nation's exports will continue to earn international currency. It's important, absolutely essential, that Canada pay the interest on its existing debt. You have to commit — publicly pledge — to do so."

"You're right — even though we have to savage our social programs and every other goddam program on our books."

"Even though," Weinstock acknowledged.

"As you know, that's a seventy-six-billion interest hit, a hit this year that creates a deficit of sixty-six billion," the PM reminded Weinstock. "Which means again that, apart from the interest, this year the government's revenues will exceed its expenditures by 10 billion."

"As for your domestic leaders," Weinstock added, "they've gone underground as of today, at least for the moment. You can probably get most of them out of their holes by using a high, I mean really high, interest rate."

"But not the international lenders?"

"Interest alone won't do it. But if you can get your budget right — and, as I said, you're heading in the right direction with it — if the budget turns them on and the interest rates, real interest rates, are high enough . . ."

The PM had to make his point emphatically. "Even if we turn on the international markets, the money taps, Chairman, Canada has to stop borrowing money — stop right now!"

Weinstock snorted. "Well, you've already done that, but somebody else made the decision for you."

There was a pause in the conversation as Black turned and spoke quietly into Weinstock's ear. He nodded, saying, "Go ahead."

Black then addressed the PM. "You have to decide, Mr. Prime Minister, if your budget is designed for the purpose of stopping, eliminating the need for borrowing. Or if it's designed to get the borrowing tap turned on again."

Carter joined in. "The stop-borrowing budget could be a helluva lot different than a borrow-again budget, right?"

"You got it." Weinstock grinned, his eyes looking directly at Carter's. As a long-time Harvard economics professor with a world-class reputation, he still retained the odd teaching trait in large meetings. "So, tell me, Ms. . . ."

"Carter . . . Ann."

"Tell me, Ann, what would the differences be, the basic differences, between a stop budget and a borrow-again budget?"

She smiled. "Will I get a fail mark if I give the wrong answer, Professor?"

"The worst you can get is an F."

"Okay. The stop budget means exactly that: cutting sixty-six billion out of our operating programs so we can pay the interest on our debt. To do that, we have to destroy our social support structures, stop foreign aid, cut the military to next to nothing, fire tens of thousands of civil servants. The blood and gore will be enormous."

She stopped to write something. Two or three words. Carter looked at the PM as if for approval, then directed her remarks again at Weinstock. "If we do the stop-borrowing scenario we have to tell ourselves we don't give a damn about the political consequences."

Black asked, "Have you people enough political guts to do that?"

Ann frowned. "Let me reserve on that question. There's a path opening up in my mind . . ."

She went on. "A borrow-again budget has a large political component: one political eye on the taxpayers, votes, the other eye on what will please, give confidence to those goddam mysterious world-market gremlins."

Someone coughed and Carter frowned at the disturbance. Weinstock waved his hand for her to continue.

"What they'll be looking for is not a stop budget but something that shows we really mean business — like cutting the deficit from sixty-six to thirty-three billion. So a borrow-again budget is political, a two-eyed political monster.

"For us it would be much easier, much more palatable than a stop budget. That was the route taken in the 1995 budget." She lifted her head to look at Weinstock. "How am I doing, Professor?"

"F so far. But you aren't finished yet, are you? You've got that note you scribbled."

Carter nodded. "You're a perceptive O.F."

"O.F.?"

"Old fart."

The room broke up. A welcome few seconds of relief from the tough going.

"What I wrote was 'interest, why pay all.'"

Black asked, "What do you mean by that?"

"Just this. The world knows we're bankrupt, we can't pay. So why don't we use an ancient bankruptcy technique and make the creditors an offer?"

Greco nodded his agreement. "That's sure worth considering."

"The offer fits the stop-borrowing concept. Don't offer, just tell the foreign creditors — and the domestic ones too — we're not going to borrow any more money and we're going to pay you interest, but only twenty cents on the dollar."

She stopped and scribbled again. "That would mean our interest payment would be about fifteen billion and the deficit would be only five billion instead of sixty-six. I can find five without batting one of my lovely eyelashes."

No smile from Weinstock. He was too busy analysing her suggestion.

"Well, Professor, what do you think?" Carter asked.

The Chairman leaned back in his chair, stuffed his hands in his pockets, and straightened out his legs while he put together his response. "Go to the head of the class, Minister. The screams will be loud, particularly in Japan.

But if the decision is to stop borrowing, what have you got to lose?"

He didn't really expect an answer to that question. The American shifted in his chair, forehead furrowed as he thought, then said, "Prime Minister, there's something going on in my head, an idea that I'd like to put to you. It's a possible solution. But as I said earlier — no offence to your people here — I'd like to talk to you privately after we wrap this session up. We can have that nightcap in my suite, okay?"

"Sure. As a matter of fact, we can adjourn this meeting right now." The PM looked around the table. "You people will be back here at eight in the morning, please. I'll be in the IMF lion's den in Washington, so Ann will be in the chair."

13

11:50 P.M.: The Chateau Laurier Hotel

Chairman Weinstock carefully poured a glass of white wine for the Prime Minister and another for Abbi Black. For himself he took a hefty shot of Jack Daniel's bourbon with lots of ice. The management of the Chateau Laurier certainly knew how to stock a bar in the royal suite. He took the glasses of white wine to his guests seated in chairs around the flaming fireplace.

As Weinstock settled himself into the third chair that formed a semi-circle around the fireplace, he said, "That was a useful session Mr. Prime Minister. You seem to have the bull by the right horns. So if you don't mind, we'll grab a ride with you tomorrow morning back to Washington. Cheers!"

"Cheers." The Prime Minister responded, lifting his glass, taking a sip from it, wondering why Weinstock had suggested this private meeting. At the same time his eyes took in the remarkable face and figure of Abbi Black. She lifted her glass only partway and said nothing.

"Absolutely. I will be delighted to have you along. I just have young Camp coming with me. I'll have a car waiting for you here at the hotel at five."

"Five o'clock?" Weinstock was startled. "God, it's five minutes past twelve right now."

"That's okay, Mr. Prime Minister," Black said softly. "We'll be up, checked out and ready to go by five. I'll make sure of that."

"The Chairman is probably not a morning man, is he?"

"How did you guess?" Black laughed.

"I'm no conversationalist between five and seven in the morning,"

Weinstock admitted. “I just need my *New York Times* and coffee fix.”

“I’ll get a *Times* faxed to the aircraft.”

“Wonderful. Just the front and editorial pages — and the business section, please.” Weinstock sat back, rolling the bourbon glass between the palms of his hands. “The reason I wanted to talk with you, Mr. Prime Minister —”

“Richard, if you don’t mind — at this late stage would you please call me by my name?”

“Okay, Richard, and the same for us.” Weinstock smiled, sipped from his glass. “The reason I wanted to talk with you privately is that my solution would be a terrible shock for your team. Terrible. You can take it but it might be too much for them.”

He took a sip of his drink, then began: “The fact is that even if you made a ten-billion surplus each year it would take Canada ninety years to pay off its debt. Even if you stop running deficits now, you’re going to have to find billions of dollars each year to pay interest. You might get away with a 20-percent interest payment to your debtor this one time. But I can tell you, you won’t get away with it a second time — not unless foreign governments are prepared to subsidize or indemnify their institutions and private lenders who have bought the Treasury bills, bonds, or whatever other paper Canada’s been flogging.”

The PM remained silent, wondering what the Chairman was going to say next.

Weinstock took a long swig of his bourbon. “You have seventy-six billion dollars in interest apparently on the books for this year. Suppose that forty billion of that amount is to be paid out as interest to your foreign holders. That money, that forty billion, has to be in foreign currency that Canada has to buy in the international money markets. But your dollar is at fifty cents to the American buck at this stage! Frankly, Richard, I don’t see how Canada can do it. You haven’t a hope in hell of getting out of this mess, unless . . .”

“Unless what?” The PM was hunched forward on the edge of his seat.

“There is only one solution. In fact, I’ve been trying to think of other alternatives, but I just can’t.”

Weinstock looked at Black, then back at the Prime Minister. “I have run this by Abbi because it is so off-the-wall, I wanted to get the reaction of a rational, disinterested person before I gave it to you. And if you react positively, I'll start to implement my idea immediately. It will be top priority. Hey, let me get you another glass of wine. You're gonna need it."

The refill was quickly poured. Weinstock topped up his own glass, sat again and began to describe his solution — as he called it.

The Prime Minister sat transfixed and shocked as he listened to the Weinstock plan unfolding. His mind was saying, "I can't believe what I am hearing, but what he's saying may well be the only solution."

Weinstock was finished. "Is there anything else, Abbi? Have I missed anything?"

"I don't think so. I think you've covered all the points. The proposition isn't complicated. But to implement it will be an absolutely enormous challenge, mind-boggling."

Badly shaken, his mind reeling at the consequences of the Weinstock plan, the PM had only one question. "What about the IMF?"

"You're seeing them tomorrow morning. They'll tell you what they can and can't do. I'm not gonna try to tell you what I think they're gonna say. Frankly I don't think they have the wherewithal to bail you out. Not even close. You heard what Abbi said about the Mexico numbers and the IMF."

Black added, "It sounds to me that, logically, Al's plan is the ultimate solution, no matter what the IMF does or doesn't do."

"Understood." The PM got up and walked to the fireplace and put his empty wine glass on the mantle. Turning to Weinstock, he said, "It seems to me that if I give approval in principle to your plan it would in no way interfere with what we're doing, developing a very tough budget, recalling Parliament, putting the budget forward on Wednesday, that sort of thing."

"Absolutely not. In fact, my plan is predicated on your continuing with all your spending reform steps — if I may use the word reform. I mean, your action has to be as drastic as possible right now. Go and see the IMF. See what you can get out of them, whether it's money or ideas. Get whatever you can."

In an unconscious gesture that showed the pressure he was under, the PM lifted his hand to rub his forehead for a moment. "I wish I had time to kick your plan around with my Cabinet colleagues."

"You really should do that," Black encouraged him. "You'll be back in your office by, what, one or two tomorrow afternoon? You could run it by the team we met with tonight, and perhaps one or two of your Ministers."

Weinstock added, "I'll need to have word by tomorrow afternoon at the outside, because if you say go, the work necessary to put this together — the ramifications internationally and otherwise — will be incredible. We're gonna need all the time we can get."

The PM nodded. "I hear you." He drew a deep breath, straightened his back, warming as it was against the fire. "I'll tell you this, Al. I think your plan has merit. But I'm going to have to present it to my people, see how they react. Meanwhile, between now and, say, tomorrow at noon, if you two can work up a business plan, a list of the steps that you and I would have to take, jointly and independently, and a timetable, then I'll have something concrete to discuss with my people. I'll call you after that meeting."

"Okay. By tomorrow afternoon I'll have the business plan ready. Abbi and I'll have the meat on the bones of the Weinstock Solution."

It was time to leave. The PM said, "I want to thank you again for coming here on such short notice. You two must be tired — I know I am. I really must go."

The Chairman stood up and shook the Prime Minister's hand, saying, "You're a brave man, Richard. The lashes across your back will be beyond beleif. But you've got a great country, almost as good as the United States. It's worth taking the lashes for."

"I'm like your President. I'll take the lashes and I'll carry the can, and I won't drop it."

He took Black's hand and kissed her on both beautiful cheeks. "Thank you, Abbi. See you at the airport." As he went out the door he stopped, looked at both of them, and said, "There have been a lo
in this hotel since it was built and a lot of choices m
Probably none as important as what we've talked about tonight. Thank you. You're both terrific."

Day Three

Tuesday, January 30, 2001

14

Early Morning: Ottawa–Washington, D.C.

For the two Americans the trip from Ottawa to Washington began as dark, frigid, snow-ridden agony, until they got on board the comfortable Challenger aircraft. For the Prime Minister and Simon Camp, the below-freezing temperature was normal. Nevertheless, getting into the cocoon of the warm jet was a relief for the near-exhausted Prime Minister.

The faxed sections of the *New York Times* were waiting for Weinstock, as was a steaming mug of excellent coffee. As soon as he settled into his seat he shared his newspaper with Abbi Black. She declined the coffee in favour of orange juice.

Shortly after getting airborne, the steward served breakfast. When that was out of the way, the Prime Minister put his seat back and went to sleep, while Weinstock conferred with Black and busied himself making notes on a foolscap pad.

As the Challenger started into its final approach to Dulles Airport, the PM woke up and apologized to the two Americans for sleeping when he should have been spending at least some of the time with them.

"No problem." Weinstock smiled. "Obviously your ass is dragging and you need all your batteries at full power when you meet those bastards at the IMF."

Black gave Richard the radiant smile that he found so attractive. "We have that plan almost finished — the action list for the . . ."

"The Weinstock Solution."

"Yes, the Weinstock Solution. Exactly."

Weinstock cautioned, "But it's still preliminary, so we're not going to show it to you now. But if you come back to me with the positive answer this afternoon, Abbi and I will have it ready by then."

He looked quizzically at the Prime Minister. "Richard, are you really sure you want to go with my plan? I mean it's a ball buster. Remember those lashes I was talking about. I'm not kidding!"

The PM gave Weinstock a rueful look in return. "As I told you, it's a decision I can't take by myself. But there really isn't much choice."

"You got it, my friend. Your choice is zero, zilch, nothing . . . unless there's something the IMF can put on the table."

"I'm sure that if there's nothing they wouldn't be letting me come down here."

Weinstock shook his head. "Don't be *too* sure about that."

"You and Abbi are driving into town in the IMF limo with us. Simon organized that with you, didn't he?"

"He sure did. We can talk on the way."

It was five minutes to eight when the PM and Camp stepped out of the limousine to walk through falling snow into the impressive front entrance of the International Monetary Fund headquarters. As they stepped inside the foyer, they were met by a distinguished-looking grey-haired gentleman in his formal banker's uniform: a navy blue, double-breasted suit and grey tie. His grey hair was combed straight back, horn-rimmed glasses perched squarely on his flushed face. This precise-looking person spoke just that way — in precise, measured tones — as he offered his hand.

"Prime Minister, I am Aubrey Farnsworth, the executive director of the IMF. Your token Canadian member of the IMF executive hierarchy."

"Yes, but the word 'token' doesn't apply to you, according to my briefing notes."

Farnsworth smiled. "It's because being Canadian, Prime Minister, I am naturally modest."

The PM introduced Camp. That done, Farnsworth said, "The Managing Director is waiting for you in his office. As you know, Mr. Tromso is Norwegian."

The three men walked to the elevator, the PM nodding and saying, "Yes, so I understand."

When the elevator reached the top floor of the tall structure, Farnsworth took them to the Managing Director's suite. The Canadians removed their heavy winter gear, which a respectful secretary deposited in the cavernous reception area closet. Farnsworth led them to the tall double doors of the spacious office of the man who headed one of the world's primary institutions for planetary economic and financial stability.

The IMF head man rose to his full six-foot-four height in order to greet his Canadian visitors. He strode from behind his desk, a warm Scandinavian smile on his long, leathery face, saying in perfect American-accented English how delighted he was to see the new Canadian Prime Minister, the head of government of a brotherly Arctic nation.

The PM studied the man in front of him. The high, narrow forehead was topped by a sparse scattering of wispy, combed-straight-back white hair. Below that forehead were slender black eyebrows, slitted green-irised eyes, puffy below-eye pouches, and a punched-in, once-aquiline nose.

Leif Tromso was known as a pleasant, cultured man who had an aloof Scandinavian innocence that was apart from the politics and ethnic hostilities that historically permeated the old Europe as well as the new.

The urbane Tromso had four hectic years behind him as head of the IMF. He had succeeded the volatile Michel Camdessus when that Frenchman's second term came to an end on February 1, 1997. Camdessus had endured a falling-out with his principal clients, the G-7 (the U.S., Japan, France, Britain, Germany, Italy, and Canada), in late 1994, when the IMF had refused a G-7 proposal to add only $23.4 billion (U.S.) to the international monetary system.

Instead, Camdessus had lobbied for $52 billion in SDRs, special drawing rights, to support the rapidly expanding economies of Asia and Latin America. He argued that the $23.4 billion proposed by the G-7 was simply not enough.

The G-7 stood fast. Negotiations collapsed. The ultimate loser was not the G-7 but Camdessus himself who, isolated by his falling-out with the G-7, became a lame duck during the remaining two years of his term.

Tromso had been the restructured G-7's compromise choice and in his four-year stint had been successful in accommodating the wishes of his principal funding masters in the crucial objective of providing money and credit to support international economic growth.

The restructured G-7? It had become the G-12.

By 1998, with Québec out of Canada, the wheels had fallen off the Canadian economic wagon. At least six other national economies were bigger than Canada's. Québec was so small it couldn't even make it to the middle of the developing country list.

The additional six countries with economies bigger than Canada were Russia, Brazil, Mexico, China, India, and Indonesia. So it was that in 1998 Canada dropped out of the Group of 7, which then became the G-12, with the six above added.

With the greeting courtesies quickly disposed of, Tromso motioned the PM and Camp to his conference table. As they settled into their chairs Tromso, sounding like a funeral undertaker, expressed condolences to the Canadian Prime Minister. He gave full sympathy to Canada for the murderous assault on its fiscal and monetary stability by the notoriously ruthless Japanese.

"Mind you, Prime Minister, the Japanese action comes as no surprise. In fact the only surprise is that it didn't happen earlier, much earlier."

"Really?" The Prime Minister could not conceal his surprise.

"Oh yes. The IMF began a Canada deathwatch back in 1995, when your federal debt broke 600 billion. The IMF . . . we calculated even then that your debt, deficit, and interest — the terrible trio — were so high and still rising that sooner or later the world markets were going to . . . how do you North Americans put it?"

"Pull the plug."

"Yes, pull the plug. I mean your situation was beyond redemption even then."

"And now?"

"Far, far worse," Tromso frowned and averted his eyes. "In fact, as I just said, Canada — at least as far as the IMF is concerned — Canada is beyond redemption."

He looked directly into the PM's eyes. "Your debt is far beyond the resources of the IMF. I mean, we're used to dealing in twenty-five- or fifty-billion figures, special drawing rights, SDRs. And we have to spread our resources over a whole range of growing economies to help them increase their productivity and their trade of goods and services with the rest of the buying-and-selling world."

The PM nodded. "I hear you."

"Now you come along with your unbelievable debt. God knows, it's been growing and spreading like lava coming out of a volcano." Tromso shifted uncomfortably. "Why, for God's sake, didn't your government come to grips with this deficit debt problem in 1994 or even earlier?"

"There wasn't the political will." That was the best explanation the PM could offer. "The politicians of the mid-'90s knew they had to kill the deficit dragon. But they didn't have the guts, the political courage, to do it. Talk about it, yes. Do it, no."

The PM sat back and concentrated on his words before he spoke again. "I can understand where they were coming from. They had inherited a massive debt, an enormous annual deficit. It was the deficit that was, and still is, the monster, alive and growing. But it was made up of organic parts that Canada's body and soul could not live without. Take away or cut down to next to nothing any one of those organic parts and the nation — its society, its economy — might well die. Take away the social net — pensions, unemployment insurance, universal government health care — take those away and there would be social disaster, revolution."

"Yes, but isn't that exactly what *you* are faced with now?" Tromso's huge hands spread and lifted as he gestured his point.

"Exactly what I'm faced with now. But there is a difference, a critical difference between then and now."

"And what is that?"

"An outside force, Japan, is attacking Canada. When a country is attacked, like Hitler attacking France, England, Russia . . ."

"And Norway."

"Yes and your country," the PM acknowledged. "When that outside attack is made against *your* people, *your* country, then anything goes. Your people will make all the sacrifices necessary to defeat the attacker. It's war."

Tromso nodded. "The Japanese have attacked again."

"Exactly. And they've made it clear they're not going to take any prisoners. So —"

"So your people, your politicians — you as prime minister — all of you will recognize that there is no choice."

"No choice whatever. The government of Canada has to immediately — and I mean immediately — bring in a new budget, a spending program, including interest, that does not exceed its revenues."

Tromso smiled. "Which is the precise message I was going to give you, Prime Minister."

"Are there other messages, Mr. Tromso?"

"Several." The Managing Director looked at the list on the desk in front of him. "The first is simply that Canada's federal debt of one trillion, a thousand billion, is far beyond the financing provided by our G-12 member states."

The PM looked Tromso in the eye. "You mean there's no way you can give us any meaningful assistance." It was not a question.

"Those are good words: 'meaningful assistance.' Which means none at all. Well, almost none. Back in the mid-'90s my predecessor, Camdessus, lost the fight to get SDRs for fifty-some-odd billion to be spread among developing, producing countries everywhere. Fifty billion is one thing. Nine hundred is quite another. You do understand."

The PM looked rueful. "Of course I understand. But what would you think of a paltry five billion or perhaps ten? Could you find that amount — U.S., of course. Could you justify that for Canada?"

Tromso was silent.

The PM went on. "Canada has credits for megabucks we've advanced to the IMF even when we had to borrow to get the money. That was part of our G-7 obligation."

"But you were dropped from the G-7 brotherhood."

"Sure we were. But the money we advanced to the IMF has never been repaid, the SDRs and that sort of thing."

"So is that all you want, five or ten billion?" Tromso sounded polite but skeptical.

"Yes, ten. For now, that is."

"Why so little?"

The Prime Minister of Canada explained the theory. The money would be used for making payments to the Canadian government's foreign creditors — so defaults could be avoided on the short term.

"So all I need right now is ten billion U.S. maximum."

Upon entering the Managing Director's office the PM had been surprised and he showed it. Tromso was alone. He should have had his Executive Director and all his departmental heads in the office to assist in dealing with the Canadian crisis. The Prime Minister decided to raise the question, late as it might be.

"I thought you'd have your top people here. I mean, I have an unparalleled disaster on my hands."

"A disaster you didn't create." Tromso was sympathetic.

"Exactly. And I'm here to ask for help. So I expected —"

"Of course you did. But this is something I can handle myself. The reality, my dear Prime Minister, as I've said, the reality is that your debt is so far beyond my SDR limits —"

The PM interrupted: "To which Canada has contributed, as I said, since the IMF was formed."

"True. But my SDR budget for this year, my total lending capacity, is about one twentieth of your federal debt. There is no possible way I can find the massive funding you need."

"Even through an appeal to the G-12 countries?"

"No. My people have been sounding out the national banks of every G-12 country. We started this morning as soon as we heard what the Japanese government had decreed."

The Norwegian was distinctly uncomfortable. His eyes shifted, a sign of nervousness. "We met for an hour this morning just before you arrived. We went over everything. And rather than having a dozen of the best economic brains in the world confront you, they and I decided I should handle the situation on a one-to-one basis, so to speak." Tromso acknowledged Camp's presence with a lifted eyebrow towards the young Canadian. Camp had found a remote chair well down the conference table but within earshot.

The PM showed his frustration, his irritation. "So if there's nothing the IMF can do for Canada, why did you let me come all the way down here when I should be in my office in Ottawa trying to stop my entire country from going over the cliff, falling into the abyss?"

"Because we may be able to do enough to help you survive, help you take the first step back from the abyss you're tottering beside as we speak.

An abyss that spells the economic death of Canada."

The PM hunched forward, elbows on the table, a wry expression on his face. "So what help can you give us? A euthanasia treatment IMF style?"

Tromso smiled. He wanted desperately to lift the Canadian's spirits. "No, no, my dear Prime Minister. We can give you a short-term line of credit of that ten billion U.S. you just asked for, to do with what you have to do. That *is* what you want, isn't it?"

"Realistically, is there more?" The PM didn't expect the answer he got.

"Well yes, there is more." The Managing Director's smile appeared again for a moment. "We propose that Canada appoint the IMF to be its official international agent to find a single group or a consortium that would use all its resources to get the debt plus its interest charges out of the way, so to speak."

"A long time to repay the debt?"

Tromso said, "No. There's no way Canada — even with Québec taking its share — no way it can repay its debt. Its foreign debt is, what, about four hundred billion?" He waited.

The PM did not respond.

"I don't know how your country with only twenty-eight million people could ever generate enough productivity, enough tax revenue, to pay down the debt even over fifty years while providing a starvation minimum of services to its citizens."

An alarm bell had been sounding in the PM's mind. "Have you been talking to Al Weinstock?"

"Of course. He called me after you had your session with him at the Chateau last night."

"I thought so. Some of the things you're saying sound like his ideas."

"With variations perhaps." Tromso put his hands flat on the table. He was ready to tell it "like it was."

"I concur with the Weinstock Solution. Furthermore, my dear Prime Minister, the IMF is prepared to act as an intermediary — an agent, if you will — to implement his plan."

"That's very generous of you. What would your percentage, your fee, be?"

"Nothing. Absolutely nothing. In the interest of the world's economy and the stability of its financial markets, I believe it is the IMF's duty, its obligation, to help Canada and its people find a way out of this incredible dilemma."

"Understood. What else is there?"

Tromso opened the leather file folder on the table in front of him. He took a foolscap agenda sheet from it which he handed across to the PM. "This sets out the conditions under which the IMF would be prepared to provide Canada with the interim ten-billion-U.S. line of credit to assist in making due interest payments on your foreign debt. Not your domestic debt, just the foreign. Is that clear?"

"Crystal."

"Very good. Now, what is required here is an enormous amount of restraint and discipline."

"What you mean is a very tough budget, right?"

"Of course. You know the problems we've had with the Russians. Incredible. From 1994 until now they've been bringing in budgets just to satisfy the IMF. Promises. No extra credits to industry and agriculture, no printing of money, spending cuts — the whole ski jump, as we say in Norway."

The PM snorted. "And you've done it every time, given them new money, new credits, and they haven't —"

"They haven't kept one of their bloody promises. Not one. But pressures from the Western world, the G-7 and now the G-12 . . . we've had no choice." Tromso leaned forward. "But the amounts, Prime Minister, the amounts the Russians have received are — how do you say it in America — pistachios?"

"Peanuts."

"Yes, peanuts compared to your debt. Five billion to the Russians one year, eight the next. And here you are at one trillion. You see the problem, Prime Minister?" Tromso's eyebrows arched as he asked the question.

"Of course I see the problem. And as Weinstock has already told you, we're working on a slash-and-burn budget. We'll finish it this afternoon —"

"And you'll present it to your House of Commons tomorrow morning." The Norwegian nodded, "Yes. Chairman Weinstock told me about it. It sounds as though you are on the right path. Your deficit target is . . . what is it again?"

The PM confirmed the target and the time frame for achieving it.

"Good," Tromso acknowledged. "Now, to the second item. I'm sure you haven't addressed it in your budget."

The PM slipped on his glasses for a moment, read the topic, took off the spectacles and laid them down on the table.

The item was "Reduce the number of levels of government."

"I know what this says. What does it mean so far as the IMF is concerned?"

"It means that Canada with its central, its provincial, its territorial, its regional, its municipal governments and its countless school boards, I tell you Canada is the most overgoverned country in the Western world. The duplication of services and those extra layers of government are excessive, unnecessary."

"But we had to have our provinces, just as the United States had to have its states. That was the only way to go when Confederation was put together in 1867. The different regions had to have their own governments."

Tromso nodded. "True. But this is 2001, not 1867. What the IMF is saying is that you have to get rid of one level of government. I mean an expensive level."

"This is part of the Weinstock plan, isn't it? A natural result?"

"No. My offer of ten billion with its terms assumes that the Weinstock Solution won't happen. On the other hand, if Weinstock does come about our ten billion will be repaid to the IMF and getting rid of a level of government will be easy, almost automatic."

"Do you have any particular level of government in mind? They're all expensive."

Tromso lifted his shoulders in a shrug. "That's up to you to figure out. If the Weinstock Solution is adopted the answer will be clear."

"But, Christ, do you know how difficult it would be to do away with *any* level of government? We'd need amendments to the constitution. We'd need referenda. We'd need time — months, years!"

Tromso, elbows on the table, put his fingertips together. "No, no, Prime Minister. You don't understand. We will decree that a level of government has to be abolished. All you have to do is say which level of your too many governments it should be. I'll be perfectly frank. It should be in the provincial area of jurisdiction."

The PM was astonished. "And if we can't, or don't?"

It was a gentle smile, no malice. "Then no ten-billion line of credit from the IMF, and no IMF as your agent to serve your cancerous debt. No assistance in putting together the Weinstock Solution."

The Prime Minister of Canada was an experienced, articulate negotiator. A hard-nosed, face-to-face dealer for his clients in transactions involving tens of millions of dollars. High-stake dealings. But this eye-to-eye, less-than-equal, one-sided laying out of terms and conditions was something else again. He had no room to manoeuvre. And Tromso knew it. He said: "Include the concept of cutting out a level of government in your budget statement tomorrow morning. That's what I'll be looking for."

The PM was beside himself. "It's bad enough that I have to stand up in the House tomorrow morning and dictate, yes, dictate, the cuts I'm going to make." He coughed, a sign of tension he had developed over the years.

"But to demand that we terminate a level of government?" He shook his head at the impossibility, the incredulity of doing such a thing."

The Managing Director put on his paternalistic face. "I really don't see that you have any choice."

"Good God, as I said, to do something like that would take years of negotiations. Years, if we could do it at all."

"I understand what you're saying. All that we at the IMF can expect is that tomorrow you make two promises, but not Russian style.

"The first promise will be to cut spending dramatically. Deficit cuts and their timing will be critical. From what you've told me, your budget plans — the extent of the cuts — will be acceptable, at least in principle, to your Cabinet."

Tromso paused to make a note on his copy of the two-item agenda sheet. He wrote the words "Weinstock Solution."

"The second promise — the elimination of a level of government — may or may not be in your budget, but you'll have to deal with it sometime during your presentation to the House of Commons. That's how you deal with a budget, isn't it? You present it to the House for debate?"

"Yes. For debate, amendment, and approval."

"Good. So you can deal with the elimination of a level of government —"

"If we decide to accept your ultimatum."

Tromso was firm. "You're not listening to me, Prime Minister. I'll say it again. You have no choice. You absolutely must have our ten-billion line of credit. You absolutely must cut a level of government if your Canada is to avoid total economic and financial collapse. A collapse that will take the newly sovereign Québec down with Canada."

The PM shook his head in frustration. "I'm listening to you, Mr. Tromso. I just can't come to terms with what I'm hearing. It's bad enough to deal with the elimination of a level of government *plus* a budget that will strip the financial flesh of every person, every corporation, every government in the country. The Weinstock Solution is far more complicated to deal with."

Tromso leaned back in his chair. His face and composure serene, he calmly said, "All those things are for you to decide. It is our function to build the hurdles, then to place them. It is for you to decide if you can run as well as jump over them. And, yes, you have very little time."

"Little time," the PM agreed. "In fact, I've run out of time. I must get back to Ottawa as soon as possible. I've called for a new session of Parliament to begin at four this afternoon."

"Yes, I know."

"I have to prepare the Speech From the Throne for the Governor General to deliver in the Senate chamber. But it's going to be in English only. No French now that Québec's gone. And I and my colleagues have to finish the budget, sell it to our Reform PC caucus, get it printed and ready for tomorrow's ten-o'clock presentation in the House."

The Canadian Prime Minister stood. He extended his hand to the Managing Director of the IMF. "The hurdles the IMF have put in place on the track, the odds against getting over them, are impossible. But yesterday's shot by the Japanese will make us run harder and faster. We might just surprise everybody — even you, sir."

"That would make me very happy, as well as surprised. And what about the Weinstock Solution? It will take weeks to put in place. I can work with the Chairman today; and we can talk with all the decision-makers. There's nothing for you, for Canada, to lose if Weinstock and I get on the telephone and talk to the people who count."

The PM would have liked to say no, an emotion-driven no. Instead, logic was in charge. "I think you should do it. But on one condition."

"Which is?"

"Do not say I've asked you to do this or that I approve in principle, that I accept the Weinstock Solution."

"Of course. You want to be in a position to deny everything, if you can. Correct?"

"Absolutely."

"Good. I will call Chairman Weinstock immediately — as your secret and undisclosed agent. I will tell him to start to work on his list and I'll do mine."

"His list? You mean the two of you have already decided who . . .?"

The answer was a slight, self-pleased smile on the long Nordic face of the Managing Director of the International Monetary Fund.

"That should not be a surprise, Prime Minister." Tromso paused for effect. "The first Weinstock call will be to his friend, the President of the United States."

15

12:05 P.M.: Parliament Buildings

A few minutes after twelve noon the Prime Minister and Camp entered the Parliament Buildings by using the Speaker's entrance at the rear north side of that towering and formidable structure overlooking the icy Ottawa River. The two men hurried through the Speaker's corridors, then up the secret Macdonald staircase in order to avoid any meeting with the press scrum waiting at the main entrance.

The crisis had put the media on total alert. They were swarming over any politician or bureaucrat who moved within range and might have some word, even a hint, of what was going on. The PM was satisfied that, so far, his early-morning foray to Washington had been carried off without the media's knowledge.

The PM glanced at his watch, thinking the budget had to be finished by six o'clock, seven at the absolute latest, so it could be fed into his secretary's word processor. The entire document would be printed and photocopied in the necessary hundreds right there in the Prime Minister's office. He was determined there would be no leaks!

He wondered how his team had fared without him. They would have put in four hours of what he hoped was solid, constructive work. He prayed they were almost finished and that he would have to make no (or a few at worst) decisions to break deadlocks.

Then he had to prepare the Speech From the Throne for the Governor General to read in the Senate chamber, known as the Red Chamber. The speech was intended to be an outline of the legislation and policies the government of the day planned to put forward and implement during the session of Parliament that was to begin. Usually it was long, too long; but this one would be short the PM promised himself. Two pages maximum would be his target. The problem was to find time to get the goddam thing done!

He was almost running when Camp, ahead of him, opened the door to the Prime Minister's offices.

"George!" the PM shouted. "Bring your book, any messages, faxes. Are they still going at it in the conference room?"

"Yes, sir."

As he opened the door to his private chambers, he said, "Simon, ask Ann and Mario to come to my office. Give me five minutes with George first."

He threw his overcoat on the chesterfield as he rounded his desk. George came in loaded with a stack of paper.

The PM sat in his low-backed swivel chair. "Quite a pile you've got there. What are most urgent?"

"Well, sir, I think you should see these first — faxes from Washington, the President and London, England."

"The Prime Minister?"

"No, the Chancellor of the Exchequer."

The PM asked if anything had arrived from the Japanese or the Germans.

"Nothing from either, sir, but there's a peculiar one from the IMF, from Leif Tromso."

"I'd better see that first."

The PM took the fax from George and read: "Have initiated Weinstock Solution action. Approached most senior U.S. contact first. He is in favor and will support attack on Hill. Weinstock and I working together. Top priority. May need a conference call. Trying to resolve before you present budget."

"Shit," the PM muttered through clenched teeth.

"Sir?"

"Nothing, George, nothing. It's just that I'm being sucked into a great Niagara Falls whirlpool. I'm going to fight it to the end. But right now I'm headed straight towards it and there's not a goddam thing I can do about it."

That was over George's head. "Yes, sir." He handed his boss the faxes from the U.S. President and the British Chancellor of the Exchequer.

The PM read them, his eyebrows arching in surprise as he told himself that Tromso really had been busy.

"A fax to Tromso, George. A two-liner. 'Ready for a conference call any time, any hour between now and eight-thirty tomorrow morning. Your efforts as agent much appreciated. Regards.'"

He reached for the pile George had put on the desk. "You're sure there's nothing here that can't wait?"

"Right now I'm not sure of anything."

"Join the crowd. I'm going to meet with Greco and Carter now to find out how far they've got with the budget. As soon as they leave I'm going to write the Speech From the Throne . . ."

"Dictate it?"

"No, I'll do it by hand. It'll be short. Tell Her Excellency's secretary to stand by. We'll fax it to her so it can be retyped in plenty of time. They'll have it by two-thirty at the latest."

"She has to leave Rideau Hall by three-thirty to get here at four. Should be plenty of time."

"Okay, George. Tell Simon I can see them now."

When his frazzled, obviously exhausted Treasury Board President and his drained, pale Minister of Finance were seated in chairs across the desk from their leader, Carter asked, "How did you get along in Washington?"

The PM smiled. "Okay. But I don't have time to go into that now. I'll fill you in later." Much later, he thought. "I have to write the goddam Speech From the Throne and I've only got half an hour to do it."

"At least now you don't have to do it in French too," Greco commented.

"Thank God. So I want you two to fill me in: what progress have you made?"

His colleagues looked at each other. Then Carter turned to the PM, rolling her eyes upwards in aggravated frustration. "I've never been through anything like this in my life. Nobody can agree on anything. The bureaucrats are the most opinionated, know-it-all bunch I've ever met, and they're fighting against every cut that affects their pay and their turf. I mean, it's unbelievable."

The PM leaned back in his chair. "Does that surprise you? These are the people who've actually been running the day-to-day policy-making and operation of the government! Not the inexperienced ministers put in their hands to mould and direct for a short period of political time."

He came forward to the edge of his chair, jaw out, eyes fierce. "The deputy ministers are the reason we're in this mess. They overpowered, seduced, misled their ministers all during the Trudeau years, then Mulroney's and even in Chrétien's time."

The PM was putting into words thoughts he'd had for years. "They're the people responsible for the government spending far more than it takes in year after year. They're responsible for creating this monstrous near-trillion-dollar debt."

"Well," Greco protested, "it was the mainstream parties — or what used to be mainstream — the Conservatives as well as the Liberals — who allowed this to happen, created or condoned the policies."

The PM waved his hand impatiently. "Of course they created or condoned the policies served up to them on silver platters by their highly paid, highly experienced deputy ministers." His legal background became evident as he made his last point. "Look. In negligence cases it's customary to apportion fault between the plaintiff and the defendant. In the case of the fault for the deficits starting in about 1975 until today, the politicians' contributory negligence is about at max 20 percent, with 80 going to the bureaucrats.

"So I'm not surprised to hear they're fighting cuts in their budgets." He was impatient to hear what had happened while he was in Washington. "Just tell me what decisions you've been able to make and the areas where you're hung up."

In a half-hour session Carter and Greco took the PM through the list of items resolved and those unresolved. He accepted all the decisions agreed upon. As to the eight matters that his team had been unable to decide on, he quickly and arbitrarily made his judgments. Some of them were such harsh and drastic cuts that both Greco and Carter raised concerns. But their PM was adamant.

"I keep telling you: there is *no* money. We have *no* choice." Then he smiled for the first time. "Okay, you two. You're doing the best you can. I'm not being critical, believe me."

Carter returned the smile. "This is a high-stress time, Richard. Look, if we're going to get this budget done by six, Mario and I have to stay with it. We can't take the time to go to the Red Chamber for the Speech From the Throne, and we may not be present for the opening of the House."

"Right. I'll join you in the conference room when I've drafted the speech. Might even run it by you. I plan to have it finished by half an hour from now. It'll be in the Governor General's hands by three. So I'll join you when it's done and I'll leave for the Senate at quarter to four. The opening session of the House should begin about four-thirty. That won't take long. I'll tell the House what's happening and what the plan is for presenting the budget tomorrow. Then I'll be back here, probably around five-thirty."

"Just in time to mop up the buckets of bureaucratic blood on the floor."

"Yes, buckets. We'll finish the session at about six. Then the ball will be in your court, Ann."

She was baffled. "What d'you mean?"

"I mean you're then going to write the budget speech — with my editorial input, of course."

"Oh my God!"

He laughed. "Well, you won't have to do all of it. You'll write the main body of it, what we're going to do ministry by ministry. Okay? I'll write the lead-in. I'll set the scene and the targets. Then I'll do the finish. We'll put together what you've written and what I've done and we'll have the budget speech ready for typing, although . . ."

He hesitated. "I don't think I'll have the last few pages typed. I'll just use my written notes."

Greco, ever practical, looked puzzled. "Why do that? Why not get everything typed?"

"Simple. I don't want anyone to know what I'm going to say when I'm finishing."

"Not even us?" Carter was shocked.

"Not even you, or Simon or George."

"But why?" It was Greco who got the question out first. He looked pleased with himself: Carter was always so quick on the draw.

"Because there are certain things going on right now as a result of the Weinstock visit and my meeting at the IMF. Really there's so much up in the air. I'll bring you two in on the situation at the right time. So let's just leave it that I may or may not have the finish of my speech typed. In fact, I may not even know what I'm going to say until tomorrow morning."

By the expression on the faces of his two ministers he could see that his answer was not satisfactory. But he refused to say more. He waved a hand at them with a smile. "Now if you two will get back to work, I'm going to write the Speech From the Throne!"

As Carter and Greco made their way out, the PM was on the intercom to his secretary. "Hold all my calls, George, except those from the President, Tromso, or Weinstock. Got that? And tell the G-G.'s people the speech —"

"I've already told them it will be there by two-thirty."

"That's right, I did ask you to do that earlier, didn't I? Must be losing it. Oh, and send in some strong black coffee, and, yes, I'd better have a salmon sandwich — you know how I like it. Have to keep up my strength, eh, George?" He laughed as he hung up the phone.

He reached into the desk drawer to pull out half a dozen sheets of his favourite three-hole, lined, looseleaf paper. Next from the drawer came a bottle of washable blue ink. He filled his broad-nibbed fountain pen — he detested ballpoints — wiped off the end with a piece of facial tissue and put the ink bottle away. The ritual completed, he was ready to write.

That ceremonial preparation, which was as automatic as the pre-service ball-bouncing a seasoned tennis player uses, allowed the PM to focus on how he would open the speech; what he would say in the hard, brutal message to the citizens of Canada. He knew instinctively that the people, the media, were panicking — and the morning editions of the *Globe and Mail* and the *Ottawa Citizen* had confirmed this. He knew, too, that he must give them confidence in his government, his decisions.

It was not just the whole country that was shaken by this crisis, he thought. It was the whole G-12 world. Like sheep, or lemmings, the American and European foreign markets were following the Japanese lead. All reports he had received indicated no dealings whatever in Canadian government paper — except to sell. Discounts were running at over 50 percent as investors world-wide tried to unload their Canadian securities. Also affected were the stocks and bonds of wholly or partly Canadian-based corporations: communications, automobiles, mining. And, as the PM had noted with satisfaction, the big Canadian banks. No wonder there was panic. Somehow he had to get control of the situation.

He put these thoughts aside and pulled the first sheet of paper towards him. The writing took much longer than he expected. It was twenty-four minutes past two when the PM finished. He had filled, double-spaced, ten foolscap pages in his highly legible, vertical handwriting. After re-reading what he had written, making a few minor changes here and there, he wasn't totally satisfied. He never was. But time had run out and it was the best he could do.

He called George in. "Here it is. Read it over, please, for any errors, words I've left out." Sometimes his thoughts moved ahead of the pen, with the result that a word or part of one might not reach the paper. "Fax it to Rideau Hall, as is. Don't take the time to type it."

"Yes, sir. It's certainly short." George couldn't resist the comment.

"Yes. In baseball terms it's a bunt. The budget's going to have to be a home run!"

George left the PM's office. Within seconds there was a knock on his door. It was Greco. "Prime Minister, may I have a word with you privately?"

"Of course. Come on in and have a seat." The PM admired his Finance Minister. He was a man who thought before he spoke, a man who chose his words carefully. The PM was curious to know what Greco wanted to speak about in private. He didn't have to wait long.

As he settled into one of the chairs at the PM's desk Greco said, "There's an approach, it's somewhat radical I must admit, Prime Minister, but it may be the answer to our debt problem."

"Right now I'll listen to anything. I mean, Christ, the only things I've got going are the Weinstock Solution or a sixty-six-billion spending cut over eighteen months. Either one of them can cause a goddam revolution."

"Well, you haven't told us what Weinstock's solution *is*. But I've been talking to an old friend of mine, Sir Robin Buchanan. We met in Barbados years ago."

Greco described Sir Robin as a tall, wily Scot, a chartered accountant who lived in Bath, England.

"Know it well," the PM interrupted, wondering where all this was leading. "Gorgeous city."

"I had lunch with Sir Robin in Bath just before the election campaign started. He's been following our debt build-up, and thinks it's a bloody disaster. He's been casting about for an answer and, frankly, I think he has one. I called him about half an hour ago to talk it over again."

"Yes?"

"Sir Robin's idea revolves around the assets in Canada as held by our banks, insurance companies, the resource, industrial, service, and other companies whose shares are listed on our stock exchanges — Toronto, Montreal, Alberta, Vancouver. And the large private corporations whose shares aren't listed."

The PM listened intently, breaking in three times with questions, making notes as Greco talked and explained the idea.

After a monologue of about five minutes Greco was finished. "That's it. That's the Buchanan proposal." He sat back and put away the notes he had consulted in presenting the idea. "It could be modified, changed. But I think it's worth serious consideration. I mean, any alternative to this budget-slashing we've been doing — a sixty-six-billion cut in eighteen months? Holy Christ! As we've all said, the federal government won't be able to provide services of any kind to any Canadian."

"Except the service of collecting taxes. Okay, Mario. I'm impressed with this proposal, your presentation. I need asset numbers. Turn your people loose on it right away. They should be able to get that information you need from Stats Canada. They'll have it all on their computers. But for God's sake, don't tell your people why you want the data. Don't breathe a word to a soul."

"Absolutely."

"I'll need those numbers by nine tonight. No later. That'll give me time to work it into my budget speech if I think . . . what's his name again?"

"Sir Robin Buchanan."

"Yes, if the Buchanan proposal will be an alternative. But Mario, why didn't you raise this sooner?"

Greco looked rather sheepish. "Well, the pressure's been so great since yesterday morning. And I'm a new boy on the block . . . Besides, Robin's idea seemed so extreme. Well, I just didn't feel comfortable enough to raise it. D'you understand?"

The PM rose from his chair and nodded. "Sure I do, Mario. Now let's go back to the conference room and see if we can finish off the budget."

When the PM and Greco walked into the room, the cacophony of loud, arguing voices stopped in mid-shout as all eyes turned to see who was entering. Faces around the table were puffy with exhaustion, tempers were short-fused, consensus was defined as "fight!" The pressure was almost visible, like steam rising from a boiling kettle.

"Hi, people." The PM gave a half-wave. "The ogre is back." A tension-softening grin was manufactured for the soothing benefit of all the bear-pit participants.

"How did it go, sir?" Smart asked, his hair dishevelled, his tie loose, askew at his thick neck.

The PM lowered himself into his chair. "It went as well as it could, in the circumstances. The IMF are prepared to give us a ten-billion U.S. line of credit. That's about it." He waited for the reactions he knew would come.

"Is that all?" Jane Smith's voice registered the shock everyone else felt.

"That's all. But there's more."

"Terms and conditions," Simpson added knowingly.

The PM threw him a sharp glance. "You got it. Two conditions. A tough sledge-hammer budget —"

"We're going to have that." Carter sounded confident.

"Goddam right we are! The second condition . . ." He paused. The silence was painful in its intensity.

"The second condition is impossible!" He swept a hand across his furrowed forehead in a gesture of frustration. "We'll never be able to do it."

"For Christ's sake, Richard, what is it?!" Carter shouted. She was at the end of her high-strung tether.

The PM grimaced as if he was in pain. He was. It was mental agony. In a gruff voice he muttered, "The bastards say we're the most overgoverned nation in the Western world. The overlap, the duplication of services between the federal government and the provinces, is costing Canadians billions every year."

"Can't quarrel with that," Greco said. "So, what are the conditions?" He wanted to say, "For God's sake spit it out, man," but he resisted the urge.

"We have to get rid of one level of government in the provincial area. The provinces are out of our jurisdiction — but that's the condition!"

No one uttered a word. The stunned look on every face said it all.

Simpson leaned back in his chair. Stuffing hands in trouser pockets, he blew out a long breath. "Holy Christ! As you said, that's impossible. The provinces can't agree on anything, let alone self-immolation."

"Suicide," Carter agreed.

"Yes, suicide," the PM repeated. "The problem is — and make no mistake — the IMF is deadly serious —"

"And God knows we need the ten billion." There was no doubt in Carter's mind.

"The problem is, I'm going to have to say yes or no to the condition. And if I say yes, then which level will be stuffed in a taxpayer's coffin and buried?"

"Cremated is a much better way to go."

"Yes, Ann. Even better environmentally." The PM looked at his watch. "The Supreme Court of Canada allows one hour for arguments from both sides. I'm giving you people ten minutes. Tell me why we shouldn't get rid of one level of government, or why we should. And if we should, then which one should it be? I'm going to go around the table. Jane, I'll start with you."

Jane Smith shook her head as she said, "No thank you, Prime Minister. I really don't think I'm in a position to comment on what is a political question. I'm a civil servant, not a politician. It's up to you and your ministers to decide. We can advise you, the civil servants around the table . . ."

The PM looked to Carter and Greco, then to Smith. "But that's what I'm asking you to do — advise us."

Smart sided with his colleague: "Sorry, sir, but I agree with Jane. It's up to you people, not us. All three of you are highly educated, experienced, knowledgeable Canadians. You're elected, we're not."

The PM tapped the table in an unconscious gesture of impatience. "I won't force the issue. Alright, Mario, which level of government should be eliminated?"

Greco looked at notes he had been making. "Look, Richard, this question has come right out of the blue. No warning. So my answer is out of the blue. But I'll give it anyway."

He turned to Carter, asking if he should go ahead of her: "Okay, Ann?"

"Be my guest. Who knows? I may even agree with you." She patted his hand.

"Alright. This is what I think . . ."

Greco spoke for several minutes in his measured, precise, unemotional way. He concluded, saying, "Let me sum up.

"My first point is that any nation must have a central government — if it is to be or continue to be a nation. The United Kingdom has always had a central, unitary government. It has no provincial or state legislatures. So why should Canada have them?"

He sat up straight and had a sip of his can of orange drink.

"Provinces being regional in jurisdiction were necessary at Confederation in 1867 because of the vastness of Ontario, Québec, and the Maritimes, the long distances between their regions, the lack of communications. Those factors have disappeared — all except the vastness, which has been shrunk by aircraft, satellites, the automobile, radio, television, the telephone, the computer, and all the other magic inventions that now exist."

Greco tapped his index finger on the table to emphasize his conclusion. "Prime Minister, there are many other considerations, but the level of government that should disappear is that of the provincial governments. They are redundant in 2001."

The PM had intently listened to every word. But he gave no sign that he was persuaded. "Ann, what about you?" While he was saying that, he was preparing himself for a long eloquent argument from Carter in favour of eliminating the central, federal government.

He was astonished when he heard her say, "I agree with Mario. That's it!"

"Your argument is compelling, Mario," the PM admitted. "I have to buy it." Then he looked to Carter. "What's next?"

"Okay. The next thing is the caucus," Carter said. "The budget second. The caucus first. When are you going to present all this stuff to our caucus? The budget, the bank legislation, the IMF . . . ?"

"We have to finish the budget, Ann. We don't have time for a caucus until the budget's wrapped up. The earliest we can do it is eight tomorrow morning. For security and protocol reasons I won't be telling them what's in the budget, but I can explain everything that's in the Speech From the Throne. But I can't deal with the IMF conditions or the Weinstock proposal."

"Of course not." Ann took over again. "That stuff belongs in the budget volcano."

"Volcano?"

"When you do the budget, Richard, Vesuvius will look like a minor-league eruption."

"And that's what the Speech From the Throne will do for the Senate." His face had a malicious grin. "So it's eight tomorrow morning." He looked for Camp. "Simon, call the whip and the House leader, wherever they are."

"Either in their offices here or on an airplane, sir."

"Well, tell them it's caucus tomorrow morning at eight. And tell them to explain to our new people what party discipline *really* is."

Camp was about to retreat to the corner with his telephone when Smart said, "Prime Minister, there's the matter of electing the Speaker of the House. That has to be done before Her Excellency does the speech."

"Thanks for reminding me. The problem is most of our members aren't here yet. Only a few of them have been sworn in."

"Those who're going to get here in time will all have to be sworn in by four. May I make a suggestion?"

"Certainly."

"Pick the person you want —"

"From my own caucus." It wasn't a question.

"Of course. Put a second and third choice on the list. Then ask the PM — sorry!" He made the natural mistake of referring to the leader of the party that the Reform PCs had defeated as the prime minister.

"It's okay, Peter. You'll get used to my being the PM."

The Clerk of the Privy Council still looked embarrassed. "Again, sorry, sir. I will take the list to the Leader of the Opposition. He's in his new office, I know."

"My old one," Smart replied soberly.

"Exactly. In these emergency circumstances I'm sure he'll agree to one of the three being Speaker. The vote can take place as soon as the House assembles. It'll be a formality."

"Usually is. The three names in order of priority . . . I've only talked with Dagon about this informally. I'm sure he'll accept." Leon Dagon, from North York East riding, had lots of experience in the House. "Then Mary Hartman — she's had a lot of time. And the third . . ." He hesitated. "Why do a third? Go with two."

"Yes, sir. I'll let you know if there's any problem."

The PM turned to his Chief of Staff. "Simon, find Leon and tell him what's happening. I'd like to speak with him. Same with Mary Hartman. If you can't get through to them, simply say you're authorized to ask if they'll stand. Got that?"

"Yes, sir."

Then it was back to the budget.

At twenty-one minutes to four, George Pearce came in with a note for his boss that read: "Tromso is on the line."

The PM stood up briskly, surprising those who had not seen the secretary enter. "I have to leave you all again. Have to get ready for the opening at four o'clock. Ann, you and Mario stay here and finish this off. You're almost there now."

Both Carter and Greco nodded their agreement.

"I'll see you back here around five-thirty. We've got to get that budget finished."

"We'll do it with you, boss." Carter snapped him a salute and grinned.

The PM liked the woman's spunk. Tired as they all were, she never let an opportunity pass to quip, challenge, or bring the group back to reality. "You've got it, Ann. And Mario, I think you'd better be here with Ann and me. Can't be alone with this gorgeous creature. There might be charges of sexual harassment." He chuckled.

"By whom?" was Carter's quick retort. Laughter, applause, and shouts of "*Touché!*" followed the Prime Minister out of the conference room.

16

3:55 P.M.: The Senate Chamber

Standing a few feet away from his chair of privilege on the floor of the Senate just to the right hand of the elevated Speaker's chair, the Prime Minister watched his newly anointed ministers and the House members who had just been sworn in, as they gathered at the distant bar of the Senate chamber inside its entrance door.

Following ancient British tradition, members of the Canadian House of Commons could enter the Senate chamber only as far as the elaborately carved ceremonial bar. From that limited vantage point only a handful of members of the House could see and hear the proceedings and the King or Queen's Speech From the Throne.

The Red Chamber was filled on both sides with the distinguished senators all appointed by former prime ministers. The crisis had brought every senator who could travel, even under physical duress, to Ottawa to hear and ultimately deal with what the new government proposed to do about the situation.

There were about thirty Conservative Senate members remaining from the Mulroney days. There were no Reform party people, no Reform PC party appointees. The majority were the senators appointed by the previous party in power.

The new prime minister made his way to his chair at two minutes to four. He watched the gabbing senators at or making their way to their seats. The odd one saw this man of new power and nodded or waved to him. None of the senators moved to approach. Either it was too close to the beginning of proceedings or it was not politic so to do. It didn't matter.

This place beside the Speaker's chair was the furthest the member of parliament from Calgary had ever penetrated the Senate chamber. He had walked past its ornate doorway countless times. He had stood at the bar at previous openings. But he had never gone into the Red Chamber to inspect it, to look around when it was vacant. As he stood there, he asked himself: Why not?

The answer was clear. He simply had little respect for the institution or for its political appointees, people who were handed a high-paid, part-time plum to savour until the age of seventy-five. This mainly for being bag-persons or intimates of the prime minister of the day. This was their reward for service to the party, but usually for another performance — that of flattering that prime minister's ego and organization.

As the newly elected Prime Minister looked around the Red Chamber what he saw did not change his mind. The Senate was an irrelevant, costly body created by John A. Macdonald and the Fathers of Confederation. It was done during their last wheeling-and-dealing sessions at the Westminster Palace Hotel in London, England, in December of 1866, when they were negotiating the final provisions of what was to become the British North America Act.

Macdonald and his colleagues obviously had some compelling reason to create for Canada a cracked-mirror image of the House of Lords. But, as the PM reasoned, at the beginning of the twenty-first century there was no justification whatever for the existence of the Senate, and certainly not for its high cost.

In the balcony above the dais on which stood the towering, throne-like Speaker's chair, the military trumpeters stood rigidly at attention, caps on squarely, banners with the Governor General's coat of arms hanging from their instruments. When word came that Her Excellency was about to enter the chamber, they would perform their musical signal.

For security reasons it had been arranged that she would not enter through the front door of the Senate, but rather through the Speaker's entrance.

The moment of four o'clock arrived with the carillon of the Peace Tower of the Parliament Buildings pealing the hour. The doors from the Speaker's chambers opened. There the Right Honourable Pearl McConachie stood in radiant white, her long, form-fitting gown reaching to the scarlet carpet.

Her sleeved arms were partly concealed by a purple cape that sat on her slender shoulders. The wavy blond hair was fetched upwards, seemingly encased in a delicate, glittering tiara.

As he gazed at her the PM felt something was missing, some quality of this vice-regal person that was so appealing. It came to him. There was no smile on that usually smiling, beautiful face. At that moment no one but he in the chamber suspected, let alone realized, why McConachie was not smiling.

Everyone there would understand in just a few minutes.

In unison the military trumpeters brought the gleaming instruments to their lips. The vice-regal fanfare began, echoing through the vast chamber. The Governor General moved slowly to the dais, mounting its few steps to stand in front of the Speaker's chair. At that point, just as she turned to face the members of the Senate, all of them standing. She did so just as the final notes of the fanfare sounded.

The PM could see her eyes looking at the grey-headed members of the Supreme Court of Canada, resplendent in crimson robes with white fur at the neck, seated in chairs in front of and below her on the floor of the Senate.

Then she turned her head to look at him for a moment. No smile, but a slight move of the head.

At the appropriate moment she sat, whereupon all the senators and others followed suit.

After the Governor General was seated, her military aide, the same young air force captain in full uniform wearing the golden aiglets of his post, stepped up onto the dais. He handed her the leather folio containing the speech written by the Prime Minister of Canada.

Once more a glance from her to her immediate right to the eyes of the handsome author of the disturbing words she was about to read. She would utter them as if they were her own, even though everyone watching and listening knew that the words were his, not hers.

She touched the tiny microphone fastened at her bodice. Its wires went to the portable transmitter strapped to her lower back, unseen under the cape. The transmitter would send her voice to the earphone system discreetly placed at members' seats throughout the chamber so that those hard of hearing could grasp what she was saying. The room was hushed, the silence fearful.

Her Excellency, The Right Honourable Pearl McConachie, began to speak:

"Honourable Members, I bring you greetings from His Majesty the King. He has asked me to convey to you his best wishes for a successful and fruitful legislative session."

She paused to allow murmuring between senators to die down, then disappear.

"This session of the Parliament of Canada promises, alas, to be the most difficult, the most traumatic, the most negative and destructive of all sessions since the inaugural session in the fall of 1867."

There was no muttering, no noise. The omens made and promised by those opening sentences had immediately focussed the attention of every listener.

In brief, terse prose she recited the events that had developed into the crushing financial crisis the country faced — a situation that all present knew only too well.

"Honourable Senators, it is for these reasons of massive crisis for the nation that my government has petitioned for and has been granted this emergency call of my new Parliament."

The Governor General shifted slightly. The PM knew she would be exceedingly uncomfortable and nervous as she read the paragraphs that were to follow.

"In view of the calamitous national debt which my new government has inherited, and because of the action against Canada decreed by the government of Japan, action which is being copied by the financial markets of the United States and Europe, my government has no alternative but to invoke draconian budgetary actions.

"It must introduce legislation designed to cauterize and staunch the heretofore unstoppable flow of money out of the federal Treasury. It is a flow which has far exceeded its revenues and brought the nation to the verge of economic collapse.

"My government will therefore put before Parliament for its approval legislation which will, among other things, do away with redundant as well as obsolete Crown corporations.

"It will introduce legislation requiring Canadian banks to continue to extend credit to the government of Canada. The banks have agreed to restore credit that was removed yesterday, but my government considers it prudent to have compulsory legislation in place.

"Legislation will be proposed that will terminate my government's speculative participation in enormously expensive major energy and public works programs.

"New policies must be established that bring into line with reality the heretofore excessively generous contributions to foreign aid of funds which Canada does not have and have had to be borrowed.

"In keeping with the absolute need to curtail spending, my government will introduce severe temporary limitations on immigration that will allow into the country only those persons — and their spouses and children — who are designated as needed in Canada for their special skills."

The Governor General paused. Not a sound did she hear. It was as if every person in the room was holding his or her breath.

"Tomorrow, my government will introduce a force majeure budget that will have the objective of doing what no Canadian government has had the fortitude to do since the 1970s. The objective of my government is to respond to the external forces that have stripped Canada of the ability to borrow from international sources.

"Accordingly, the goal of my government is to impose such spending reduction as to reduce the deficit to zero over eighteen months."

Those words turned the decorous chamber into an angry hive of buzzing senators. The sound escalated to a roar as the senators began to absorb the impact of what they had just heard.

Civility went out the window as appalled members on both sides of the chamber stood up, arms and hands gesticulating, and shouted out accusations and curses: "They can't do that, it's ruin!"; "The economy will collapse!"; "That stupid bastard ought to be strung up!"; "Never, goddam it, never!"; "There's the Frankenstein who created this monster! Hang the sonofabitch!"

Eyes glared at the Prime Minister, fingers pointed at him as his political enemies, now in full howl, were joined by some purported allies.

The shock wave rolled over them, stunned them. They ought to have guessed there was more to come.

Finally, the Gentleman of the Black Rod, the ultimate keeper of discipline and the enforcer of the rules against disorderly behaviour in the Senate chamber, decided to act.

He pushed his black tricorn farther down on his head, stomped one of his high boots noisily against the carpeted floor between the cowering justices of the Supreme Court and the defiant, not-to-be-humiliated Governor General.

Pounding his rod furiously against the floor at the urging of the Senate Speaker at his side, Black Rod shouted his demand that all honourables cease their noise and take their seats. This performance continued for some three or four minutes before the participants in the débacle, apparently exhausted by their emotional efforts, gradually quieted down and slumped back in their seats, some still growling in anger.

Her Excellency was in no hurry. The speech was brevity itself. She would take her time.

When, in her experienced judgment, a sufficient level of near-silence was reached, she signalled she was ready to begin again. The signal was a brief, gentle clearing of her throat.

"Honourable Members, in keeping with the objective of a zero deficit within eighteen months, the annual budget of the Canadian Armed Forces will be reduced by more than 50 percent."

She waited for the reaction. There was a bit of buzzing but no shouting. Her Excellency knew the situation would be otherwise with the next words.

"In affirmation of the statement to the media made yesterday by the first minister of my government, legislation will be introduced and all necessary steps will be taken to terminate within six months the huge annual expenditure of some one billion dollars of public monies by the Canadian Broadcasting Corporation and the existence of the Corporation itself."

That did it. The roar of protest was immediate and prolonged. Shouting, screaming members were on their feet again, arms flailing like Don Quixote's windmills. Vile epithets spewed from their mouths, directed at the perpetrator of this cultural murder. The Prime Minister remained motionless, defiant. He looked out of narrowed eyes at the tumult, but did not respond to the abuses, the vicious looks flying at him like arrows from both sides of the chamber.

He glanced only once at the Governor General, perhaps his only friend in the hostile Red Chamber. Her face was impassive, composed, but he could almost feel her heart pounding.

Again Black Rod was compelled to intervene. The commotion took much longer to die down. Finally, sufficient quiet reigned for the Governor General to resume.

"Honourable Senators, my new government is pledged to retrieve this superb nation of Canada from the edge of the abyss.

"My government has arranged with the International Monetary Fund a short-term line of credit of ten billion U.S. dollars. The IMF does not have the resources to be able to offer assistance that will address Canada's debt of a thousand billion dollars and our deficit of sixty-six billion.

"Nevertheless, my government must have that small IMF line of credit. But before my government can gain access to that line, the IMF has stipulated that two conditions be met."

Silence, except for a smoker's cough.

"The first condition is that my government must bring in a budget that reduces spending to an acceptable level in relation to revenue. As stated earlier, my government will propose a zero-deficit budget."

Again moans and buzzing, but of low intensity and duration.

"However, the second condition is much more difficult and may be impossible. Even so, my government will attempt to meet that condition."

The PM could see the self-possessed, winsome woman steel herself for the next onslaught that was bound to come.

"The condition is that because of the cost of duplication of services as between the provinces and the federal government, there is an unacceptable waste of money and resources. Therefore one level of government, either the provincial governments or governments created by the provinces, must be eliminated."

As Pearl McConachie uttered the word "eliminated" the chamber erupted into a chaotic uproar of even greater magnitude than the preceding outburst. The honourable senators, young and old alike and of both mainstream parties, were convulsed with rage. Some even left their seats to move threateningly, fists raised, towards the Prime Minister, only to be restrained by their saner colleagues.

The Prime Minister observed some honourable senators turning on each other as ancient animosities were let loose. Their frustration at being trapped in the terrible financial crisis exploded into violent rage at the ruthless measures this novice prime minister was proposing.

Just as the melee was about to turn into physical violence, a dozen Mounties in full red-coated regalia marched in through the Speaker's entrance to spread out in a semicircle in front of the dais. The Governor General was still seated, calmly watching these distinguished women and men make videotaped fools of themselves.

The arrival of the RCMP force, summoned as it was by the Speaker after the first outburst, had an immediate calming effect. The senators, still grumbling and casting poisonous looks at the PM, returned to their seats.

None of them knew what was coming next. If they had, they would never have allowed the final paragraph to be read by Her Excellency, the Right Honourable Pearl McConachie, PC, CC, CMM, CD.

"In conclusion, Honourable Senators, my government has decided that this chamber is both redundant and of too great an expense to the people of Canada."

She could hear the mounting furor as she rushed to read the final words.

"Accordingly, my government will introduce legislation and take all necessary constitutional steps to abolish and terminate the Senate of Canada."

Pandemonium on a scale never before witnessed in the history of Canada's Parliament was explosively set loose by those cruel, pragmatic words written by the Right Honourable, the novice Prime Minister of Canada.

17

4:22 P.M.: Parliament Buildings

The two Mounties and the Parliamentary security guards assigned to the PM made a flying wedge with the PM in their centre as they moved down the long floor of the Senate chamber, past the bar. They turned to the right, down the wide marble hallway, through the towering rotunda of the Centre Block to the first elevator. The RCMP pair immediately commandeered it. At his office floor the two Mounties escorted the PM to his new quarters past startled MPs and staff. They were perplexed at seeing in the apparent custody of the police the man they were just starting to recognize as prime minister. The PM did not stop to greet or wave at colleagues or in any way acknowledge their presence.

Of course he had expected the senators to be furious, outraged, at being "terminated." They would suffer a loss of prestige, influence, not to mention money. Nevertheless he was shaken by the degree of violence and hostility shown by so many of the normally conservative and well-behaved members of the usually somnolent Senate. But then he remembered a similar nasty but not nearly so prolonged event. It was the G.S.T. fight that had occurred in the Senate back in the early '90s. That issue between the Conservatives and the Liberals in the Red Chamber had produced screaming, shouting and even fisticuffs among the honourable members.

The uncivilized behaviour he had just witnessed was distasteful to him. Worse, though, was the personal animosity directed at him. It was unjustified, distasteful, but there was nothing he could do to change that. Not for the moment anyway.

At the door to his suite of offices the senior Mountie, an inspector, said, "Here you are, sir. The Commissioner has instructed us to stand guard here until further orders. There will be two of us at all times. We will be with you wherever you go inside the Parliament Buildings. Our plainclothes people will look after you if you have to go anywhere outside."

It was a matter-of-fact announcement, not a request for permission.

The PM didn't object. "That's fine, Inspector . . .?"

"Johnson, sir. Eric Johnson."

"Yes. When I'm planning to do anything, go anywhere, my staff will let you know."

"Yes, sir. I have my phone and Sergeant Fraser here has his walkie-talkie."

"Next to his gun." The PM nodded his approval as Johnson opened the door for him.

"George, get Simon and my ministers in here. Any messages?"

"Your wife called. No message — just wanted to wish you good luck. And Mr. Tromso called ten minutes ago. Urgent."

"Okay. Get his secretary on the line."

He had just settled in at his desk with paper and pen in hand when the phone rang. George had the IMF secretary on the line. She was getting Tromso and Weinstock on a conference call. The PM activated the tape recorder. He didn't want to miss anything during what promised to be a very important three-way conversation.

Tromso's Norwegian voice and Weinstock's New York–accented tones came through clearly. The courtesies were out of the way quickly.

"We are making progress, my dear Prime Minister," Tromso began. "Yes, indeed we are. All of the appropriate people, the decision-makers here, support the Weinstock Solution. Let us tell you who they are and our impression of their reactions."

Tromso began his report. The PM quickly stopped note-taking. It was easier to rely on the tape.

Tromso had made eight negotiating contacts. Only one was negative.

"Why was he against it?"

"It is too complicated for him. He thinks it will take months of haggling and negotiations. And he couldn't understand why the IMF is involved, why I'm trying to get support for the Weinstock Solution. I tried to explain to him that the IMF's role is to maintain international stability and we have to do everything in our power to help Canada at this time — even if it means lobbying American politicians."

The PM grunted. "I can understand his problem. So are you telling me the Weinstock Solution is acceptable in principle?"

Weinstock came in. "I'll give you the answer to that. But I want to tell you about what I've been doing, my calls. Five of them. None negative. I'll start with the head man."

He talked at his typical rapid-fire pace. The PM absorbed it all, his eyes wide with astonishment at what he was hearing.

"So there you are." Weinstock's voice was loud with the excitement of his and Tromso's success. "The answer is yeah! The Weinstock Solution — the only solution for getting rid of your goddam mountain of debt — is acceptable in principle."

"There will have to be an enormous amount of haggling and negotiations — just as my negative contact said," Tromso cautioned. "And it will take time, much time."

"Plus stainless-steel balls and backbone," Weinstock added. "So the ball — if I can use that word again — the ball's in your court, Richard. If you decide to go for it, when will you know?"

The PM answered without hesitation. "It'll take me at least a week. But I'll have a better idea after I've delivered the budget speech in the House."

"How's it coming?"

"We're almost there. As I told you, and as the world now knows, my target is a zero deficit in eighteen months."

Weinstock reacted. "And like I told you, I'll be goddamned if I know how you're gonna do it. That's sixty-six billion Canadian in spending cuts. Impossible!"

"I grant you it will take a miracle, or close to it. I appreciate what you two have done. Thank you both. There are hard decisions for Canada to make. You gentlemen obviously appreciate that."

Tromso responded. "Of course we understand. In terms of world economic stability it is our duty to try to help you solve the crisis."

To which Weinstock added, "Don't forget that stainless steel backbone."

As soon as they were off the line, the PM switched off the recorder. Before he had time to reflect on the conversation Camp brought in Carter and Greco. They were smiling.

The Finance Minister announced, "We've done it! The budget's in the bag."

Carter added, "Well, we think we've got it in the bag. What an ordeal."

The PM looked approvingly at his two hard-working ministers. "I can imagine. That's the best news I've had all day. Sit down and tell me about it. We've got twenty minutes until the House opens. What about the Speaker, Simon?"

"No problem. The former prime minister agreed. Dagon's in the Speaker's office right now, getting his gown fitted." The Speaker of the House, when performing his or her duties in the House, wore a black silk gown with winged collar and tabs, similar to the legal gown of a lawyer who had achieved the distinction of being appointed a Queen's or King's Counsel.

Greco asked, "How did the Speech From the Throne go? I gather they gave you a rough time."

The PM gave a quick description of the tempest created in the Red Chamber when the senators heard the tough legislation the new government would propose. Carter and Greco looked shocked. "What a lousy way to start out," Carter said sympathetically.

The PM shrugged and changed the subject. "Tell me about the budget."

"The good news is it's finished. We're ready to write the text for you. It won't take long. We have most of it done already," Carter said. "The bad news is that it's a disaster. You can't do a sixty-six billion cut in spending in eighteen months without . . ."

"A total, unmitigated disaster," the PM filled in. "But you've got it done. That's the main thing. Are you satisfied? Can we go with it?"

"We have no choice, Richard. No choice at all." Carter never pulled punches. "Some economists think we can cut to a percentage of GDP like Martin did. But that still piles on the debt."

"What I want now is a Cabinet meeting tonight. The House opens now. Make it nine for Cabinet. Simon, can you do it?"

"Yes, sir, but . . ."

"But what?"

"I recommend you don't use the Cabinet room. You'll have the media hanging all over you. I suggest your conference room."

Carter moaned, "I can't stand another ten minutes in there!" Greco's face showed his agreement.

"We'll have to bring in some extra chairs. Maybe thirty ministers. We can do it." Camp was confident.

"We'll use the Cabinet room," the PM ordered. "To hell with the media. Get George and his assistant to track everybody down."

"No problem, sir. We know where all of them are. They didn't leave town after the swearing-in."

"Do it." The PM looked at the ceiling for a moment, trying to collect his thoughts, then looked at his watch. "We have to open the House session in fifteen minutes. If you two have a budget, then release your people. Tell them they're sworn — no, they have an absolute duty to Canada — to say nothing about what's gone on. Any leaks will cost them their jobs. I mean that!"

"I'll tell them," Carter offered, and started towards the door.

"And in the next ten minutes I have to decide what I'm going to say when the House convenes."

"After that Speech From the Throne you'd better wear a bullet-proof vest," was Carter's parting remark. "I'll be back in a minute."

Camp checked his watch. "Time to go, sir."

Greco rose, straightened his tie, ran a hand over his hair. This would be his first appearance in the House, and he was nervous. "How are you going to handle this, Richard?"

"Simple. Welcome the Speaker. Say a few words about how the Japanese have skewered Canada. Comment on the Speech From the Throne. Introduce the bankers' bill for first, second, and third reading. The Opposition have to go with it."

Greco agreed that it was important to have the legislation in place anyway.

Carter came briskly into the office as the PM continued: "Then a statement that the budget will be presented to the House in emergency session at . . . I had originally said nine tomorrow. Better make it ten. I need time for the caucus."

"Good idea," Greco agreed.

Now it was time to go down to the House. The new Prime Minister was about to make his debut before his peers. It should have been an exhilarating moment for him. But the stark reality was that the country was collapsing under the weight of its ever-increasing indebtedness. If Canada was to have any hope of financial survival, he would have to carry out decisions that even Solomon would have found almost impossible to make. This enormous weight of responsibility dramatically robbed him of any sense of excitement and pride of accomplishment. But not totally robbed.

18

5:00 P.M.: The House of Commons

Followed by Carter and Greco and flanked by the two RCMP officers, the Prime Minister made his way along the corridor and entered that special Sir John A. office with the clandestine circular stairway that led to the curtained corridor behind the government benches on the west side of the House, to the Speaker's right.

A cluster of new Reform PC members were trying to help each other find the seats that had been assigned to them by the Speaker's office. Their babbling and pointing to the seat charts that had been given to them stopped as soon as their PM and his entourage suddenly appeared in their midst as if out of nowhere.

Ever the politician — and now the leader — the Prime Minister paused to shake hands all round and introduce Carter and Greco. Typical of his usual courtesy, he included the RCMP pair, and then asked Carter to help the neophytes find their seats.

"Me? This is the first time I've sat on this side of the House myself!" She laughed. "Of course. You and Mario go ahead."

The PM glanced at his watch. In five minutes the new Speaker would enter the House, the mace marched in ahead of him, and the first session of the next Parliament would begin with himself in the prime minister's hot seat. The hottest seat in Canada.

As he looked down he noticed something he had never seen before. His left hand had a visible nervous tremor. He held out both hands in front of him. Both were shaking. Only slightly, but shaking they were. That couldn't be happening to him!

Of course it could. The unrelenting tension of the last two days was obviously taking its toll on his nervous system and every other part of his body, including his overloaded brain.

The moment was at hand. He was about to part the curtains and enter the House for the first time as Prime Minister. He squared his shoulders and told himself, "Go for it, you dumb bastard! Give 'em hell, and if they don't like what you have to ram down their throats, screw them all!"

He went through the curtains, stopping briefly on the top step of the stairs that went down to the floor of the House between the members' carved-wood benches and desks.

The members of the House, new and veteran, were milling about or already seated at their assigned places. The enormous vaulted chamber was filled with the voices of just over two hundred involved, adrenalin-charged Canadians. They were talking, chatting; some even laughing.

The question on everyone's mind and lips was, what was the government, the new Prime Minister, the Cabinet, going to do about this catastrophic financial crisis? The government was bankrupt. And the Speech From the Throne, did you hear it? No? Well, let me tell you! Unbelievable!

As the PM started down the steps, he looked up at the spectators' galleries ahead of him and to his right. They were packed. People up there were pointing at him and telling each other, "There's the Prime Minister!"

To his left and above the ornate, high-backed Speaker's chair square on its dais — teen-aged pages would soon be sitting on the steps up to it — the press gallery was crammed full of jostling media people, each wanting to be in the best seat in the House.

When the PM was halfway down the steps, a sudden hush spread throughout the chamber as the members and spectators realized that he was there. He was among them, the main person on whose shoulders rested the survival of Canada. In a sense they were awestruck, moved to silence as they turned to stare at this lone figure making his way for the first time to the front bench, to the seat and desk where all the prime ministers of Canada before him had sat or stood during their respective periods as first minister.

No one, none of his own party on each side of the short stairs, reached out to shake his hand. No one patted him on the back. Nor did anyone speak to him as he slowly made his way. It was as if all of them were afraid. Suddenly he was untouchable.

By the time he reached the bottom step the entire House was silent. All movement had stopped, all eyes were focussed on the haggard, grey-haired, still handsome, truly distinguished-looking man from the West.

Then it began. On the government side a member clapped her hands to applaud her leader. Immediately the applause came like a wave from all sides as nearly all — but by no means all — members of Parliament and spectators rose to their feet to give welcome and praise to the Prime Minister.

He was in the centre of the nation's bear pit. The Speech From the Throne had been the signal to ready the dogs for an attack on his government. As in the ancient sport of bearbaiting, the members would be unleashed on the Prime Minister. Tomorrow he expected to face the most vicious attack, participate in the most acrimonious, destructive debate, ever waged in the House of Commons. The very vitals of Canada — what remained of it with Québec gone — would be ripped open with ruthless savagery and exposed to the danger of dissolution and collapse.

The applause that was filling his ears today would soon turn into bitter, slanderous shouting, questioning, arguing. The bear pit would probably be beyond the control of a Speaker who had never before faced the House.

As the Prime Minister moved from the aisle to his front row and centre seat his mind was turning over those pessimistic thoughts about what lay immediately ahead of the House and himself.

He sat. Greco came in from the other aisle to sit on his left. Then Carter joined him, sitting on his right. This was temporary seating for the two ministers. He needed them by his side during this brief opening, and while he delivered the budget speech the next morning. He would rely on them to provide information and answers and, when appropriate, to stand and respond to questions directed at the Prime Minister. He and his little team of Carter and Greco were as prepared and ready as they could be in the extremely brief time the crisis had allowed them.

But it was the rest of his Cabinet and his caucus that he was worried about. At that point in time he had no idea how they individually or collectively had reacted to the jolting punches of the Speech From the Throne.

Even more troublesome was that there hadn't been time to convene a Cabinet meeting, let alone a caucus meeting, to lay out his radical budget and other related proposals.

Cabinet. He had called a Cabinet meeting for nine that evening. And caucus at eight tomorrow morning. The budget would be printed by that time and he'd have the opening and closing of his speech ready.

As their Cabinet colleagues settled into their front bench and second row seats to the left and right of the Prime Minister, Carter and Greco passed the word to them about the timing of both the Cabinet and caucus meetings.

Carter caught the eye of the whip as he came through the curtains. He went down the aisle to her and bent over to listen. He got the caucus timing message and said he would make sure every Reform PC member would be there, even if they had to be wheeled in on a stretcher!

At precisely five o'clock the Speaker's procession entered the House through the massive brass and glass doors at the south end of the chamber. Everyone stood as the black-uniformed Sergeant-at-Arms marched in the lead with the crown-headed mace of authority on his right shoulder. Following him was the new Speaker, Leon Dagon, his ceremonial tricorn sitting squarely on his head, his black robe billowing about his short body as he walked at the smart pace set by the Sergeant-at-Arms.

At five minutes past the hour of five o'clock in the afternoon of Tuesday, January 30 of the year 2001, the newly installed Speaker of the House of Commons of Canada, Leon Dagon, the Reform PC member from North York East, mounted the dais to the Speaker's chair. He turned to face the House, the signal to the Sergeant-at-Arms to carefully lay the mace into its oak rack that stood on the floor in its customary place in front of the dais.

That done, the Sergeant-at-Arms bowed to the Speaker. Then he walked formally, with upright dignity, down the floor of the House, skirting the long, narrow tables at which the Clerk of the House and his black-gowned staff sat. Then he disappeared through the entrance doors.

The House of Commons was in session.

All members resumed their seats, with the exception of the Prime Minister. When the rustling noises subsided, the Speaker removed his tricorn — a relic of parliamentary antiquity — signalling that the House was indeed in operation. He handed the tricorn to a waiting page. He then recognized the only person standing by saying, "The Honourable member from Calgary North."

That said, the Speaker gingerly lowered himself into the seat of authority. He appeared relieved that the initial formalities of the difficult post into which he had been thrust with little or no warning had apparently gone so well.

The Prime Minister of Canada's first words were of tribute to the Speaker for accepting the delicate, onerous function at all, let alone on such short notice.

"I believe, Mr. Speaker, that the Honourable Leader of the Opposition, the gentleman across the floor, who until so recently stood for so many years where I now stand — I believe, Mr. Speaker, that he joins me in congratulating you."

The PM looked for and saw the nod of assent from the leader opposite.

"I might say, Mr. Speaker, if the actions and reactions we observed earlier, during the reading of the Speech From the Throne in the Senate chamber are any indication of the type of emotions that will be brought to flash point in this House as the government presents the budget then, Mr. Speaker, I respectfully suggest that you take steps to ensure the security and safety of all honourable members of this House. Mr. Speaker, I suggest that you request the Commissioner of the RCMP to provide an adequate number of his officers in position just outside the entrances to this venerable chamber so they can move immediately, should it be necessary for them to assist you in either maintaining or restoring order."

That statement evoked shouts from the Opposition: "Shame! Shame!", "Fascist pig!", and the like.

The Leader of the Opposition, appearing quite uncomfortable in his new role (an enormous comedown from his post as prime minister, which he had held since the secession of Québec), stood and looked to the Speaker for permission to speak.

The PM immediately sat in order to give way.

"Mr. Speaker, I, too, stood at the bar of the Red Chamber as Her Excellency read the Speech From the Throne. I, too, witnessed the reaction of some if not most of the honourable senators to what I consider to be the most inflammatory, reckless, ill-advised Speech From the Throne since the first day of July 1867, the birthday of Confederation."

The government benches exploded with fury: "You caused this mess!"; "Go home and play with your boats!"; "You goddam hypocrite!";

"World's biggest spender, sit down!" A multitude of other epithets flew across the floor, colliding with retorts returned at full volume.

The Speaker stood. He called "Order" again and again. The PM sat quietly, elbows on his desk. Carter, the experienced parliamentarian, was letting fly at the Opposition in a distinctly unladylike manner. Greco was moved to silence by this appalling new experience.

The Opposition Leader remained standing, waiting for the furor to subside. Finally it did.

"Mr. Speaker, now that the juvenile and for the most part inexperienced members on the other side of the House have regained control of themselves, at least temporarily, I support the advice the Leader of the Opposition — sorry — the Prime Minister has given you concerning the RCMP."

He looked smugly to his left and right at his own members. "There's really no telling what the Cabinet or the new backbenchers over there are capable of doing once they lose control!"

With that riposte he sat down to a thunder of desk-thumping by his followers, which was overridden by roars of anger from the government side.

The PM was on his feet, his finger pointing at the Opposition Leader. His voice was filled with cutting sarcasm. "Lose control, Mr. Speaker? Lose control? The leader of the party that has brought Canada to bankruptcy is talking about *my* government losing control!

"Mr. Speaker, that honourable gentleman and his entire party lost control of government spending years ago. They've been out of control for as long as they've been in power. They lost control of Québec, they've lost control of governing, and they lost, totally lost, any vestige of control of the deficit and the debt!"

He paused to relish the thumping of desks by his members.

"My honourable friend the former prime minister and his suckophants — yes, Mr. Speaker, *suck*ophants — have come within a hair's-breadth, a microsecond, of destroying Canada. Why? Because they lost control of themselves, lost control of the civil servants, the bureaucracy. And they didn't have the guts, didn't have the intelligence, the fortitude, to take back the control they lost."

Those words provoked screams of anger from the benches across the floor, countered by cheers and pounding from the people surrounding the PM. He waited, then went on.

"Mr. Speaker, I wish now to attempt to lay out a program for the orderly and urgent conduct of the business of this House in this moment of absolute and profound financial crisis."

Muttering, but nothing more than that, came from across the floor.

"At this time I will move the first, second, and third reading of a bill to ensure bank credit availability to the government of Canada."

When those formalities and votes were completed, the Prime Minister continued.

"At the opening of tomorrow's session I will present to the House for its consideration and debate an emergency budget as referred to in the Speech From the Throne.

"I must tell you, Mr. Speaker —"

"Why are *you* doing the budget? Why isn't your rosy-cheeked Finance Minister doing it?" came the derisive words shouted from the opposite back bench. The PM thought, "That arrogant asshole, that know-it-all!" The interruption had come from the member from Winnipeg who had been Minister of Revenue in the defeated cabinet.

The Prime Minister's response was calm. "My Finance Minister, Mr. Speaker, like the shouter of that question, is from Winnipeg. There the similarity between the two honourable members ends. The honourable member opposite brought with him as Minister of National Revenue in the former cabinet the experience, literally, of a used-car salesman. The result was unmitigated catastrophe for Canada. On the other hand, my Minister of Finance has a rich and broad experience in the financial world and in banking.

"Above all, my Finance Minister recognizes his own limitations, something my friends on the other side of the House are totally incapable of recognizing — their own limitations."

A blast from across the floor was led by a shouted assault: "Idiot!"

The PM pressed on. "My Finance Minister has not had any experience in this House. The budget that will be delivered tomorrow is so complex, so full of harsh and heartless actions and absolutely mandatory steps, that it would be unfair and inhumane to ask anyone — anyone who has not been in parliament before — to deliver this government's first budget."

He bent down to listen to Ann Carter for a moment. He straightened up, thought about what she had said.

"Mr. Speaker, my colleague, the President of the Treasury Board, reminds me that the Minister of Finance and she will take full part in the debate that will follow the budget. Mr. Speaker, in addition to the budget, and as supplementary to it, I will be putting forward alternative proposals. Those proposals will be designed to get the nation out of this death-by-deficit-and-debt box into which the party now in well-earned opposition has locked the nation and thrown away the key."

The furor over that shaft was short-lived.

"Mr. Speaker." The PM wanted to finish this off. The urgency to write the final draft of the budget spurred him to say, "Mr. Speaker, I move that this House reconvene at ten tomorrow morning."

The Speaker seized that motion with alacrity. He stood, saying, "A motion by the Prime Minister that this House reconvene tomorrow at ten o'clock in the forenoon. All those in favour say yea."

The yeas from the government side were strong and conclusive. The nays asked for were few and weak.

"Motion carries," the Speaker announced. A page delivered his tricorn, and the Sergeant-at-Arms appeared as if by magic to hoist the mace on his shoulder. The mace, the Sergeant, and a much-relieved Speaker departed the House.

The PM had only one thing on his mind. "It's five-thirty," he said to Carter and Greco. "It's back to my office. You and I have to get that goddam budget speech done."

"Do we have to have this Cabinet meeting tonight?" Carter asked plaintively.

"Absolutely. No choice." He turned to face the horde of Cabinet ministers and members descending on him with smiling words of congratulations on how he'd handled those bastards, and himself.

19

5:40 P.M.: The Prime Minister's Office

Flanked by the RCMP officers, the Prime Minister and his two ministers arrived back in his office to find that Camp had a call waiting for him. It was Weinstock on the line. "Tell him I'll call back in a few minutes," the PM said, then turned quickly to Carter.

"You and Mario use the conference room. Bring in whomever you want from your staffs. I'll work in my office. George'll look after my typing. Get one of your own people in to do yours."

He loosened his tie and his mind worked at top speed to organize the many things he still had to do that evening. "Remember: secrecy and security. We're going to produce and print everything right here. George has brought in two more big photocopying machines and a ton of paper. Okay?"

"The Cabinet meeting's at nine," Carter reminded him. "How're you going to handle it?"

"Carefully. It will be a briefing. I'll tell them what's happening and what the budget will look like. Then I'm going to ask for their blind, unswerving, unquestioning support in caucus and in the House — or else."

"What about the people who don't like what they're hearing?" Greco asked.

"I can guarantee they won't like it. None of them will. But if anyone's got a better idea I'll listen."

"But not for long," Carter guessed.

"You've got that right. There's no time left. We've got three hours before Cabinet. I won't let the meeting go beyond an hour. That'll get us back to the drawing board by ten. I want us to finish the text, the whole thing, your part and mine, by midnight. Edited, on the word processor, the original ready for copying."

"How many?" Greco, always thinking in terms of numbers, asked.

"What?"

"How many copies will George run?"

"Five hundred. One for every member of the House and the Senate plus the press gallery."

"The press gallery. What about their traditional preview — the lock-up?" Carter raised that question.

"I've told Simon to arrange it for eight tomorrow morning. That'll give them two hours before they're let loose and I'll just be getting on my feet."

Carter, with Greco nodding his agreement, said, "Sounds good. We'll have some sandwiches and coffee sent in, maybe around seven-thirty. God, I don't even remember what, if anything, I ate for lunch." She laughed. "I could go for Chinese in a big way tonight — how about you, Mario? Oh, well, maybe for breakfast." Another chuckle and a wave of the hand: "Well, we're off. See you in the cabinet room at nine. Come on, Mario."

The PM smiled after her and went into his private office. "Simon, get Weinstock back on the line. Use the videophone. He's got one, hasn't he? And make sure the line is secure."

In four minutes the two men were speaking with each other, their talking heads clearly displayed on their respective videophones.

The garrulous Chairman of the Federal Reserve Board went right at it New York style: "Hiya, buddy! How're you doin'? Hope it's going alright. Got your budget finished? When're ya gonna give it to 'em?"

The PM gave Weinstock a quick status report.

"Great!" was Weinstock's judgement. "That's exactly the kinda budget the Japs and the world money markets wanta hear."

"So what's new from your end?"

There was a broad smile on the Washington face. "Tromso and I've been making great progress. As far as I'm concerned you've got a done deal. If you've got a recorder, turn it on . . ."

"It's already on."

"I thought so. Anyway, here's the deal. I'll give you the details. You're clear to go public with it anytime you want. If you think you can buy the deal, that is."

"That decision is not mine alone to make. As I told you it'll take probably a week to sort things out. If I put your solution forward as an option it will be at the end of the budget speech tomorrow. I have a Cabinet meeting in about three hours, but I don't think I'll run it by Cabinet. In fact, I haven't run it by anybody."

Weinstock was puzzled, even surprised. "Shouldn't you let Carter and Greco in on this thing? I mean it's so big, so important. It would change everything up there."

"Which is why I've kept it to myself. I don't want anyone panicking. And I don't want any goddam leaks. So what's the deal, the Weinstock Solution?"

It took Weinstock a full five minutes to lay out in detail the terms and conditions of his proposal, which had been refined and now agreed to in principle by all the main players.

When the Chairman declared he was finished, the Prime Minister was so overwhelmed by the consequences, the impact, of what he'd heard, that he used the last word almost always used by a pilot whose plane, out of control, is about to crash and take him to his certain death.

Shaking his head at the magnitude of the now fully developed plan, he muttered, "Shit!"

He thanked Weinstock for the man's remarkable all-out effort, said good-bye, and turned off the recorder. The PM was about to give Camp the Weinstock tape for George to transcribe but he decided not to — just yet. Its contents were too volatile. Even George might have a heart attack, go into convulsions when he heard it.

In fact he decided not to include either the Weinstock Solution or the Buchanan proposal in the typed material. He would write out the text and photocopy it himself. But he wouldn't give it to George. That way there would be no possibility of a leak.

He had his own doubts about the feasibility of the two solutions. But, he reasoned, both were only ideas, propositions to be discussed and debated as alternatives to the budget. The budget, on the other hand, was government policy, subject to amendment through debate.

"Simon, I'm starting to write my part of the budget speech. I'll do the intro and the exit. Ann, with Mario, will do the main text, department by department, program by program."

"Yes, sir."

"What I want you to do is guard the gate. Screen the phone calls. Between now and the cabinet meeting, no calls, no visitors. The same after the meeting until I get the bloody thing finished."

"What about something to eat?"

"Tuna sandwich on brown, no butter. Glass of white wine. If you'll monitor what Ann's writing, then you can collect each section as she finishes it and feed it to George, or to Ann's secretary if she turns up. Do the same with me. That way everything will be on the word processor, well almost, by the time we finish writing."

"What's your target?" Camp wanted to know.

"What d'you mean?"

"Is it still midnight to finish?"

The PM nodded firmly. "Has to be. And, Simon."

"Yes, sir?"

"Bring the whole goddam bottle of wine."

20

9:00 P.M.: The Cabinet Room

The soundproofed door closed promptly on the first stroke of nine o'clock. The first Cabinet meeting of the new government began awkwardly.

The new Cabinet people, especially those who had never before been in the House, were uncertain of what to do, how to act, what the protocol was. They had not a clue as to how decisions were taken in the ultra-secret environment of a governor-in-council meeting.

The conduct of a Cabinet meeting was shaped by its chairman, the leader of the government of the day. The Prime Minister.

If he wanted voting on an issue, he got voting. If he wanted decisions by consensus, that's what he got. Most prime ministers had liked the consensus route. Why? Because he or she — the prime minister of the day — would decide if there was a consensus. And would also decide what it was.

Any nay-sayers could leave their resignations in the salver at the entrance door.

The Prime Minister laid it on the line to his Cabinet. There were no uncertain terms. There were no choices. "Think what you want, disagree all you want, if necessary shove your conscience over your favourite cliff. Remember, if you're in my Cabinet, you're in a position of power, a position from which you can influence the course of events for the better. So hear me. Stay with me."

In that first meeting the PM made it clear from the word *go* that, until further or other notice, policy and all other Cabinet decisions would be made by consensus. He would hear reasonable views on all matters to be considered by the "committee of twenty-eight" as he described it. But in the end it would be the consensus that prevailed.

Once a consensus was reached, every last one of the members of his Reform PC Cabinet — all of whom he had hand-picked from among the large crop of newly elected members of Parliament — would fully support and stand behind that consensus. They were obliged to do so, even if in their own judgement and conscience they believed it was not right.

"Understood?" the PM asked. To a man and woman all gave the same answer: "Yes."

The PM then took them step by step through the budget notes that Carter had been busy putting down on paper with Greco's help. Some ministers made notes. Others listened, some in awe, others accepting with difficulty what they were hearing. There were looks of pain, grimaces, negative shaking of heads on certain issues. On others there were nods and smiles of approval all round.

The PM had not even hinted at the Weinstock Solution or the Buchanan proposal. They were tucked in a separate compartment of his mind. They were kicking and screaming to get out, but he stood fast.

By quarter to ten the Prime Minister concluded his rapid rundown of the budget. Then it was the feisty Ann Carter who took on almost all comers who voiced their challenges, their shocked complaints. She had all the numbers, the complete rationale for each decision the PM, Greco, and she had taken as they were shaping the budget.

The experienced, vocal Ontario members, mostly from the Greater Toronto Area, had severe emotional objections to the main mandated cuts. Their vented concerns were mainly those that affected the extremely expensive social programs: unemployment insurance, the CPP and OAS, the medical care system.

The PM noted that despite all the shouting, arguing, and posturing he had not heard one single threat to resign. He would use that unspoken knowledge when he wrapped up the session.

Near the end of the hour-long meeting the PM broke up a particularly loud shouting match between the Minister responsible for the CBC (the member for York Centre in Metro Toronto) and Carter. "Kill the CBC over my dead body" was his theme.

The PM held up his hand, a signal to calm down. "You don't seem to understand. Listen to me: the country's broke. Our revenues exceed our expenses this year by sixty-six billion. And nobody will lend us the money to cover that debt. Nobody!"

"Domestic lenders, surely . . ." was the retort.

"Forget it. Canadians who have any money — do you think they're going to buy government bonds, Treasury bills, whatever, when the whole world has just cut us off?" The PM shook his head. "I have no choice. *You* as a Cabinet minister have no choice." He took a visible shot. "As long as you're a Cabinet minister, that is."

Silence.

"So we have our budget consensus, haven't we?" he asked, the thrust of his jaw and the fire in his eyes sending only one message: Don't even think of saying no.

"Good. Now, I expect to have your full support at caucus tomorrow morning. By full I mean total. No breaks in the fortress walls will be tolerated. Each of you has to get out there and sell this worst, couldn't be worse, terrible budget.

"But remember, you're selling it to caucus members only — and only at caucus tomorrow morning at eight, or after caucus. Not before."

He looked at the faces along both sides of the long walnut Cabinet table. "Do I make myself clear? If any of you can't support me, and I mean support on every point — oh, by the way, having listened to all of you I've decided to make one change, one variation." He paused.

The suspense showed on the waiting faces.

"Yes, I've decided we should go for the zero deficit in twenty-four months instead of eighteen."

Carter agreed: "It would be much more practical, much more do-able."

"Let me finish. If any of you can't support me, then in all fairness you should tell me by tendering your resignation from your ministry, from the Cabinet." He began stacking his papers, ready to shove into his briefcase. "And I must have it by midnight — in writing. If you, individually if you don't submit your resignation, I will know I have your support, no matter how bloody the caucus or the House or the media get."

He pulled his briefcase off the floor, opened it and began stuffing in the documents. "One final thing. Do not, I repeat, do not say a word to anyone about what goes on at this or any other Cabinet meeting, particularly this one. There used to be a sexist saying — it's now obsolete. You can tell when I say it. If any one of you breaks the historic code of Cabinet secrecy and confidentiality I'll have your whatevers for book-ends!"

That remark brought smiles to most faces.

"Okay, people." He returned the smiles to ease the tension. "This first meeting of Cabinet is finished. Ann, Mario, and I still have work to do, because the budget is scheduled to be finished by midnight, and my speech to go with it."

At three minutes past ten the meeting was over. The door opened and the Cabinet members filed out. To the media standing watch in the corridor, everything that had gone on in the Cabinet room was apparently conciliatory, non-combative.

That was the face put on by the participants as they emerged. In the presence of the waiting media, the Cabinet members were all smiles. They were also delighted that the Cabinet confidentiality rule absolutely barred them from talking about what had gone on in the session.

It also saved their respective "whatevers" from becoming book-ends.

21

11:14 P.M.: The Prime Minister's Office

Drained. He felt absolutely drained.

The Prime Minister had caught himself falling asleep twice, brain turned off, head bobbing, pen stationary instead of writing.

The two alternatives to the budget were difficult to deal with because they were such radical concepts. Would Parliament choose one of them over his budget? And if so, which one?

"Christ, I can't think about that now," he told himself. "I'm almost finished. The Weinstock thing is done, I'm nine-tenths of the way through Buchanan. What a complicated yet simple thing Buchanan is. Gotta keep going. Gotta finish. What time is it?

"Eleven-fourteen. Forty-five minutes left to deadline. Wonder how Ann's doing? And Mario. Whatever she . . . they're writing I'll have to accept. No problem. We've been over every item. I just have to get my part right. Okay. Back to Buchanan and the finish. This should cause a revolution on Bay Street."

The PM wrote on. No wine. No coffee. Just get it over with.

At 11:35 p.m. he was finished. Not — nor ever — satisfied, he went back to the beginning of his script and started to speed-read it through. Commas, spelling, letters he'd left out of words because he wrote so quickly, all were checked.

He took the tail end of the budget text (but not Weinstock and Buchanan), stacked it, hauled himself to his feet, and staggered out the door to George. The secretary was pounding away on his keyboard, eyes glued to his screen.

"How're you doing, George? My stuff almost finished?"

"Yes, sir. Christ, this section of the budget is long!"

"Well, this is the end." He handed two pages to George.

"I have additional notes, but they're not going to be typed. Understand?"

"Yes, sir. For your eyes only, right?"

"You got it. What about Ann and Mario?"

"They're almost finished. Maybe ten minutes more. Her secretary — she's over there — she can tell you where she's at."

"What's her name?"

"Damned if I know, sir."

"Pretty thing. And young."

"Yes, sir."

The PM walked over to the young woman. Her eyes lifted from the handwritten page to look at this older man. Good-looking for an old fart. Never saw him before.

"May I help you?" she asked.

"You may. Are ministers Carter and Greco through writing?"

"No, there's more to come, but everything they've given me so far — almost everything — is on the machine. I have maybe three minutes more typing to do. Are you part of the staff here? Security, maybe?"

The PM smiled. "Yeah, I'm security. Just checking up on what's happening."

He was content. The entire budget speech would be in printout mode before midnight. The three of them, the ministers, could do a rapid copy-edit, run the typos and changes into the machine, print out one copy, check, then print five hundred. Would that be enough? Yes, enough for the ten-o'clock session of the House. More could be run off after that.

Weinstock and Buchanan! He had almost forgotten. They were on his desk. Without a word he went back into his private office, picked up his handwritten pages, marched to George's prized photocopier. Three full copies came out of the machine.

All three copies went into the private, hidden vault in his office. The original he folded and stuffed into his inside jacket pocket. He would read and re-read it, adjust it, before, without warning, he presented Buchanan and Weinstock to the House.

Carter and Greco opened and walked through the conference room door. She had a sheaf of papers in her hand.

"Ah, Richard. We're finished!" she exclaimed.

"And right on time. Well done. Didn't think you'd do it." He bent over to kiss Carter's offered cheek, then shook Mario's hand. Both ministers looked exhausted.

"Think you've got it right?" the PM asked.

Carter answered, "Yes, just the way you approved it. But, my God, Richard, it was tough to do."

"You can say that again. And it will be tough, very tough, on the taxpayers, the lower class, the middle class, the rich, the corporations, big business, small business . . ." The Prime Minister stopped as he saw tears welling up in Carter's eyes.

"It's like, it's like murdering your own child," she whispered. "Maybe we could cut spending to 35 percent of GDP instead of zero deficit? I wish there were another way."

"I do, too, Ann. I really do." He was on the verge of telling her about Weinstock and Buchanan. "As a matter of fact . . ."

He stopped as George appeared. "Is that the end of it, Minister?"

Carter pulled herself together. "Yeah. It's all yours, George." She handed him the papers.

"Good. I'll give this to your secretary." He turned to the Prime Minister. "I've printed out your stuff, three copies, sir. It's on your desk, ready to edit. By the time you've done that" — he waved the pages Carter had just given him — "this and the rest of Minister Carter's text will be ready to look at."

"Great. Where's Simon? Tell him I need him, and another bottle of wine. Red this time, and four glasses. And George . . ."

"Yes, sir."

"You're doing a helluva job. Thank you."

The PM took Carter by the arm. Followed by Greco, he steered her to the chair in front of his desk, saying, "And so are you, Ann."

The final page was edited and delivered to George at five minutes to one. By that time George and Camp had the photocopiers going full tilt.

At one-thirty the PM insisted that his two ministers get some much-needed sleep.

"You'll need all your strength to face the House in the morning," he told them. "Thank you both. I couldn't have done this without you." Carter and Greco gave him weary, grateful smiles and left.

The Reform PC government's budget, to be presented to the House of Commons on January 31, 2001, was being put to bed in final form.

It was time for him to catch a few hours' sleep at home. The RCMP would escort him. The Prime Minister put on his overcoat and took a last look around his office. There was no turning back now.

Not unless there was a revolt by the caucus. The way the PM saw it, a revolt by his inexperienced backbenchers was a distinct possibility.

If his own members refused to support him, what then?

Day Four

Wednesday, January 31, 2001

22

8:00 A.M.: The Government Caucus Room

The PM looked over the sea of faces looking up at him as he stood on the platform of the government caucus room. Feeling only slightly refreshed from the brief, restless sleep, he braced himself for this next challenge.

It was another "first" for him and for every Reform PC party member in the room — except for two Conservatives from the Mulroney era who had just returned from the political graveyard. The first caucus ever in that special room.

Briskly taking charge, the PM thanked the caucus chairperson whom he had appointed. There would be a chair election later. Perhaps tomorrow.

He then began his talk with a description of the function of the caucus, the coming together behind closed doors to discuss in secret the issues of the day, the policies that the Cabinet was going to propose and any legislation the government intended to introduce.

Caucus was a place where backbenchers could say their piece.

He felt like a university professor talking to a class of new students. The experienced members were probably bored to tears, but as leader of the party he believed he had no choice but to deliver this lecture before he moved on to discuss the crisis and the budget.

"Because of the parliamentary principle of party discipline, it is essential that all the members of the government party vote en masse, in a bloc, for the legislation and resolutions and procedural steps the Cabinet, the government, puts before the House.

"If the government loses a vote on a money bill — in this case, the budget — confidence is lost and there must be a general election. That we cannot have!

"In extra-special circumstances, usually where the issue is one of morality and conscience, such as the death penalty, the Prime Minister may decide on a free vote, which means that members are not bound by party discipline and may vote as they see fit."

A voice came from the back. He had seen the face but he couldn't put a name to it. "Will you give a free vote on the budget, Prime Minister?"

The PM's eyes sought out those of the questioner. "The answer to your question is this: At ten o'clock this morning I will present the budget. It isn't protocol to discuss its contents with caucus, but you already have some hints from the Speech From the Throne. After I present the budget it will be open for debate. The debate will be bloody, it will be ferocious, and it will go on for days. At the conclusion of the debate the amendments to the budget that the government is prepared to accept will be made."

The PM paused for effect. All eyes were riveted on him. "At that point there will be a vote. And I can tell you right now there's no goddam way it will be a free vote!"

The questioner was not satisfied with that answer. "So what you're saying, sir, is that whether I like the budget, whether in all conscience I can support it, or even if part of it cuts right across everything I believe in, I still have to vote *for* it?"

"Exactly."

"And if I don't?"

"You're out of the party. Period. You can then sit as an independent if you so choose, or you can resign your parliamentary seat."

The Prime Minister waited a moment in order to let his words sink in.

"Okay, now I want to give you the background of this financial crisis. Feel free to ask questions or express your own thoughts to me if you want to interrupt." He looked at his watch. "I have to be out of here by nine-fifteen."

It was the voice at the back again. This time the questioner stood up, all six-foot-five of him. "Young, probably late thirties," the PM thought. "Good looking lad. One I haven't met yet."

"Sir, my name is Robert Stevens, from Vancouver where it never rains. You and I share the same profession, except that I'm a trial lawyer."

The big man put his hands on the top of the chairback in front of him. "Sir, I'm new here so you'll have to bear with me. You've said you won't tell us what's in the budget. You said it isn't protocol, right?"

"That's correct."

"So why is it the media have the budget as of eight o'clock — right now? And if they have it, why in hell can't we have it, or why can't you tell us the high points, tell us where you're headed?"

The PM didn't like the tone or the challenge. "The media are in a lock-up. They can't get out until I start my speech at ten."

"Ah, so what you're saying is, the media can't be trusted, so they get locked up. What you're *also* saying is, you can't trust us, your own party members, because we're *not* locked up. Because we'll walk out of this caucus room door, spill our guts to other press people out there in the hall. Is that what you're afraid of?"

"I've got news for you, Mr. Stevens." The Prime Minister, near-exhausted, could feel himself losing his temper. "Parliamentary history teaches us that the caucus room walls have big ears and people, even members of parliament, one's own party members, have a tendency to talk when they should keep their mouths shut."

"Well, sir, if that's the reason you won't tell us what's in the budget, then I'll extrapolate the real reason."

"Which is?"

"Which is because you don't want to be upstaged. And this caucus is just one big leak, right?"

The leader of the Reform PC party pulled himself together. He realized he was scowling, his face reflecting his anger. Bad form. He took a step back from the lectern. Then he smiled, that broad, toothy smile the nation's editorial cartoonists were already latching onto.

"Mr. Stevens, I couldn't have put it any better myself. You've hit the nail right on the head. There's no way I want the budget leaked. There's no way I want to be upstaged when I stand to deliver the toughest, most important budget this country's ever seen."

He was coming alive now, his arms sweeping with gestures, his voice oratorical. "I'm the leader of this party. I'm the Prime Minister of Canada. In this hour of crisis, the worst since Confederation in 1867, Canada, the people of Canada, and this party need to see strong, credible leadership in their prime minister."

He shook his finger at the neophyte member from Vancouver. "Let me tell you, Mr. Stevens, I've put my heart and soul into preparing this budget, into trying to come up with solutions that will save Canada from total collapse.

"And I can tell you that at this moment of crisis this caucus can't, you can't, the party can't, the people of Canada can't afford to have the situation made worse by a budget leak!"

He waited for a response from Stevens. Without a word the big man sat down. "He'll probably be on his feet again," the PM thought. "That lad has a lot of potential, if he conforms."

The PM went on to describe the overall financial crisis, as he had promised to do before Stevens stood up to put his second question. In the course of the next forty minutes the bug-swept wood-panelled walls of the caucus room reverberated with the sound of the PM's strong, resonant voice and with the questions, challenges, and statements from both old and new members of Parliament.

The acting chairman of caucus told him that it was nine-fifteen. The PM had to leave but the caucus would continue in session until nine-thirty.

"I have to get out of here," the PM said, "but a couple of things before I go." He ran his hand across his forehead without knowing he had done it.

"The budget I'm about to present will rock Canada, stun everybody, including every single one of you. That's not a promise, not a threat. It's reality. It will contain a set of fiscal-restraint goals that advisors have been telling me are impossible to achieve in a short time frame — or at all."

He shrugged. "But I have no choice. However, I'll also present two other scenarios that can impact on the budget as we've prepared it, 'we' being Ann Carter and Mario Greco and I." He nodded toward the two sitting together in the front row.

"The final thing I have to say is really a plea. I ask for your trust and faith. I ask you to maintain your loyalty to Canada and for your continued allegiance to the Reform PC party. I ask for your full *but positive* participation in the debate. I implore you to recognize and honour party solidarity and discipline when it comes time to vote."

The integrity and sincerity of the leader of the party impressed everyone in the caucus room. They literally leaned forward to hear his parting words.

"To conform to party solidarity and discipline may be the most difficult decision, the most testing act, of your life. But if you fail, you may well destroy this government and you may well destroy the last chance to save Canada."

23

10:00 A.M.: The House of Commons

The House of Commons was packed. Not a seat was empty in the spectators' and press galleries. Not a member of the House was absent, except for a handful ill or unable to get back to Canada from remote foreign places in time for this emergency session.

The opening formalities were over. The Speaker was standing before his chair. He recognized the Prime Minister.

The thick Budget Address speech lay on the desk in front of the PM. It had been put together by George in a looseleaf, easily flipped, three-ring format. The extra-large type enabled the PM to read at standing distance without having to use his glasses.

He had marked the text in yellow to highlight the major points, although he could hardly fail to make them. In the margins were handwritten notes he had made early that morning. He might or might not use them.

This would be an unqualified ass-dragger of a speech, he thought, because it had three long components.

Long? So what? With their bureaucrats the jackasses on the other side of the House were responsible for this appalling bloody mess, he told himself. So if it took one hour or ten to put forward the cure for the near-terminal financial crisis they had negligently, wilfully, created, too bad.

As he prepared to stand in response to the Speaker's recognition, "The Right Honourable, the Prime Minister," he lifted the cover of the book that had been so meticulously crafted by George.

Following the printed speech, but not attached to the looseleaf rings, were his handwritten notes on the Weinstock and Buchanan alternatives. He tried to imagine what the response to them would be. Angry rejection?

Cautious weighing of pros and cons? Or curses and accusations of treachery, treason? He put such thoughts from him.

To the cheers and desk-pounding of his Cabinet and backbenchers, the Prime Minister of Canada slowly got to his feet to deliver the most important speech of his life. He, the twenty-second prime minister since Confederation, had before him the task of trying to save what was left of that nation, save it from self-destruction, from death by deficit.

As he waited for the supportive applause to die down, his eyes were fixed on the Leader of the Opposition and what remained of that burned-out politician's front bench, who, with the governments of the 1980s and '90s, were the architects and the builders of the present debacle. Now it was up to him, the novice prime minister, and his Cabinet members who were just getting to know each other. He reminded himself again that the majority had never set foot in the House of Commons until yesterday afternoon.

The desk-pounding and clapping subsided. The PM knew he would hear very little of that welcome noise from that moment on.

He turned momentarily to face and, with a nod of his head, to acknowledge the Chair.

"Mr. Speaker, it is my duty to place before the House this day an emergency budget of the most drastic kind."

There was a slight commotion in the press gallery above the Speaker's chair. Some members of the media who had been in the lock-up had finished filing their preliminary stories and were having a difficult time getting through the crowd to their assigned seats.

The PM waited patiently. Calm was restored in less than a minute.

"It is my duty as prime minister to propose a budget that will implement the principles set out in the Speech From the Throne that Her Excellency the Governor General so fearlessly presented to the members whose behaviour was raucous, unruly, and truly disgraceful in that other place yesterday afternoon.

"I must say, Mr. Speaker, that this government's decision to abolish the Senate was fully justified by the near-riotous conduct that required the RCMP to restore order in that chamber."

After that statement, the PM had to wait for the noisy reaction on both sides of the House to subside. He then proceeded to describe the mountainous federal debt, the deficit and the interest payments, the Japanese government's actions, and the world leaders' response that had precipitated the crisis.

"The reality, Mr. Speaker, is that as of this moment Canada's government is bankrupt. It cannot borrow money in the international markets. It cannot borrow domestically, because the citizens, banks, and financial institutions of Canada, our normal lenders to governments, have lost all confidence.

"That confidence must be restored. It can be restored only by a budget that will be followed and acted upon to the letter and number. It must be a budget that will reduce the annual deficit to zero in the shortest possible time. That time frame was stated in the Speech From the Throne as eighteen months. On reflection, the government has decided that time will be twenty-four months."

He reached for his water glass. The Opposition benches were silent. In every waiting mind in the House of Commons there was a single theme: sixty-six billion to zero in two years! How was he going to do it?

Fifty-five minutes later they knew how he was going to do it.

The budget proposed the most drastic downsizing ever of a Western government:

The first principle was that the federal government would reduce its activities to those defined in the original British North America Act that Sir John A. Macdonald and his colleagues had crafted with their British masters.

"In keeping with that position, this government will retain its obligations for External Affairs, Defence, Justice, Communications and Culture, Transportation, Immigration, and for social programs that are national in nature.

"Therefore the following departments will be eliminated and with them all subsidiaries, boards, and Crown corporations related to those departments: Agriculture; Energy, Mines and Resources (Natural Resources Canada); Environment; Forestry; all regional agencies; Consumer and Corporate Affairs; Industry, Science and Technology; the National Research Council of Canada and the Natural Sciences and Engineering Research Council; the Canadian Space Agency.

"There are some ten agencies that will be terminated, including the

Export Development Corporation and the Federal Business Development Bank, with a projected annual saving of $320 million."

The Prime Minister's throat was dry. He signalled for his glass to be refilled. The chamber seemed very warm, or was it just he himself?

"Under the heading of Transportation, Transport Canada's budget will be cut from 3.6 billion to 1.5 billion, with appropriate down-sizing of Marine Atlantic and Via Rail. The major expenditure of 220 million for 'Policy and Coordination' will simply vanish.

"The Communications and Culture — including Heritage — budget of 3.6 billion will be reduced 1.2 billion, with the immediate termination of the Canadian Broadcasting Corporation, the National Film Board, and Telefilm Canada. That leaves 2.4 billion in the current C. and C. allocation. That amount will be halved so the budget of Communications and Culture will be 1.2 billion." A few feet-shuffling noises were heard, but the PM did not pause.

"It follows that the multicultural program and the Official Languages funding will be dropped, for a saving of nearly 400 million.

"The budget of Justice at 3.9 billion will be reduced to 2.5 billion. That will have an impact on the RCMP, the Legal Aid system, the operation of the federal courts, and a broad range of services.

"At External Affairs the Canadian International Development Agency and certain other agencies will be terminated, for a savings of 3.3 billion.

"Canada's entrenched social programs plus transfers to provinces total 115.4 billion. The total of 115.4 billion will be reduced by more than a half, that is, by 60.5 billion. The impact on UI, on OAS, and the CPP will be reflected by a cut by one half in all those programs. The same will apply to all transfers to the provinces under the Canada Health and Social Transfer program."

That announcement prompted shouts from the Opposition and negative head-shaking and muttering from the Prime Minister's own backbenchers, who were hearing all of this for the first time.

The PM went on: "The budget for general government services now at 6.6 billion will be reduced by two billion, with appropriate adjustments being put in place as will be decided by the Governor-in-Council.

"And finally, there is Defence. From the current budget amount at nine billion there will be a reduction to 6.2 billion, effective April 1, 2002. The Regular Force will be reduced to 20,000 personnel. The Reserve Force will be increased to 40,000, will have its own budget at 15 percent of the 6.2 billion, and will have its own command. The armed forces will have one year in order to reshape themselves."

Carter tugged at the PM's sleeve. He bent down to listen to her whispering. Nodding his agreement, he said, "Mr. Speaker, my learned colleague, the Honourable President of the Treasury Board, has asked that I say a word on the timing of these dramatic and highly distasteful cuts and terminations.

"They will, with certain exceptions such as Defence, take place within the next fiscal year, which begins on the first of April 2001, just two months away. The reduction implementations will carry on, where necessary, in the fiscal year of 2002–2003, so that there will be a zero deficit for the fiscal year 2003–2004 and thereafter.

"The zero deficit target will be achieved in that fiscal year because the government will have carved at least sixty-six billion out of its annual expenditures."

He turned first towards his benches on his right, then left to face his other members. Then he addressed the Chair again.

"Mr. Speaker. That is the government's proposed budget. It is there for the debate of this House. It contains draconian measures that will effectively destroy the ability of the federal government to deliver services to the citizens of Canada. Health care, old-age pensions, education assistance — every program will be at prejudice, if not destroyed.

"Let me tell you, Mr. Speaker, I detest every word, every number, in this budget. I would do anything, anything within or even beyond reason, to avoid making these drastic cuts.

"What troubles me deeply is the fact that these cuts are necessary so that Canada can pay the horrendous annual interest on its mountain of debt, interest in the amount of seventy-six billion.

"If there was no interest to pay today, it follows that instead of a deficit of sixty-six billion with no lender available to bail us out — except for ten billion from the IMF, but I'll come to that in a moment — instead of that deficit, the government would have a surplus of ten billion and I would not be presenting a death-by-deficit budget to this House."

Suddenly he felt slightly dizzy. He had been on his feet for over an hour. Swaying, he picked up his glass of water, but it slipped through his fingers and crashed onto the desk. The dizziness was accelerating. He slumped into his chair muttering to Ann, "A recess. Stand and ask for a recess."

She was more concerned about him than about what he was asking her to do. "My God, Richard, are you alright?" Her arm went around his shoulders to steady him.

He shook his head groggily. "Nothing like this . . . I'll be okay."

"Mario, get Dr. Andrews. He's one of our people way down at the south end."

A deep male voice spoke from the aisle behind Carter. "I'm not at the south end. I'm right here."

Carter immediately moved away from the Prime Minister so that Andrews could get to him.

She stood up. "Mr. Speaker, the Prime Minister has suffered a slight spell. If the Honourable Leader of the Opposition will agree, I would move a half-hour recess."

The Speaker got the nod of assent from the Opposition Leader, who immediately walked across the floor to the PM. "Sorry, Richard. The strain of this goddam situation's enormous." Then to Andrews: "What do you think?"

"Chances are he's just run out of steam. But we'll get him out into the hall, just back there, and I'll take his blood pressure. His pulse is a little fast. I think he's just exhausted."

"I hope that's all it is." Then the Opposition Leader was gone.

Greco and Andrews on either side of the PM, with Carter following, helped the ashen-faced PM up the stairs, past the curtains, and steered him through the milling members into the nearest chair.

Carter, eyes wide with alarm, whispered forcefully at Greco: "Pray, Mario! Pray!"

24

11:40 A.M.: The House of Commons

"Mr. Speaker, I'm pleased to inform you and this House that the diagnosis of Dr. Andrews, the Reform PC member from Newfoundland — the riding name escapes me for the moment — Dr. Andrews says that exhaustion, lack of food, and a high level of stress disrupted my overloaded cardiovascular system momentarily. The high pressure gave way to low pressure — blood that is.

"But I'm fine now. Some soup and a shot of cognac have done the trick." That brought applause from both sides of a civil House.

Civil, at least for the moment.

"I am obliged to my honourable friend across the floor for his consent to the recess and for his personal concern."

That salute was acknowledged by a brief smile and tip of the head.

"If I may continue with my address, Mr. Speaker . . . it is appropriate to keep in mind that the national debt — that is, the federal debt, quite apart from the provincial and municipal indebtedness — is now over nine hundred billion and is reaching for one trillion dollars. That's one thousand billion dollars no matter how you look at it."

The PM then told the House that he had had a meeting with the IMF yesterday morning. That news brought a flurry of activity in the press gallery. He said he had been offered a line of credit to Canada of ten billion U.S. on two conditions: a very tough budget and a commitment to do away with one level of government in the provincial sector.

"Crafting that drastic budget, doing away with the Senate, and closing down departments that overlap with provincial jurisdictions should be sufficient to meet those conditions.

"However, even with that ten billion U.S., and even if we had no interest payments today, with the result that we had a ten-billion-dollar surplus on our hands, and even if we had a similar surplus of ten billion every year for the foreseeable future, it would take Canada how long to repay the federal debt?"

He paused to let the answer to the question be calculated by every listening mind.

"Mr. Speaker, Canada would need nearly one hundred years to repay that debt, wipe it off the books.

"So, are there alternatives to this oppressive budget and, if so, what are they?"

Movement and whispering in the House began to subside as the Prime Minister's words began to seize the full attention of everyone, including his own members and in particular Carter and Greco, neither of whom had been consulted about other options.

"In fact, I'm going to outline two alternatives to the budget I have just placed before the House. I will provide the House with each of these proposals, and if they are of substance and worthy of discussion, they can be included in the budget debate as it moves along."

He now had the rapt attention of every person in the House.

"I have a duty to put both concepts before the House and the people of Canada, but I do so without indicating a preference for one or the other."

The PM turned the pages in his book until he came to the beginning of his handwritten notes.

"The first alternative I choose to call the Weinstock Solution."

He then proceeded to explain the entire Weinstock advisory participation — the attendance of the Chairman of The Federal Reserve Board at the meeting on Monday evening and the midnight conversation over drinks at the Chateau Laurier.

"His advice centred on Canada's total inability to repay its debt, even if Canada had a ten-billion-dollar annual surplus.

"Chairman Weinstock suggested a solution and asked my permission to explore it. I agreed because it is my duty to examine every opportunity to get us out of this catastrophe."

Now the PM was perspiring. He pulled the handkerchief out of his upper suitcoat pocket. Wiped his brow as Carter urgently asked if he was alright.

"Sure," was the answer.

"Mr. Weinstock then enlisted the assistance of Leif Tromso, the Managing Director of the International Monetary Fund, and he supported the Weinstock Solution. He also volunteered to do everything in his considerable power to sell the idea to the powers-that-be. Weinstock and Tromso — both of them working the phones yesterday — obtained preliminary approval of those powers.

"I should say now that it is also implicit in the Weinstock Solution that one level of Canadian government would be eliminated." He gave a Trudeau-like shrug. "It would be at the provincial level."

Loud gasps were followed by murmuring and negative head-shaking.

"The Weinstock Solution has the strong support, in principle, of the President of the United States and of the top leaders of both parties, Republican and Democrat, in the Senate and the House of Representatives.

"The solution is simple. The United States will assume all of Canada's federal and provincial debt and pay all the interest thereon" — the PM drew a deep breath — "provided that Canada agrees to give the United States free and unfettered access to our most valuable commodity, of which Canada has the world's largest supply — fresh water."

He paused, waiting for an outburst. Nothing.

"I wish to make it clear, Mr. Speaker, that the President was emphatic — the United States does not want to take over Canada. The Americans have enough domestic problems as it is, without having, as it was put to me, the Canadian can of worms dumped on them."

"Screw the Americans!" That shout came from one of his own backbenchers, far to the PM's right. It was greeted by cries of "hear, hear" from both sides of the House.

"Mr. Speaker," the PM went on, "I must say that we owe a debt of gratitude to the Americans for offering to come to our assistance at this hour of total crisis. Even so, I recognize that there are some deep-seated anti-American emotions that are alive and well in this House. Indeed, they were the main engine in the creation of the Dominion of Canada in 1867."

His eyes went briefly back to his notes.

"There are other conditions in the Weinstock Solution, Mr. Speaker. I am sure that all honourable members will find them to be of — how should I put it? Yes — of controversial interest.

"The next Weinstock condition is that the United States should have the right — free and clear of any involvement or participation by the government of Canada — the right to negotiate directly with the government of British Columbia for that province to become a state of the United States of America."

The PM pressed on in the midst of a rumbling of voices on both sides of the House.

"As I understand it, for security and defence reasons the Americans would want British Columbia as a land bridge between the state of Washington and Alaska."

He glanced across the floor of the House to see the Leader of the Opposition shaking his head negatively while furiously scribbling.

"Mr. Speaker, I must tell you there's more. The final condition of the Weinstock Solution is that Canada must give up its ongoing battle for something the Americans can't understand — the battle for our cultural sovereignty."

That opening of the final condition brought a hush to the House.

"The Americans demand a complete abandonment of all Canadian legislation and policies that protect our book publishing, radio, television, and newspaper industries against foreign — that is, American — ownership, and also they want the dismantling of all Canadian-content rules for radio and television broadcasting."

The silence was palpable. The normally garrulous politicians on both sides of the House were speechless. Flabbergasted. That included Carter, Greco, and every Reform PC member.

They were, all of them, looking at the Prime Minister as if he had just shouted "shit" at the Cardinal in the middle of a Roman Catholic Mass.

"Mr. Speaker, as you may have noticed, I have developed a fit of perspiration. That, coupled with my earlier seizure, compels me to ask the indulgence of the House once again. I would move for a brief recess, please. Say fifteen minutes?"

The PM waved Greco away and brushed past Carter who was still seated. He was up the steps and through the curtains before any members of his party could stop him to ask questions. The agitated buzz of voices followed him as he retreated down the hall to the door of Sir John A.'s staircase.

25

12:16 P.M.: The House of Commons

Actually it was twenty-one minutes later that the Prime Minister made his way back through the curtains and down the steps to his seat in the packed House. He ignored the angry or quizzical stares that greeted his return.

The signal was given to the Speaker to enter the chamber. The PM was back and ready to go. The proceedings resumed when Leon Dagon was in place and once again recognized the Prime Minister. It would be the final piece of the budget presentation.

During the last break the experienced members of the House had told each other and their newly elected colleagues that they'd never heard a budget like this one before. And that Weinstock Solution! Christ, it was right off the wall. But it had to be looked at carefully. Maybe a referendum would be necessary. After all, Canada's water to the United States — were the provinces and Canadians ready for that now? And the cultural issue and the B.C. condition?

And they asked themselves and one another, "What's the second alternative to that nutcracking budget the PM has put on the table?" A budget designed to seduce the IMF and the world's lending markets. A budget that would absolutely emasculate the federal government and the hundreds of agencies, institutions, and educational facilities. Unbelievable, it was so bad.

The Prime Minister had some soothing words for Carter and Greco. Then he was on his feet once more. Some thought he still looked a little grey, a trifle wobbly.

"Mr. Speaker, I am obliged to you for your kind indulgence. I have put before the House this government's proposed budget. I have laid before you a scheme — the Weinstock Solution — that even my closest colleagues and staff have known absolutely nothing about."

He flipped the pages of his handwritten notes to the beginning of the final selection.

"Similarly, they have known nothing about the second alternative. No one, that is, except the honourable member who brought the germ of the idea all the way from Bath, England." The PM nodded slightly at his Finance Minister. "The idea sprang from the fertile mind of a well-known, brilliant Scot who is an experienced business-oriented chartered accountant. This man has lived in and served the community of Bath and the national community of the United Kingdom since the 1950s.

"The second approach to Canada's monster debt is the brainchild of Sir Robin Buchanan. I have yet to meet this distinguished gentleman, but he should know that I am grateful to him for his contribution."

For the first time he put on his half-spectacles, the better to see his own handwriting.

"Mr. Speaker, I will refer to this alternative to the budget as the Buchanan Plan, even though Sir Robin has provided me indirectly with only the seed of an idea around which I have developed the full-blown plan that must withstand the test of debate.

"I present it to the House and to the people of Canada — and, for that matter, to the money-lending markets of the world — as a viable alternative."

The PM hesitated. He was trying to size up the mood of the House. Was the Opposition getting ready to leap at his jugular, challenge his political credibility? He could only sense that they were listening.

Wait till the Buchanan Plan was fully on the table. God, he could hear the banks and insurance companies screaming blue murder.

The Prime Minister was showing his exhaustion. He was stumbling over the odd word, fidgeting with his spectacles as he read from his text, then occasionally improvising.

Presenting the budget and the Weinstock Solution had been painful in the extreme. He had detested every word of it, as had every old member and new of the anguished House.

Perhaps the Buchanan Plan would provide an unexpected light at the end of the tunnel. Perhaps. Like the Weinstock Solution, it would require stratospheric leaps of faith by all parties, by all members of Parliament, and by the people of Canada.

He glanced at Carter. Her eyes were deep-set with fatigue, but she was sitting erect on her front bench seat, supportive, confident in him. He straightened his shoulders and focussed his attention on the notes in front of him, even though every nerve of his tired body was sending distress signals to his brain. The brain rejected the messages, countersignalling the body to pull itself together.

The other message came from Carter, whose look said, "Keep going, Richard, you're doing fine."

Doing fine? A compartment of his mind challenged that. It said to him that no one had ever had to walk through the minefield of decisions that he had to guide the House of Commons through. Here he was, the first minister, telling these elected men and women how their beloved country would be torn apart, piece by piece, and how it could be stitched back together again.

In the Senate, his speech had provoked sporadic responses of indignation, shouts of denigration, disbelief, grief, and pain. But here in the House, his words had produced violent emotional reactions. Everyone knew there was no choice. The debt, deficit, and interest payment dragon had to be slain, no matter how deep the national pain and humiliation.

He looked around the House defiantly but his eyes saw none of the listening, waiting spectators. His mind zeroed in on the notes before him.

"In essence, Mr. Speaker, the Buchanan Plan contains the following elements:

"First, it recognizes that there are multitrillion non-government assets of Canada. Those assets can be marshalled in a way that could, in the short term, relieve the government of Canada of the massive interest payments on its federal debt."

He sensed a stirring among the members, an even sharper attention to his words.

"I remind the House that the interest payment for this fiscal year of 2000–2001 is an earth-shaking seventy-six billion dollars.

"Mr. Speaker, let me take us through the mechanics of the Buchanan Plan so everyone can see how it would work.

"I'm going to use Statistics Canada figures found in its current *Quarterly Financial Statistics For Enterprises.*

"The total assets of all Canadian industries are now 3.247 trillion dollars. Those assets have grown from 2.197 trillion since 1994.

"Of that 3.247 trillion, approximately 1.61 trillion of assets are attributed to the finance and insurance industries that have thrived in the Canadian business environment."

A raucous remark from across the floor caused him to stop and cast a quick look in that direction.

"May I remind you, Mr. Speaker, that the federal debt that is killing Canada is 914.5 billion and rising by the deficit of sixty-six billion — if we could borrow the money, which we now can't. So we are close to the one-trillion mark, which is about 30 percent of the 3.247 trillion in assets of all Canadian industries.

"I will come back to that 30 percent figure later."

He told the hushed House that it would be useful to demonstrate the Buchanan Plan by taking Canada's chartered banks as an example. He said that these banks had assets of 1.1 trillion, up from 611.8 billion in 1994. Under the plan each bank — and all other industries — would be required to assume a portion of the national debt equal to 30 percent of its assets.

"The bank would have an option," the PM explained. "It could pay off its share of the national debt so that there would be no interest payable to the lenders, whether foreign or domestic. Or the bank could simply assume the debt allocated to it and be responsible for paying the interest charges.

"If the bank assumed the debt and paid the interest, the interest would be a deductible tax item. There would also be a small tax incentive credit of, say, 1 percent."

Time for a break of a few seconds. A sip of water. He hung onto the glass with both hands to cover their shaking.

"On the other hand," he continued, "if the bank paid off its debt share, it would in effect be using its assets to invest in that share of Canada's national debt. The bank would be entitled to a fair rate of return, which would be in the form of a tax credit to be applied against its income tax payments."

He could see from the expressions on many faces, that the members were rapidly doing mental calculations.

"The amount of that fair rate of return tax credit would not be difficult to calculate," he told them. "Since banks consider a 5 to 7 percent rate of return reasonable, a tax credit of one-half that amount would put them in the same rate-of-return position. Banks customarily pay their customers between 3 and 4 percent interest for the use of money. That amount is of course taxable in the hands of the customer. So a tax credit in the range of 2 percent would likely be a fair rate of return. The credit would remain in place until the entire national debt was retired."

He whipped off his spectacles as he turned toward the Chair to apologize. "Mr. Speaker, I regret the use of so much detail, but it is necessary to put every aspect on the table in order to make the Buchanan Plan as clear as I can."

To sum it up, he said that the fundamental objective of the Plan was to raise enough cash annually to pay the interest on the enormous national debt. The collateral objective was to run substantial revenue surpluses in order to pay down the debt to zero within thirty years, or better still, in twenty.

It was time to shift the focus away from the bank example.

"I have used the banks with their enormous asset bases as the example of how the Buchanan Plan would work.

"The industrial segment of our economy comes in with an asset base of 1.63 trillion. That's just a little more than the financial and insurance institutions at 1.61 trillion." He explained that those combined assets and a continued high rate of productivity would immediately generate Buchanan Plan revenues sufficient to pay the current seventy-six-billion interest charges. All private corporations and all corporations listed on the Canadian stock exchanges would be participants in the Buchanan Plan and the Canadian assets of private foreign corporations in Canada and of those listed on a Canadian stock exchange would also be subject to the Buchanan Plan.

"To elaborate further," he told the House, "if the Plan was implemented tomorrow and the interest of seventy-six billion was covered by it, and if not one single cut was made in government spending — in other words, if the budget I have introduced did not exist — then there would be an immediate surplus of ten billion dollars."

Another sip of water. A pause to let that point sink in. He was surprised at how few verbal jabs had come from the other side. Some, but not many.

"Mr. Speaker, let me try to put the Buchanan Plan principle in the simplest terms. I put this forward with a major caveat — Buchanan requires refining and testing by experts. What I give to the House is the bare bones of the idea.

"One — the federal debt is rounded to one trillion.

"Two — total assets of all Canadian industries are rounded to three trillion.

"Three — therefore the debt is 33 percent of the assets, rounded to 30 percent.

"Four — a qualified private or listed Canadian corporation or the Canadian assets of a foreign corporation would pay as a special levy interest on the value of 30 percent of its assets.

"Five — as an example, a company with assets of one million would pay an interest levy on 30 percent of its assets, rounded to 300,000 dollars.

"Six — the interest rate applicable to the 300,000 dollars would be 7.6 percent, which would generate a payment of 22,800 dollars.

"Seven — the interest rate is obtained by dividing the amount of the national debt of one thousand billion by the amount of the interest payable on that debt, namely seventy-six billion.

"Mr. Speaker, I stress that no corporation must buy a piece of the federal debt. There will be no need to find the capital to purchase that debt.

"What is required of a corporation is that it will pay the special interest levy during the period in which the government's surpluses are paying down the debt. It follows that as the debt is paid down, the annual interest levy will decrease."

The PM stopped to read the note that Carter had just scribbled and handed to him. It read, "Great stuff. Even I understand it now!" He looked down at her, nodded his thanks, then turned back to his notes.

"Mr. Speaker, if it is the Buchanan Plan that is accepted by the House, I will propose that the budget I have put forward today be altered so that the spending cuts will be to twenty billion, not the horrendous sixty-six billion. That would provide a surplus of thirty billion, to be applied to pay down the national debt. That debt of nine hundred billion plus would take thirty years to pay off. Therefore, that would be the maximum lifespan of the Buchanan Plan. As I said earlier, twenty years would be better.

"And that, Mr. Speaker, is the Buchanan Plan."

The PM gathered his waning strength as he neared the end of his speech.

"Mr. Speaker, this new, this novice government, upon which has been dropped the worst financial disaster in Canada's history, has presented to this House three solutions to this unprecedented crisis. There could well be others."

He swung to face the whole House, his body language confident, his voice again full and strong.

"To sum up, Mr. Speaker, the budget I have presented calls for spending cuts of sixty-six billion dollars in twenty-four months. It requires a massive downsizing of the federal government. With this budget Canada can probably survive economically but our way of life will be severely affected.

"The first alternative to that budget is the Weinstock Solution, in which Canada's national debt and provincial debts are assumed by the United States of America in exchange for our water and a pledge to achieve a zero deficit.

"The second alternative, the Buchanan proposal, by legislation would co-opt the assets of the country's private and listed corporations to assume the interest payments on the national debt. There would be a collateral commitment of the federal government to budget only surpluses and to use them to pay down the federal debt to zero within thirty years or earlier."

He was within a few seconds of finishing his gruelling task.

"Mr. Speaker, my motion to endorse the budget and to debate these proposals will be made by the President of the Treasury Board. Debate can commence tomorrow."

The Prime Minister of Canada collapsed into his seat while each and every Reform PC member of the House jumped up to give their leader a roaring, standing ovation.

Across the floor the Leader of the Opposition was trying to sort out what his opening response would be. He was relieved of the immediate pressure when the Speaker declared the luncheon recess with the House to be in session again at 2:30 p.m.

26

2:30 P.M.: The House of Commons

When the House resumed after the lunch break the recently deposed prime minister rose to open the response of the Opposition to the incredible proposals that his successor had placed before the House.

The Leader of His Majesty's Loyal Opposition did not outwardly show any hint of his intense distaste for his new, unwanted post. He was out of power and all its trappings. It had been a demeaning, humiliating experience since the night of the general election. So much so that he had seriously considered resigning. In fact he had not yet put that option aside.

He was a tall, distinguished looking man in his early sixties. He had a full head of wavy grey hair. Now heavy of body, his lined, round face was recognized by everyone in Canada. As he stood, he was satisfied that what he planned to say in his preliminary statement would be well received — if anything anyone said in the House in this hour of shocking reality could be well received.

On the other hand, the thoughts he was about to put into words were moulded by his recognition of two facts. The first was that he and his party and its leaders before him — all of them, but he in particular — were responsible for the existence of this economic calamity. Since he could not avoid that responsibility, he would have to temper those words.

The second fact he told himself to recognize was the obverse side of the responsibility coin. He was no longer responsible for government policy. Instead, it was his function to challenge and test the policies being proposed by the new government. Criticize, challenge, contest, oppose: those were the operative words of his new mandate.

There was also the obligation, moral on his part, to not oppose, but support, policies with which he and the remnants of his party agreed, policies that he considered to be in the best interests of Canada.

He looked up to his right at the press gallery high above the Speaker, who was also standing, ready to recognize him. There was noise, movement, confusion. Some media people were trying to make their way back into the crowded gallery, having rushed to file their stories on the Prime Minister's three proposals, each one sensational in its own right.

The chamber was also filled with the noise of members on both sides of the House still talking excitedly with their colleagues. All of them were shocked to the depths of their souls by the magnitude, the ramifications, of the plans the Prime Minister had put before them.

The Speaker waited until the commotion died down as members saw that he was standing.

"The member for Windsor-Walkerville," the Speaker said, thereby recognizing the Opposition Leader and giving him the floor.

"Mr. Speaker." Then he waited a few moments for total silence throughout the House. Now it was his turn. Every eye was on him. The floor was his alone.

"Mr. Speaker, it would not be an overstatement to say that we have just listened to the most appalling speech ever delivered in this House, and . . ."

The shouts and screams of protest from the government benches were instantaneous as the Prime Minister's supporters erupted. Some stood, waving their arms, pointing, shaking fists as they spewed threats and invective at the members across the floor. "Traitor! You're the cause of this!", "You sonofabitch!", "It's all your fault!" were but a handful of oaths and insults that were replied to in kind from the Opposition front as well as backbenches.

The Prime Minister remained in his seat, impassive. He made no effort to restrain Carter, who was standing, leading the verbal assault against the former prime minister directly across the floor of the House.

The Opposition Leader considered sitting down until the uproar had subsided, but decided to remain defiantly standing.

Finally Speaker Dagon, alarmed by the ferocity, the signs of potential physical violence, summoned the Clerk of the House to the chair. Bending over to shout into the man's ear, he gave the Clerk an order.

The Clerk immediately moved to the Sergeant-at-Arms and spoke to him. The two of them walked quickly out of the House through the door on the Speaker's right. In less than a minute they came back into the chamber followed by the Commissioner of the Royal Canadian Mounted Police and some twenty of his most senior officers, all in full red-jacketed uniform. As prearranged, the Commissioner took up a position immediately to the right of the Speaker's chair. His officers, moving smartly, positioned themselves with half their numbers on each side of the chair. They stood at ease, facing the mace, the long desk of the Clerk and his staff, and the long expanse of red-carpeted floor that divided the benches of the government on the Speaker's right hand from those of the Opposition on his left.

The entry of the RCMP had a small dampening effect on the enraged members. As the police officers appeared, Speaker Dagon began his ritual call, bellowing "Order! Order!" into his lapel microphone. He had removed it from his gown and held it to his mouth for maximum volume. He continued his call for order until he could see and hear that the presence of the RCMP was taking effect. Members sat down. The shouting stopped. An uneasy, tension-filled atmosphere filled the place.

Judging that the situation was under control and the still-standing Opposition Leader could now continue, the Speaker, with a nod of the head, signalled him to continue.

"Mr. Speaker, it is not my intent to disrupt the proceedings of this House by the use of inflammatory rhetoric."

He could hear groans and muttering from the government benches.

"But as you are aware, Mr. Speaker, like my late father before me, who was one of the most eloquent —"

"And verbose!" a voice shouted from the other side.

"— orators ever to stand in this House, I sometimes use graphic words which, if taken out of context or if reacted to before I have completed my thought, can be totally misleading.

"Such was the case when, some ten minutes ago, I used the word 'appalling' to describe the Prime Minister's speech this morning."

He let an expected rude, momentary interjection pass.

"When I used the word 'appalling,' Mr. Speaker, I did so meaning no criticism of the Prime Minister or of the three proposals in his speech. I will make comments on those proposals shortly.

"What I meant by saying that his was the most appalling speech ever delivered in this House was simply that all of us on both sides of the House must be appalled by the fact that such a speech has had to be made at all. We must be, all of us, appalled at the enormity of the economic disaster that has befallen us."

"You did it to us!" Carter, sitting on the edge of her seat next to the Prime Minister, couldn't contain herself.

"Mr. Speaker, the Honourable President of the Treasury Board has said that I did it or my government did it, I'm not sure which. Whatever, there's no doubt that my government is largely responsible for this crisis. No question about it. But we are only partly to blame.

"As I see it, the whole country, all of its citizens, shares as much of the blame as the governments that I and my immediate predecessor have led over the past years — or for that matter the government that preceded it in the 1980s and early '90s. All of us share responsibility."

He raised his arms towards the government benches, then turned to his own members, a gesture that included everyone.

"Why have I said that all of Canada's citizens share in the blame? Because they would never accept the reductions in social and other government services, reductions in pensions, health care, and unemployment insurance benefits that would have resulted if we had reduced the deficit to zero, as the Prime Minister now is forced to do."

His fist hit the desk. "The people said no! So it was politically impossible for us to do what is proposed in this appalling budget."

He knew there would be — and there was — another, but relatively tame, uproar when he used that "appalling" word. It passed in a few moments and he went on.

"I say to you, Mr. Speaker, that the proposed zero-deficit budget is now possible, not because of the political will of the Canadian people, but because Canada is being attacked by outside forces that will destroy our nation unless we fight back against them.

"Canada is at war, a war of survival. If we are to survive, we must be prepared to make sacrifices and to work together for the common good."

He could hear the beginning of hand-clapping from behind and to each side. His members, all of them, were now on their feet, their applause expressing full support for their leader's statement.

Across the floor, many of the Reform PC members wanted to join in. They looked to see how the Prime Minister would react. As he watched, he asked himself what he should do. The answer was instant and obvious. The offer to cooperate and "work together for the common good" could not be scorned.

Nodding his approval, the Prime Minister got to his feet and joined in the growing applause, its noise now thundering within the chamber as all his people rose to take part in the spontaneous salute.

When that was finished and all honourable members had settled back into their seats, the former prime minister continued. There was no smile on his face. The situation was too grave for even a thought of satisfaction.

"Mr. Speaker, I am humbled by this rare demonstration of response to words intended to express my intent that, from our side, there should be every effort to achieve a nonpartisan approach to defending Canada against the assault of external as well as internal economic forces that are in fact on the verge of destroying the nation."

He paused to savour a further round of applause, this time not standing and only from his own benches.

"That is to say, Mr. Speaker, that my party will not be critical of any action, any policy, that the government puts forward in the battle to defend Canada in this crisis. On the contrary, we reserve the right to fight against any proposal the government makes, if we consider it to be contrary to the interests of the people of Canada."

More Opposition applause, but now almost perfunctory.

Carter leaned over to speak in a low voice into the PM's ear: "Where do you think he's going?"

He shrugged. "I haven't the slightest idea. He's a clever bastard. He could throw a bomb any minute now."

Standing at his seat in the middle of the front benches of the Opposition, the Leader paused and shifted on his feet. He picked up and looked at the notes he had made when the PM was speaking. He put them down, saying, "Mr. Speaker, I now wish to deal with the three topics the Prime Minister has put before this House. Each of them has consequences of enormous gravity. Each of them is appalling — and I use that word again advisedly — appalling in its own right.

"With your permission, Mr. Speaker, and that of the Prime Minister, I would like to put some questions to him. His answers will help me and my colleagues to better understand the nature of his proposals and where he really intends to go with them."

Speaker Dagon stood and said, "I have no objection." He looked at the Prime Minister, who rose long enough to say, "I would be happy to attempt to respond to any questions, Mr. Speaker."

Dagon nodded to the Opposition Leader, then sat down.

"Thank you, Mr. Speaker. The first question I put to the Prime Minister may well be the only one, depending on the quality of his answer . . . Prime Minister, the usual practice in this House is that when the government of the day presents a budget, that budget is firm and fixed policy subject to reasonable amendments that emerge during debate and are acceptable to the government.

"Today you have presented a budget, saying this is government policy. But you have also said that this budget for a zero deficit in twenty-four months is so draconian . . ."

"So appalling!" Carter shouted across the floor.

"Yes, Mr. Speaker, so appalling that it might not be government policy, that there are two alternatives that are worthy of consideration.

"You then laid out for us those two alternatives: the Weinstock Solution and the so-called Buchanan Plan." He looked to the chair. "In fairness, Mr. Speaker, I recognize that the Prime Minister has said that he has not had the opportunity to put either alternative to his Cabinet or his caucus."

Then his eyes went back to the Prime Minister, who was watching his every move, listening intently to every word.

"The Prime Minister has given the House one solution that in effect means the cession, the sale, of Canada's main natural resource, our precious fresh water, to the United States, the abandonment of Canada's cultural sovereignty, and the potential loss of British Columbia, in consideration of the U.S. taking over the nation's mountain of debt. Then he has presented the other solution, which calls for the industrial, commercial, and financial sectors of Canada to pay the interest, some seventy-six billion a year, on the national debt until the debt is eliminated twenty or thirty years from now."

He turned again briefly toward the chair. "Mr. Speaker, I reserve my comments on the proposed budget and on Weinstock and Buchanan until a more appropriate time in this debate, and I can assure you that neither my colleagues nor I will be reluctant to be forthright in our criticisms and our contributions."

He again faced his adversary. Leaning forward, the palms of his hands flat on his desk, he put the question that was at the front of the mind of every person in the House except the Prime Minister.

The Leader of the Opposition raised his voice. His words cut clearly through the tension-filled, hushed House of Commons as he put into words what everyone craved to know.

"My question to the Prime Minister is this: When you present the Weinstock Solution and the Buchanan Plan to your Cabinet and your caucus, which of the two do you intend to recommend?"

As he sat down, there was no outbreak of applause from his supporters. Instead, the House remained silent. The place was caught up in taut apprehension by the uncertainty of all members about what the answer would be. Because in that answer could well be found the destiny of Canada.

27

3:12 P.M.: The House of Commons

The Prime Minister was slow getting to his feet. He needed precious long seconds to decide how he would begin his answer and what the conclusion would be.

"Mr. Speaker, I am obliged to my honourable friend for his offer — I think I can call it that — his offer of a nonpartisan approach in resolving this crisis. And I am obliged to him for putting the question to me."

He was using the time of that preamble to think out the substance of his response.

"First, Mr. Speaker, let me say that as I see it, we have three choices: the draconian budget, Weinstock, or Buchanan.

"A budget there will be, you can be sure of that. If it is the Weinstock Solution, the budget will be totally revised as we await the American funding and the Treaty that would implement Weinstock."

There was much mumbling and grumbling as those words sank in.

"If it is Buchanan, then the budget will be altered to provide much less hurtful and stringent cuts in government social and other services and to provide for the surplus with which to begin to pay down our brutal debt."

The PM leaned over to speak to Carter. She immediately poured a glass of water for him. He lifted it with both hands to take a sip.

"Mr. Speaker, I must put a caveat on my answer to my honourable friend's perceptive question. And he above all others here will understand the caveat. It is that regardless of whether I recommend Weinstock or Buchanan to my Cabinet and my caucus, the decision of my government as to what to do, what to accept, can be very different from what I am going to tell this House that I will recommend."

He looked across the floor for approval from the former prime minister, who gave it by vigorously nodding his head.

The Prime Minister said, "Mr. Speaker, let the Hansard record show that the Leader of the Opposition has signalled his agreement with that proposition."

He permitted himself a fleeting smile at his predecessor.

"Now, Mr. Speaker, the Weinstock Solution. It may well be that my caucus and my government will decide that we should take the United States' offer. Our culture is swamped by the Americans. Eighty percent of our exports are to the U.S. We rely on American military might for the defence of Canada. Countless reasons will be put forward to support accepting or rejecting the Weinstock Solution."

There were shouts of "hear, hear" and desk-banging applause from both sides of the House.

"As to the Buchanan Plan, Mr. Speaker, I expect a negative reaction from the business community and particularly from the banks, insurance companies, and Canada's communications giants. That's where the greatest assets are, just as that's where the largest cash flow is. It is my reading of the situation that the proposed Buchanan utilization of the nation's assets and cash productivity base is something the private enterprise and Crown corporations of the nation can afford. What they cannot afford is for Canada, the government of Canada, to collapse into financial bankruptcy."

He shrugged as the next thought passed his lips.

"On the other hand, perhaps the business community — and by that I mean all of the private and listed corporations as I defined them earlier — the business establishments would want us to accept the Weinstock Solution and cede our water to the Americans."

The PM picked up his glass with one hand. His nervous tremor was gone. No need now for the second hand to steady his lifting the water to his mouth.

"Mr. Speaker, I have nearly reached my direct answer to my honourable friend. But before I tell you and this House what my recommendation to my Cabinet and caucus will be, there is a significant element, an exceedingly important factor, that is in play in my thinking process.

"When I tell you what it is, you will see immediately whether my recommendation will be Weinstock or Buchanan."

The Prime Minister stopped. He turned to face the Speaker in his chair and the scarlet-clad contingent of RCMP officers standing stiffly at ease.

"An oversight on my part, Mr. Speaker. I should have recognized the unique presence in this chamber of the Commissioner and the senior officers of the finest police force in the world!"

That salute was greeted by applause and shouts of approval from both sides of the House.

"I might say, Mr. Speaker, that I had earlier considered asking you to relieve the Commissioner and his officers from their uncomfortable and perhaps even embarrassing duty of being present in the House of Commons to assist you, Mr. Speaker, if necessary in keeping order.

"However, when the question was put to me by my honourable friend and I elected to answer it, I also elected not to ask that the RCMP be excused, because I am uncertain, indeed perhaps fearful, of what the reaction might be."

Knowing that statement would put everyone's teeth on edge, the PM began a turn to face the Opposition benches again.

"Mr. Speaker, if Weinstock was to be implemented, the negotiations for a Treaty would take months to sort out. Earlier I said it would take about six months to implement Weinstock. On reflection, it would probably take a year or even eighteen months to have the national referendum that I think would be required and to negotiate with the provinces and territories. Perhaps a plebiscite, a binding vote of the people, rather than a non-binding referendum, would be the necessary vehicle.

"Furthermore, it might well be necessary to hold plebiscites in each of the provinces and the territories. What I am saying is that if it is to be implemented, Weinstock will require changes that will have to be directly mandated by the citizens of Canada over and above a mandate from the Parliament of Canada.

"Mr. Speaker, I am not saying that those changes could not be made or that successful plebiscites could not be held. I am simply saying that to implement Weinstock there must be changes, including constitutional change."

Another sip of water to give himself precious seconds to organize his thoughts.

"On the other hand, Mr. Speaker, the Buchanan Plan requires no constitutional change, no referendum, no plebiscites. Buchanan requires only the legislation of this House as approved by the other place and Royal Assent. It is within the power of Parliament to deal expeditiously with Buchanan, to deal with it immediately on an emergency basis!"

He was about to answer the question.

"Mr. Speaker, the government of Canada must deal with this crisis today, tomorrow, not months down the road, when it may be too late. This is the greatest emergency in the history of Canada. As my honourable friend the Leader of the Opposition said, this is war!"

The Prime Minister shifted his feet and drew himself up. "Mr. Speaker, my answer to the question of whether I will recommend Weinstock or Buchanan to my caucus must be prefaced by the observation that the proposal that I do *not* recommend will still be alive as a safety net, should the one I recommend be dead on arrival."

His long pause was calculated.

"Mr. Speaker, there are those who will say that the Buchanan Plan will not work, that the gearing ratio of the banks is twenty-five to one, which means that the true assets of the banks are not 1.1 trillion dollars but only 4 percent of that. They will say that the Buchanan Plan would destroy the integrity of the Canadian banking system and the industrial sector."

He nodded his head as he spoke. "Yes, there will be much controversy over whether the Buchanan Plan will work. And perhaps at the end of the day Buchanan will be modified beyond recognition. But the Buchanan Plan is a start, Mr. Speaker, a point of departure.

"Mr. Speaker, my answer to the question of the Honourable Leader of the Opposition is this: I will recommend to my Cabinet and caucus the adoption of the Buchanan Plan or a variation of it and the enactment of necessary legislation to give effect to it. At the same time I will recommend that the Weinstock Solution be adopted as the backup plan, with immediate preparation of all constitutional and legislative steps necessary to put it into effect if the Buchanan Plan fails or in some way is not feasible."

The Prime Minister of Canada prepared to sit down. But he had to have the last word. "Mr. Speaker, I am confident that this House, with all of the experience and wisdom that exists on both sides, will make decisions that will ensure the survival of our beloved country, Canada."